THE PRIMAL HUNTER

VOLUME 2

WRITTEN BY
ZOGARTH

ILLUSTRATED BY
SENCHIRO

vault

VOLUME 2

WRITTEN BY
ZOGARTH

ILLUSTRATED BY
SENCHIRO

AETHON BOOKS

vault

EDITORIAL
ADRIAN WASSEL — CCO & EDITOR-IN-CHIEF
DER-SHING HELMER — MANAGING EDITOR

DESIGN & PRODUCTION
TIM DANIEL — EVP, DESIGN & PRODUCTION
ADAM CAHOON — SENIOR DESIGNER & PRODUCTION ASSOCIATE
NATHAN GOODEN — CO-FOUNDER & SENIOR ARTIST

SALES & MARKETING
DAVID DISSANAYAKE — VP, SALES & MARKETING
SYNDEE BARWICK — DIRECTOR, BOOK MARKET SALES
BRITTA BUESCHER — DIRECTOR, SOCIAL MEDIA

OPERATIONS & STRATEGY
DAMIAN WASSEL — CEO & PUBLISHER
CHRIS KANALEY — CSO
F.J. DESANTO — HEAD OF FILM & TV

THE PRIMAL HUNTER, VOLUME 2, MAY, 2025 COPYRIGHT © 2025, ZOGARTH. ALL RIGHTS RESERVED. "THE PRIMAL HUNTER," THE PRIMAL HUNTER LOGO, AND THE LIKENESSES OF ALL CHARACTERS HEREIN ARE TRADEMARKS OF ZOGARTH, UNLESS OTHERWISE NOTED. "VAULT" AND THE VAULT LOGO ARE TRADEMARKS OF VAULT STORYWORKS LLC. "AETHON BOOKS" AND THE AETHON BOOKS LOGO ARE TRADEMARKS OF AETHON BOOKS, LLC. NO PART OF THIS WORK MAY BE REPRODUCED, TRANSMITTED, STORED OR USED IN ANY FORM OR BY ANY MEANS GRAPHIC, ELECTRONIC, OR MECHANICAL, INCLUDING BUT NOT LIMITED TO PHOTOCOPYING, RECORDING, SCANNING, DIGITIZING, TAPING, WEB DISTRIBUTION, INFORMATION NETWORKS, OR INFORMATION STORAGE AND RETRIEVAL SYSTEMS, EXCEPT AS PERMITTED UNDER SECTION 107 OR 108 OF THE 1976 UNITED STATES COPYRIGHT ACT, WITHOUT THE PRIOR WRITTEN PERMISSION OF THE PUBLISHER. ALL NAMES, CHARACTERS, EVENTS, AND LOCALES IN THIS PUBLICATION ARE ENTIRELY FICTIONAL. ANY RESEMBLANCE TO ACTUAL PERSONS (LIVING OR DEAD), EVENTS, INSTITUTIONS, OR PLACES, WITHOUT SATIRIC INTENT, IS COINCIDENTAL. PRINTED IN USA. FOR INFORMATION ABOUT FOREIGN OR MULTIMEDIA RIGHTS, CONTACT: RIGHTS@VAULTCOMICS.COM

TABLE OF CONTENTS

Chap. 24	Palate of the Malefic Viper	1
Chap. 25	Enjoying Life	15
Chap. 26	More Skills!	29
Chap. 27	Evolution	41
Chap. 28	Base-Building	53
Chap. 29	It's Just Logical	65
Chap. 30	Preparations for Evolution	77
Chap. 31	Professional Evolution	89
Chap. 32	A Very Weird Encounter	101
Chap. 33	True Blessing of the Malefic Viper	115
Chap. 34	Manipulation	129
Chap. 35	Blood of the Malefic Viper	139
Chap. 36	A Battle of Life & Death	153
Chap. 37	Leave Nothing Behind	165
Chap. 38	Broken	179
Chap. 39	Powershot	191
Chap. 40	Defect & Meeting	205
Chap. 41	Clash	217
Chap. 42	Twin-Fang Style	231
Chap. 43	Big Pig II - Steeltusk Edition	243
Chap. 44	"Partners"	255
Chap. 45	Shadow Vault & Instincts	265
Chap. 46	Unexpected Encounter (1/3)	275
Chap. 47	Unexpected Encounter (2/3)	287
Chap. 48	Unexpected Encounter (3/3)	299

Chapter 24
Palate of the Malefic Viper

Jake focused as he felt the mana flow through his body and into the reddish mixture in the bowl before him. He felt that this would be the one. After nearly twenty failed tries, this had to be the one.

For nearly a full day, he had been attempting to make health potions. He had been very positive initially, believing that it would be a cakewalk, considering his experience with the mana potions. But oh boy, was he wrong.

Much of the process had become far more straightforward than his first attempt to make a potion. But the mana injection still stumped him. He had to do it in a way that would bring forth the natural healing properties in the red lavender and successfully combine it with the Evergreen Grass.

It was changing the mana's properties by filtering it through the bowl and into the herbs. Normal mana was relatively easy to control, but it became more problematic when Jake had to transform it. The herbs and moss served as catalysts for his mana, binding itself to them.

The ultimate purpose was to make the liquid in the batch resemble the energy called health points, also known as vital energy. The herbs themselves already contained a lot of this energy, but he had to bring it out and make it into an actual potion.

To be perfectly honest, Jake still wasn't entirely sure how the whole thing worked; he just went by what the books said and what felt right during the moment. He had long learned that a lot of the crafting was "feeling" what to do more than just following some step-by-step guide. As long as your underlying methodology was serviceable, chances were you wouldn't go all wrong. At least with inferior-rarity potions.

Luckily, this time, he didn't fail. With a final push, the liquid gave off an invigorating smell, and he barely managed to contain his excitement as the system messages appeared.

*You have successfully crafted [Health Potion (Inferior)] – A new kind of creation has been made. Bonus experience earned.

'DING!' Profession: [Alchemist of the Malefic Viper] has reached level 5 - Stat points allocated, +2 Free Points

'DING!' Race: [Human (G)] has reached level 7 - Stat points allocated, +1 Free Point

He did a mini-cheer as he bottled the health potions. He only ended up making three from the whole batch, but a success was a success. One of the primary reasons why the number of potions varied was the purified water evaporating during the brewing.

According to the books, in a perfect scenario, nearly none of the water would disappear. This would, in turn, lead to more of the energy contained in the herbs not being wasted. Jake was currently wasting a lot of precious energy, mainly because he quite honestly still sucked.

But then again, he had only been an alchemist for less than two days. He could not be expected to be a potion master instantly. On a side note, his Free Points were once again just thrown into Wisdom.

Apropos of becoming a master of alchemy. Having reached level 5 in his profession, another message appeared along with the level-up, one he had been looking forward to.

> *Alchemist of the Malefic Viper profession skills available*

Jake didn't hesitate to open the menu. The first thing he noticed was that there were far fewer skills to choose from compared to his Archer class. But that wasn't really a bad thing. All of those skills had been "filler," so to say. Useless passive weapon skills mainly, all of which he had no interest in at all, and every one of them was inferior rarity. The alchemy profession didn't have a single one of those. Instead, it had given him only six options. He started going through them one by one.

> [Pill Consolidation (Inferior)] – The path of alchemy is diverse and methods aplenty, with potion brewing but one of the major paths. Another is pill consolidation. Pills come in many forms, but most have the purpose of empowering the one who consumes it, both temporarily and permanently. Must have

> suitable materials and equipment in order to create pills. Adds a minor increase to the effectiveness of produced pills based on Wisdom.

Reading through the entire thing, Jake had to scratch his chin a bit. Pill consolidation did seem useful; however, Jake had no interest in it at all right now. He already had a hard enough time making potions, and he still had poisons to concoct on his timetable. On top of that, he was still somewhat unclear as to the differences between pills and potions. The description did offer a bit of a hint, mentioning permanent benefits. But it also compared the two "paths" as similar.

While the promise of permanent buffs was tempting, unless those permanent benefits included not dying in less than a month, he wasn't that interested. So, learning about the wonders of alchemical pills was something for later, if ever. For now, he moved on to check the next skills.

> [Geology (Inferior)] – Grants knowledge of minerals and other similar natural treasures found throughout the multiverse. These natural treasures can be combined with other materials to amplify or bring forth strong magical effects. An alchemist must be able to distinguish the magical rock from the mundane gravel, after all.
>
> [Metallurgy (Inferior)] – Grants knowledge of metallic materials and substances found throughout the multiverse. Many types of rare and powerful metals are found throughout the multiverse and can be combined with other materials to amplify or bring forth

> powerful magical effects, not limited only to alchemical products.

Jake decided to group these together as they were somewhat similar. They were like his Herbology and Toxicology skills, only for stones and metals. Well, geology did include things that couldn't strictly be defined as stones, but quite frankly, he didn't really care. He had always found geologists a weird bunch, and there was no way he was going to spend his days looking for, or studying, rocks.

Thus, he moved on swiftly.

> [Sense Herb (Common)] – Gives a passive ability to detect herbs and a rough feeling of their properties. An alchemist must be able to find the materials to craft his products, after all. Adds a minor increase to the effectiveness of Sense Herb based on Perception.
>
> [Sense Poison (Uncommon)] – Gives a passive ability to detect poisonous substances and their toxicity level. An alchemist must be able to find the materials to craft his products, after all. Adds a minor increase to the effectiveness of Sense Poison based on Perception.

These two skills were, in his honest opinion, quite necessary. It would be splendid out in the forest or anywhere else really, as finding herbs and toxic materials he could craft from likely wasn't just found lying about. Or maybe they were; he just wouldn't know without a skill to help him find them. Or he would be forced to scour through the underbrush constantly. But while he considered them essential, finding materials was not exactly a challenge in his current situation.

He would need them for sure. But the last skill made it absolutely clear he wouldn't pick any of them.

[Palate of the Malefic Viper (Rare)] – The Malefic Viper has honed its venom by devouring myriad toxins found throughout the multiverse. In the same vein, the Alchemist of the Malefic Viper can consume toxins to learn their effects and properties. Grants the alchemist immunity or resistance to most low-level poisons. Through consumption, may your power grow; through gluttony, may your Records expand.

Okayyy... was his first thought after reading it. Most of the descriptions were rather direct, but this one was quite a bit more flavorful, especially in the last part.

Based on the name, this one was clearly associated with his variant of alchemist. Thinking about the effects of the skill, the prospect of eating the blue mushrooms came as both pleasing and horrifying at the same time. He did hate the damn things, so the thought of eating the bastards was nice, but on the other hand... they were blue magic mushrooms.

Shaking his head, he picked the skill. Surprisingly, he felt nothing despite getting another rare-rank skill. He had to open his status screen and check to make sure that he, in fact, did have the skill.

Confirming that he did, he walked to the cave and looked at the mushrooms. He decided to go for the flytrap one. He picked it due to it being inferior rarity. He assumed that even if his skills didn't work like he believed, it wouldn't kill him.

> [Flytrap Mushroom (Inferior)] – A carnivorous and poisonous mushroom that eats insects to accelerate its growth.

Picking the fungus up, he inspected it closely. To call it appetizing would be a straight-up lie. Not that Jake was the best judge; he'd hated mushrooms even before the tutorial. According to him, the mere thought of people willingly adding them to salads was one of life's greatest mysteries.

He had never used them for... "recreational" purposes either, even though he had known some who did during his university days. And yes, he had been offered plenty, despite him barely ever participating in social gatherings. One guy had even knocked on his door at 4 am, randomly offering him a bag, though he was pretty sure the guy was looking for Andrew, his roommate at the time.

Oh well, no better time to do mushrooms than when stuck in a dungeon with less than a month to live, Jake thought as he threw his first Flytrap Mushroom into his mouth.

The first thing that hit him was the taste. Or more accurately, lack of taste. It was a bit chewy, but it didn't have much flavor to it, honestly. He had half-expected it to taste like chicken. The juices coming out of the shroom made sizzling sounds as it came into contact with his spit. It did not hurt or feel uncomfortable in any way; it was more akin to drinking carbonated drinks.

However, Jake did not have time to think much of it as a weird feeling of realization struck him akin to if one had been struggling with a math problem for hours, and then suddenly, something clicked, and the solution came to them.

He now knew a lot, not about the mushroom per se, but the poison it possessed. It felt familiar to him now. But he also knew that the knowledge was not complete.

A single mushroom was not enough to truly familiarize himself with its properties, far from it. And as such, his feasting began.

The cave was big. Very big. Same with the garden. Jake knew there was no way for him to use all of the ingredients found here in thirty days, even if he was several times faster at doing alchemy.

But now he was starting to get a bit worried as he chomped down Flytrap after Flytrap. He had to be honest with himself; the taste was kind of growing on him. Or maybe it was just the feeling of quite literally eating himself to knowledge and understanding that he found so intoxicating.

After eating way too many, he finally stopped. First of all because his stomach was starting to hurt from being overstuffed, and secondly, the diminishing return had kicked in hard. The first couple of mushrooms had given the most, but the later ones barely helped.

By now, he felt amazingly familiar with the little buggers. While he had no intention to confirm it currently, he felt like this familiarity would be incredibly helpful when concocting poisons later.

Feeling stuffed, he decided to go back to the laboratory. He felt a bit tired earlier from trying to make health potions, but now he felt strangely invigorated. Looking at his stamina, he noticed that it had actually gone up over his feeding frenzy. It was only a measly 2 points, but it had gone up. More surprising, however, was his mana. It had been topped up, him having restored more than 100 points.

The Palate of the Malefic Viper skill said nothing about restoring resources from eating mushrooms. And with his newfound intimate understanding of the shrooms, he knew nothing in the shrooms had the effect of restoring anything.

But thinking about it further, it did kind of make sense. While not containing a lot of it, the mushrooms most certainly did hold some mana. And him consuming them with the skill must mean that he directly devoured the mana within.

Feeling renewed, he began attempting to make his second successful health potion. He wanted to try making poisons soon, considering it was kind of the focus of his profession and all. But he decided against doing so before he got a chance to eat some moss... something he was most certainly not looking forward to.

He did try to eat some lavender too. They tasted like shit and didn't give him any knowledge. So the skill did indeed only work on toxins.

After cleaning the mixing bowl, he poured water into it before adding some Evergreen Grass. The flowers only came in later after the grass was correctly saturated with mana. That part of the process went relatively easy, far more so than before, and he quickly got to the point where he put in the red lavender.

This was the part that often stumped him. You had to inject mana into the herbs rather quickly, or it would ruin the mixture. But too fast, or done wrong, the batch would also go bad. But once again, the ease of the process surprised him.

A couple of minutes later, he stood with another successful batch, even resulting in four bottles. Without hesitation, he got started on another round and was once more met with success, only resulting in three potions this time. But it did confirm it wasn't a fluke.

Two or so hours later, and a good number of potions, he was once more greeted with another level.

> *'DING!' Profession: [Alchemist of the Malefic Viper] has reached level 6 - Stat points allocated, +2 Free Points*

As always, he put the Free Points into Wisdom. At this point, his Wisdom had become his second-highest stat, only behind Vitality.

He brought up his stat page, feeling rather pleased. He thought about how nice it would be to see his skills on the menu, which it surprisingly just... did.

Status
Name: Jake Thayne
Race: [Human (G) – lvl 7]
Class: [Archer – lvl 9]
Profession: [Alchemist of the Malefic Viper – lvl 6]
Health Points (HP): 510/510
Mana Points (MP): 324/480
Stamina: 247/270
Stats
Strength: 30
Agility: 33
Endurance: 27
Vitality: 51
Toughness: 23
Wisdom: 48
Intelligence: 18
Perception: 46
Willpower: 32
Free Points: 0

Titles: [Forerunner of the New World], [Bloodline Patriarch]
Class Skills: [Basic One-Handed Weapon (Inferior)], [Basic Stealth (Inferior)], [Advanced Archery (Common)], [Archer's Eye (Common)]

> **Profession Skills:** [Herbology (Common)], [Brew Potion (Common)], [Concoct Poison (Common)], [Toxicology (Uncommon)], [Malefic Viper's Poison (Rare)], [Palate of the Malefic Viper (Rare)]
> **Race Skills:** [Identify (Common)], [Endless Tongues of the Myriad Races (Unique)]
> **Bloodline:** [Bloodline of the Primal Hunter (Bloodline Ability - Unique)]

He had gotten a lot more skills since he'd entered the tutorial, and it was oddly satisfying to see his growth laid out before him like that. He was still doubtful if just dumping everything into Wisdom was the correct decision. Perhaps it was in this dungeon, but assuming he survived the challenge, he would barely have grown in his Strength, Agility, and Perception.

But then again, it was still early days. Poisons were bound to increase Jake's offensive prowess significantly.

As he was pondering on the future, he felt a rumbling in his stomach. A rumbling that quickly got worse. This was the moment where Jake learned why this dungeon had a toilet.

Turned out that eating a bit over a hundred mushrooms and having that be your only diet for two days wasn't the healthiest of diets. What followed was Jake spending the better part of an hour stuck on the toilet, contemplating his prior mushroom-eating madness. He hoped the moss would be gentler on his bowels.

After the less than pleasant experience, he also learned why the bathroom came with a shower. Because he sure as hell needed one.

Before the tutorial, he'd been the kind of person that took a shower pretty much every day. If he went to the gym or had done a lot of archery, it often resulted in two that day. During holidays, he could get a bit lazy about it, but he doubted he had ever been dirtier than these past few days.

The positive part of his toilet tour, however, was his stomach feeling way less stuffed. He was not quite ready to eat the moss, but he was getting there. The mental exhaustion was also starting to get to him. His need for sleep had been significantly reduced, but he still had to rest occasionally.

With that in mind, he grabbed the book Poisons: The Elementary and went to bed. When he woke up again, he would make some more potions, eat some moss, and finally get started on concocting poisons.

Chapter 25
Enjoying Life

Jake had never been a huge fan of salads. He could do cucumbers, tomatoes, and a bit of lettuce in a burger here and there, but the mere thought of living off salads was horrifying to him. One should understand why he didn't find his current meal the most pleasant with that in mind.

He was currently sitting in the library with a bowl in front of him filled with water and moss. He had tried to eat the moss, but it was honestly disgusting. Not the taste—it was fine—but the texture and the aftertaste of dirt.

Instead, he plucked it, rinsed it with water, and used the cleaned mixing bowl to eat from. It was a rather disgusting-looking soup. He didn't even have a spoon, so he had to use his hands to eat out of it.

However, the torturous meal was made acceptable by the feeling of knowledge and improvement from eating it. It was the same as with the Flytrap Mushrooms, though he made sure to control himself and not overeat.

After his wonderful meal, it was back to making potions. He had started alternating between health and mana potions to break the monotony. Not that it mattered much. He was also considering if he should give making stamina potions a shot, but according to the books, it was quite a lot harder than both health and mana. And not by a little either.

Stamina potions were essentially a mix of health and mana from a methodological standpoint. Quite honestly, the book's explanations were quite terrible, and Jake had no desire to attempt it currently.

One good thing about his improved Wisdom was that he no longer needed to take notes. By now, he could easily remember everything. It was kind of weird and a bit scary when he thought about it more in depth. He had not felt anything immediately, even when gaining a lot of Wisdom at once, but it had changed him without a doubt.

He already knew that the system could directly implant knowledge, and it could obviously also improve memory. Jake had always had a relatively good memory, but now he could verbatim recall the page numbers of where everything stood in his alchemy books.

And if the system could implant both knowledge and make his memory that much better, what was to say it couldn't change something more fundamental? His Intelligence stat had also been improved quite a lot, but he hadn't felt anything directly from that. Something that he was still unsure whether to be assured or concerned about.

For some reason, he found his Bloodline far less scary, even though it clearly was the thing introduced by the system that had affected him the most. But he was aware of it doing so. He had let his Bloodline affect him; he had allowed his improved instincts to take charge during times of danger. In essence, he felt like his Bloodline wasn't changing him, but merely bringing forth who he was in a more primal and instinctual form.

But ultimately, did such existential worries even matter in the grand scheme of things? If he had been changed, he would have no way of knowing. He remembered Descartes saying *"Cogito, ergo sum*—I think, therefore I am"—and he was undoubtedly thinking far too much, so he most certainly existed in his own mind. Also, damn, the extra Wisdom made him remember random quotes.

Never mind that tangent—back to potions. Jake had needed to refill the barrels of purified water a few times already, but after his meal, he had to do so yet again. It was kind of insane that he could carry an entire barrel filled with water. It was with some difficulty, but it still clearly showed that his strength had reached superhuman levels, especially considering the difficulty mainly stemmed from how unwieldy the barrels were.

After filling the barrels and cleaning the bowl after his mossy meal, he jumped right back into it—there was an entire day of mixing ahead of him.

William walked through the forest, alone as always. Richard had gotten a bit annoying the last few days, but it was not time yet. The man still had time to grow. William also still needed him, or more accurately, what his camp could offer.

The teenager smiled as he saw a group of big molerats. He knew these things had some annoying sound attack that hurt like shit, but they were pretty weak defensively.

He took out his wand, an item he had found within the first couple of hours after he got here. He had been with a group of nine others, just like everyone else apparently had.

He had no idea who any of them were. But then again, he hadn't really known that many people before the tutorial either. His parents and his psychiatrist mainly. Oh, and the workers in the center, but they were all massive assholes.

To be fair, though, pretty much everyone was a waste of space. Everyone was either obnoxious, pretentious, or just plain old annoying. So, William had always preferred activities where no one bothered him.

Looking at the molerats, he knew that he had to wait for an opportune time to strike. And strike hard he would. Admiring the wand that made this all possible once more, he only got happier.

> [Exceptional Wand of Ferroras (Uncommon)]
> – A wand crafted by followers of Ferroras, God of Iron. The wand is made of a special kind of iron, only found in mana-rich areas. Grants the ability: [Metal Manipulation (Uncommon)].
>
> Requirements: Lvl 5+ in any class or race. Metal affinity.

This wand had been his bread and butter since he'd become able to use it, due to the skill attached. He'd discovered a box when he was bathing in a lake after seeing something glitter at the bottom. Diving down, he had found this wand. He'd been a bit sad that he could not use it right away, though. He'd needed a few levels, first using the terrible mana bolts. When he finally reached level 5, he was able to use the wand and see the ability.

> [Metal Manipulation (Uncommon)] – Allows for control of metallic objects by spending mana. This skill falls under elemental manipulation, a prevalent brand of magic throughout the multiverse. Adds a small bonus to the effect of Metal Manipulation based on Intelligence.

In concert with the many daggers he carried in his robe, this skill allowed him to dominate pretty much everything he met. His only weakness was his lack of healing outside of health potions, which was why he even bothered with Richard and his group. Oh, and his high mana consumption in combat, but he was sure that would get better with time.

His thought process was interrupted as he spotted his chance to strike. The molerats had jumped a group of badgers, allowing William to also make his move.

Focusing, he lifted the wand as seven daggers flew out of his robe and toward the closest rat. Their speed and power were far more potent than if he had simply thrown them. The daggers hit the rat in its head, cutting it to pieces.

Before any of the other rats could register that had happened, the daggers spread out, hitting the three others in their throats before they could do their screech.

The rats made gurgling sounds as they charged toward him. Raising his wand, he cast a spell toward the ground as a metal board appeared before him, blocking the rats' charge and obscuring their vision. At the same time, he lifted himself off the ground as he shot backward.

After killing a medium warrior, he had started wearing the chestpiece he had looted off the man. It was hidden beneath his robe. While it was expensive as hell to lift his whole body off the ground, it gave him excellent mobility.

THE PRIMAL HUNTER

As he dodged around, blocking off the rats with the metal barrier and having the daggers penetrate the rats over and over, he felt quite wonderful.

As his mana was starting to get dangerously low, the last molerat fell to the ground, never to move again. Checking his notifications, he was delighted to get another level.

> *You have slain [Molerat Screecher – lvl 14] – Bonus experience earned for killing an enemy above your level. 1500 TP earned*
>
> *You have slain [Molerat Screecher – lvl 16] – Bonus experience earned for killing an enemy above your level. 2000 TP earned*
>
> *You have slain [Molerat Screecher – lvl 16] – Bonus experience earned for killing an enemy above your level. 2000 TP earned*
>
> *You have slain [Molerat Screecher – lvl 15] – Bonus experience earned for killing an enemy above your level. 1750 TP earned*
>
> *'DING!' Class: [Caster] has reached level 17 – Stat points allocated, +1 Free Point*

Finding high-level beasts was still somewhat tricky, in his opinion. He had killed a good twenty-plus beasts above level 14 to get from level 16 to 17. Richard kept refusing to go further into the forest, which made William really wish for some kind of healing skill at level 20.

At level 5, he had gotten [Basic Stealth (Inferior)], at 10 [Conjure Iron Wall (Common)], and at 15 [Metallic Sight (Uncommon)]. The Iron Wall was the skill he had used in the battle before, and the Metallic Sight was the passive skill that made his entire style possible. It let William "see" through the metal he was manipulating, allowing his flying daggers to act as really shitty, yet still usable, eyes.

The only annoying thing was that he had to "attune" to the metal he was manipulating. In other words, he had to fill any metal he wanted to control up with mana, linking it to him. This was done super easily with random unranked metal but was pretty much impossible for enchanted stuff. Well, he could still do it, but the mana consumption was insane and not worth it.

It was not that it made the skill terrible in any way; it just sucked that he couldn't make a warrior cut his own head off with his sword. Oh, or make arrows do a one-eighty and hit the archer. However, the saddest was his inability to lift a medium or heavy warrior up and smash them down again, or maybe use them as living wrecking balls.

The skill was also quite mentally taxing. When he'd first gotten it at level 5, he could only control two daggers at once, and lifting even a set of armor was challenging. By now, he could do seven daggers comfortably but could push it to eight in a pinch, though it would hurt his versatility in using his Iron Wall and his own movements.

The skill was amazingly good in open combat, but he felt it worked even better at stealthily killing. Picking up Basic Stealth had been a lucky coincidence.

The group of ten he'd arrived with had been filled with the usual pieces of shit—pretentious idiots who kept talking about bullshit. None of them understood that things have changed. No, they were merely background characters—unimportant fodder for the true players in this new world.

This new reality was clearly a game made real. William had enjoyed games and books his entire life. He understood the genre. One had to embrace the system, game it where possible, but otherwise, follow its rules and abuse them for the maximum potential. It was all about min-maxing.

And yet those bloody fools kept talking about working together, staying safe, finding other humans, and finding somewhere to hunker down for the entire tutorial. Didn't they understand this was a golden opportunity? This tutorial was the easy starting area that would give one a kickstart before entering the real game.

William was not a delusional idiot who believed this world to be fake. It was obviously real. Real, and yet still a game. Which was why he had decided to think of it as an ultra-realistic virtual reality MMORPG with permadeath. So far, he had never been proven wrong in that assumption.

His initial group of ten had quickly outlived their usefulness, as the only useful person, a healer, ended up dying due to their own stupidity. A light warrior had also died, so William gracefully offered to carry his daggers if anyone needed them later. The first fight after he reached level 5, one of the other casters had suspiciously died, stabbed in the back of the neck by a dagger.

But dear William had been standing right beside the archer leading their group, so it couldn't possibly have been him. With the seed of discord planted, he'd managed to easily split the group. A little word here and there about how the third caster had asked for one of the daggers he had been carrying earlier, and then afterward finding it in said caster's satchel had only sealed the deal.

ENJOYING LIFE

It was like screwing with stupid NPCs in an otherwise well-made game. It took him only a couple of hours to kill all of them; no one had suspected the small and scared teenager. Well, except the archer at the end, who in his very last moments seemed to finally see through him. Not surprising, considering they were the last two alive.

The idiot had yelled a couple of vulgar obscenities before he, too, died.

Looking back, that first day had, without a doubt, been the best in William's nineteen years of life. Everyone had always treated him like shit his entire life, no one ever *getting* him. The worst part was that some of them even thought something was *wrong* with him.

Oh, how he had wished he could just get rid of that stupid teacher who kept pestering him in school. But he knew he couldn't. At least not without getting caught. The rules of society had held him back for so long, limited him in so many ways.

But here? No police, no law enforcement, no shrinks or therapists, no drugs being pumped into your system day in and day out to try and make you "normal." The system had fixed all the harm the drugs were doing, restored his body and soul, freeing him.

Entering that tutorial had felt like waking up from a long, hazy dream. But now William was awake, and he was aware. He understood his new reality far more so than he ever had the old one.

Currently, he was quite a bit of distance away from Richard's camp. He still needed them for now, as they had a healer and all, and some of the professions that people had started acquiring turned out to be very useful, allowing him to get his clothes fixed and cleaned.

After walking a bit, having recovered a good portion of his mana, he saw movement out of the corner of his eye. Crouching down, he snuck closer, raising one of his daggers with metal manipulation and using it to see what was going on. Three silhouettes were at a small pond—two in the water, and one person standing guard, it seemed.

The Metallic Sight skill was not good enough to see any details. But it looked like no one was looking William's way. Looking from behind a tree, he saw two females who were not wearing anything in the water, with a third woman standing outside the water in a full heavy warrior outfit.

Looking around further, he spotted a robe and a cloak folded at the edge of the water—one caster robe and one archer cloak.

No healer, huh, he thought, disappointed. He didn't recognize any of them, and a quick look around with his Metallic Sight and a dagger spotted no one else in the area.

Oh well, no reason to keep them around, he thought. The system did say that the final reward from the tutorial was based on the number of survivors. He had read that as the fewer survivors, the better. Also, humans were so much easier to kill than beasts, honestly. Because they had one fatal weakness...

As he was preparing to strike, the heavy warrior, for some reason, turned around and looked straight at him.

"Who are you!?" the woman yelled in an annoyingly loud tone.

William knew he was spotted, so he didn't try to hide. No, he could do far better than that. "I am so sorry, miss! I got lost after my team got attacked, and I thought I heard someone."

He spoke with deliberate shyness in his voice. This "shy, vulnerable kid" act worked well with older females. And work it did.

The warrior's gaze visibly softened as she saw him acting incredibly scared. "Oh, I see," she said in a calming tone, as William spotted the two naked women now getting dressed, both looking very flustered.

He estimated them to be around his own age, and likely related to the warrior based on their looks. Their mother? Aunt? It didn't matter. He started walking toward them cautiously, bit by bit, as the woman spoke again. He made sure to shiver slightly with every step. It took a long time to get that one down.

"Do you know where your team went? What attacked you?" the warrior asked as she got a little closer.

William acted scared at her coming toward him, backing away with big steps and staying in character.

"It's okay, we're not going to do anything," she said, stopping.

"O-Okay," William stammered as he stopped backing off. The woman kept walking closer to him until she got to the spot where he had backed off from.

From below the leaves, four daggers flew up, startling the woman. All of them found purchase in the gaps of her armor before she even had a chance to react. A fifth dagger simultaneously flew out of William's robe, hitting the woman in the face and killing her instantly.

The two other women were still only halfway dressed when more daggers flew for them, and they only managed to give out brief screams as the daggers struck them. They tried to defend, but neither of them had their weapons ready. It didn't take long for both of them to fall to the ground, their half-naked bodies covered in cuts.

After making sure they were all dead, William checked his notifications, disappointed. The warrior had been only level 10, with the two younger ones at 9.

"What a waste of time," he muttered to himself as he looted their remaining potions and the archer's dagger.

"Oh well, better luck next time," he said, smiling at the three mutilated corpses as he turned for the trek back to Richard's camp. His mana was beginning to get a bit low, so he would have to take a break. Sadly, the caster didn't have any mana potions left.

He could not help but whistle a happy little tune as he walked. True, it didn't reward much to kill the three of them, but it was kind of fun. Oh, how he loved this new, wonderful world.

Chapter 26
More Skills!

As he lay on the bed, Jake was proud of his progress for the day. He had mixed so many potions that he eventually had to just dump the mixtures in the sink. It was so incredibly wasteful, but he just didn't have anywhere else to put them.

While there were undoubtedly many bottles, they were far from unlimited. He was reusing the bottles after he drank the mana potions, but said potion consumption had fallen to nearly nothing after Jake had gotten his Palate of the Malefic Viper.

It wasn't that he was entirely out of bottles; in fact, he had many left. He just knew that the potions he currently made wouldn't be things he wanted to save. He also didn't know where to store them. Pretty much every surface in the lab was filled with potions.

During the day, he had also eaten two new kinds of mushrooms, one called [Reddot Stool], a small white mushroom with red spots on it, and the other identified as a [Brunneius Aqua Mushroom], a brown mushroom found growing from small puddles in the damp cave. Both were naturally inferior rarity.

Overall, his day had resulted in quite the progress.

'DING!' Profession: [Alchemist of the Malefic Viper] has reached level 7 – Stat points allocated, +2 Free Points

'DING!' Race: [Human (G)] has reached level 8 – Stat points allocated, +1 Free Point

'DING!' Profession: [Alchemist of the Malefic Viper] has reached level 8 – Stat points allocated, +2 Free Points

'DING!' Profession: [Alchemist of the Malefic Viper] has reached level 9 – Stat points allocated, +2 Free Points

'DING!' Race: [Human (G)] has reached level 9 – Stat points allocated, +1 Free Points

The only significant difference was that he had decided to save the Free Points. The Wisdom seemed to barely add anything to his mental capabilities at this point, and he was unsure if any other stat would help him in any way at the moment. He had considered Willpower and Endurance, hoping that it would allow him to stay awake longer and reduce the mental exhaustion.

But for now, he would save them. He was very close to level 10 in his alchemy class, at which point he would likely unlock another skill or some other benefit. So he had decided to wait for the last level.

He had finished the book on elementary poisons and the two basic alchemy books, and had decided that he was ready to give concocting poisons a try the next day. He had eaten the shrooms and moss he needed as ingredients, and he had even found a book describing recipes.

MORE SKILLS! 31

Said recipes mentioned the Reddot Stool and Brunneius Aqua Mushroom, which was why he had decided to munch on those.

After getting up from his bed, he headed straight for the cave to collect a good batch of mushrooms and moss. And with that, he got to work. In retrospect, Jake wasn't sure it could even be considered work, considering how easily it went.

Concocting poisons and brewing potions shared a lot of similarities. The mana injection and mixing were essentially the same, with only a few minor differences here and there. The most significant difference was the requirement to squash any elements of vitality within the ingredients while simultaneously amplifying the damaging properties.

When making health potions, the direct opposite of poison, one had to simply bring forth the already existing vital energies found within the herbs. That same vitality was found to a lesser degree in poisonous plants. They were living entities too, after all.

This vitality would lower the effect of the poison, and sometimes even wholly ruin the concoctions. This made Jake consider the silver mushrooms he had that gave Vitality when consumed. In one of the books, such cases were described, where the poison and Vitality reacted together, empowering one another. This could then go in either direction, either becoming extremely toxic or overflowing with Vitality.

Due to such ingredients' overpowering nature, new alchemists were generally recommended to stay the hell away from attempting to use them, not to waste such precious natural treasures. Reading it did give him an idea for later, but that idea was for way later.

Currently, Jake was not mixing ingredients that were hard to use. He was mixing the Reddot Stool and Brunneius Aqua Mushroom and the green moss in the mixing bowl. All of the components floated in the purified water.

Purified water was used for pretty much every kind of liquid poison. It was wholly uncontaminated and was nothing more than filler. All it did was dilute the mixture a bit, but that was about it.

The mixing itself went easy, as he had the methods described in the books memorized, and when he got to the more challenging parts of the mana injection, he was almost dumbfounded by how easy it was.

By now, making mana potions was incredibly easy for him, and he barely had to focus when brewing them. But the ease and familiarity he currently felt were incomparable. It felt like he had worked with the ingredients thousands of times before. The moss and mushrooms felt like an extension of his own body, quickly absorbing his mana and doing what he wanted, when he wanted.

The entire thing only took minutes before he was greeted by a collection of very welcome system messages.

You have successfully crafted [Weak Hemotoxic Poison (Inferior)] – A new kind of creation has been made. Bonus experience earned

'DING!' Profession: [Alchemist of the Malefic Viper] has reached level 10 - Stat points allocated, +2 Free Point

He had not expected to get a level-up so fast again. Not that he was going to complain about it. Inspecting his new creation, he was thrilled with the result.

> [Weak Hemotoxic Poison (Inferior)] –
> Increases bleeding on afflicted entities
> and makes any injuries harder to heal. The
> poison must be introduced directly into the
> bloodstream to have any effect.

According to the books, the poison was a weak type of poison that disrupted the afflicted's usual bodily balance, thinning the blood and increasing blood loss. It also, like the dagger he had, made healing the target harder. Overall, it was not a very powerful type of poison. Still, considering his current strategy in battle, where a lot of it revolved around kiting and slowly bleeding the opponent out, he didn't doubt its effectiveness.

He stored the poison in a rectangular bottle with a big bottleneck. While there were far less of this type of bottle than the regular potion bottles, there was still a cabinet containing a few hundred. This kind of bottle was designed to dip arrows, needles, and daggers into, soaking the weapon in the poison. He believed this would become very relevant when he got out of this Challenge Dungeon.

The level also came with the expected notice of new skills.

> *Alchemist of the Malefic Viper profession
> skills available*

He had five skills available. Looking at the five skills, he used the same approach as the last time he'd been offered skills and went through them one by one.

> [Transmute (Inferior)] – Transmutation is
> an ancient art used by alchemists since the
> beginning of time. Allows for the alchemist

> to attempt to transmute types of metal into ones of greater value. Must have suitable materials. Transmute does not require any additional tools or equipment, but the skill's effect can be amplified using certain catalysts. Adds a minor increase to the effectiveness of Transmute based on Wisdom.

This one was, without a doubt, nice. But totally not in Jake's lane at all currently. He was all about potions and poisons. It could prove useful down the line, but for now, it was not for him. Making gold from iron did seem awesome in the real world, but he doubted if the skill would have any use in curing him of the poison in his system. Also, who would even care about gold if people could go around making it? Basic economics, yo.

Thus, he swiftly moved on.

> [Graft Plant (Common)] – Sometimes, two plants are greater than the sum of their parts, and the perfect plant may be created, not found. Grants the ability to graft plants. Plants must be compatible. Must have suitable ingredients and equipment to facilitate the grafting of plants. Adds a minor increase to the effectiveness of Graft Plant based on Wisdom.

This one also did seem very cool, and he had read about the art of grafting plants in several of the alchemy books. Most plants could be found naturally in the world; what had surprised Jake, however, was that the system had not created the majority of them. Many plants found had initially been created by alchemists grafting something into existence more suitable for their needs.

The system had over time then integrated these plants into ecosystems, naturally growing them around the multiverse. The author of the book was unsure about how the system did so, but its involvement was inarguable, as plants even seemed to spread to other universes.

This had inevitably led to many not knowing which plants were system-made and which ones were grafted by alchemists. Jake did not know how old the multiverse was. He knew that his universe, according to modern physics, was thirteen-point-four billion years old or so. He also remembered that the system had said that his universe was the ninety-third to be introduced to the system. The other universes being older was a fair bet, in his opinion.

But despite the exciting thoughts of time and grafting, Jake quite frankly had no use for it currently. It was described as a rather advanced type of alchemy in all the books, and something novices should avoid. The main reason for grafting, a lack of suitable ingredients, wasn't an issue with him having his own garden and cave, both still nearly full despite his use over the last days. So unless he wanted to become a master grafter, he wasn't going for it.

So, with that in mind, he moved on to the next skill.

> **[Alchemist's Purification (Common)] – Attempt to purify any alchemical ingredient. Purification can help remove unwanted properties from a component, making the finished mixture purer. Must have suitable ingredients. Must have suitable materials. Purification does not require any additional tools or equipment, but the skill's effect can be amplified using certain catalysts. Adds a minor increase to the effectiveness of Alchemist's Purification based on Wisdom.**

Another handy skill. Jake assumed this was what had been done to the water he used in his alchemy, considering the name Purified Water. If grafting allowed you to create your desired plants, this one allowed you to attempt to transform the ones you already had into something more useful.

Jake had no idea what effect the skill would have on his current ingredients, however. He did not need to purify any water as there was plenty of it, and thus far, he hadn't run into any issues with unforeseen properties within the plants he used. He seriously doubted he could cleanse the vital energy out of a living thing.

Once more referring to the books, this skill was mentioned extensively as one essential to all alchemists. A lot of herbs found throughout the multiverse were borderline useless. That, or they were highly specific for only obscure recipes. Thus, purifying some of these ingredients could allow them to be used in more types of creations.

This one was most definitely a contender, but he was still unsure of its usefulness currently. He knew that he would have to pick it up at one point, but as the six skills offered at level 5 were still on his list, he could just get it later.

The next two skills were very similar, much like the Sense Herb and Sense Poison skills.

[Germinate Herb (Common)] – Germinate an herb, allowing it to grow faster and increase its quality. Germinate Herb enables the alchemist to not wait the many years usually required for the necessary herb to mature. Germinate Herb does not require any additional tools or equipment, but the skill's effect can be amplified using certain catalysts. Adds a minor increase to the effectiveness of

> Germinate Herb based on Wisdom.
> [Cultivate Toxin (Uncommon)] – Cultivate the desired toxic ingredient, allowing it to amplify its deadly toxins. On poisonous plants, this skill will also enable said plants to grow faster and increase their quality. Cultivate Toxin does not require any additional tools or equipment, but the skill's effect can be amplified using certain catalysts. Adds a minor increase to the effectiveness of Cultivate Toxin based on Wisdom.

These were also quite amazing and frequently mentioned skills in pretty much all the books he had read on alchemy, both essential skills of an alchemist who dreamed of owning their own garden. The skills were especially interesting with their usefulness in leveling the profession.

Not all alchemists had the privilege of a fully stocked garden in a Challenge Dungeon when they first started out doing alchemy. Many started simply by tending gardens of senior alchemists. This was also how many achieved their profession to begin with. Some books even had the assumption that the reader had started out that way.

Of these, Germinate Herb was, without a doubt, the most mentioned. The use of potions throughout the multiverse was considered standard practice, and someone needed to grow the ingredients used. Jake also knew that many alchemists started with the Germinate Herb skill from the beginning.

Professions came in many forms and variants. One of the books on how to properly care for ingredients and tend the garden mentioned more than ten different types of the alchemist profession that could be unlocked from cultivating different sorts of herbs.

However, the most usual way of obtaining a profession was not through effort or hard work, but through being taught by someone already possessing said profession. But many senior alchemists still had their apprentices try and learn the craft themselves in the hope of them unlocking a more powerful variant from the beginning, or perhaps just one more specialized.

Jake's Alchemist of the Malefic Viper was one such variant. It was both more powerful and specialized in poisons compared to more traditional alchemists.

More powerful variants often offered better skills of higher rarity and gave more stat points per level. The downside was that, while they could often learn pretty much all types of skills commonly available, it would usually be at a lower starting rarity and/or at higher levels.

This was also shown by Transmute, for example, being inferior rarity, and the same with the Geology, Pill Consolidation, and Metallurgy skills at level 5.

Overall, however, there was a strong consensus that variant classes were just straight-up better. The stats alone made them far more valuable all on their own.

One aspect he still did not quite understand was the constant mention of something called Records. He had seen the same word used in his [Bloodline Patriarch] title and even in the Bloodline description itself. More powerful variant classes, especially named ones like his, came with inherited Records. While he had yet to see any explanation of what exactly Records meant, from what he could deduce, having many Records was a good thing. Or maybe high-quality Records?

This made him wonder if Records was a hidden achievement system or something—another mystery he had to solve when he eventually got out of the dungeon.

Back to the skills, he didn't hesitate before picking the Cultivate Toxin skill.

> *Gained Skill*: [Cultivate Toxin (Uncommon)] – Cultivate the desired toxic ingredient, allowing it to amplify its deadly toxins. On poisonous plants, this skill will also enable said plants to grow faster and increase their quality. Cultivate Toxin does not require any additional tools or equipment, but the skill's effect can be amplified using certain catalysts. Adds a minor increase to the effectiveness of Cultivate Toxin based on Wisdom.

He felt the slightly disorientating experience of having knowledge downloaded directly into his mind. The reason why he had chosen this skill was, to himself, quite obvious.

First of all, this was the only skill at uncommon rarity. Secondly, it went perfectly with the whole poison-themed profession. It was also perhaps the only skill Jake could immediately make use of during the challenge. He could use it to gain experience and spice up his day while trying and making more potent poisons with his ingredients.

Happy with his new skill, he prepared himself to get working once more. He still had a lot of work ahead of him.

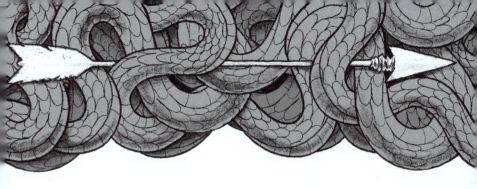

Chapter 27
Evolution

Jake got to work right away after waking up, concocting poisons like never before. The process kept getting easier and easier. After a couple of hours and a lot of poison later, he was a bit surprised by the lack of a level-up. It seemed like the experience gain had slowed down after reaching double digits.

However, one negative aspect of his increased speed was shown as his mana pool emptied. His pool was a lot higher by now, and he had honestly doubted that he would've been able to empty it with his daily poison-eating and regular mana potions.

Speaking of mana potions, it was about time he made some more. He still had a lot left, but their quality had a lot to be desired. His skills had increased significantly over the last couple of days, having learned a lot from both health potions and, of course, the poison. All of that was ignoring his increased stats.

Jake, with his increased mana usage and capacity, had tried to replenish it by eating his ancient rival. The blue mushrooms shone brightly in the cave, oblivious to the man walking toward them to devour as many as his stomach could handle.

Which turned out to be only one mushroom. Those damn blue bastards were full of mana, increasing his regeneration but also making him quite ill. His health points began ticking downward as he, for the first time, was actually poisoned. Luckily, it wasn't more than he could handle, and it did come with benefits.

Jake learned a lot about the mushrooms from that event. As it turned out, the poison in them was incredibly potent and had necrotic properties. This was obviously not a surprise to Jake, as necrosis was one of the most horrific things he knew of, quite literally rotting the flesh on a still-living being. For the mushrooms to have such an evil property was only natural.

He also had to reluctantly admit that the cursed shrooms tasted damn good, though. Not that he was going to eat any more just yet.

After a brief ingredient-collection run to the garden, he got to work once more, making mana potions. After making a few batches, he got right back to making poison. A couple of concoctions later, he finally got a level.

> *'DING!' Profession: [Alchemist of the Malefic Viper] has reached level 11 - Stat points allocated, +2 Free Points*

As he saw the message, he instantly noticed the lack of a race level, but before he could ponder it further, the system appeared once more.

> ***Race Evolution Requirements Met***
> Your body and soul have become accustomed to the energies found in the multiverse, allowing you to truly become a being of the new world. Evolution is a natural step for all multiverse entities, with nature and benefits associated with evolution dependent on all Records.
>
> **Begin Evolution now?**
> **Y/N**
>
> WARNING: Postponing evolution may have adverse effects, and no further race experience can be earned before the evolution is completed.

Well, that sure answered why his race hadn't leveled up. But thinking back, it made sense, considering what else he had seen so far in the tutorial. All beasts at level 10 and above got significantly stronger, so the same thing happening to humans was not out of the question.

But he was unwilling to spend a lot of time deliberating about the system's evolutionary process after seeing the last line. He still took minor precautions, leaving the laboratory, going to the bedroom, and sitting down on the bed.

Taking a deep breath, he agreed to the system prompt.

The second he accepted, his vision went black.

When he came to once more, he was in a black void surrounded by small bright dots. Inspecting them further, he noticed they were stars. Jake was suspended in what seemed like the middle of space as he felt his body slowly change.

Thinking back, this was possibly what had happened to him when he first entered the tutorial. The only difference was that he now was far more aware of his surroundings.

The seconds ticked by as he simply looked around and relaxed. His body felt numb, but he could still sense something changing within him. As he floated there, he also started to get a weird feeling. He felt *something*. He could not put his finger on what it was, but something was clearly present all around him in the blackness.

As he focused on the feeling, it only became more apparent. The feeling was oddly similar to the one he had when he examined the alchemical ingredients during his potion brewing. More specifically, the kind of energy he felt when making mana potions.

Suddenly, it clicked for him. This was mana he could feel. Mana was an ever-present aspect of the multiverse. Before, he'd only known it was there due to reading about its presence, but now he could finally feel it.

He had wondered if he was for some reason inept at it, as nearly all the books he had read had references to feeling mana and examining mana density as if it was something everyone could just do. It turned out he just needed to evolve.

The changes in his body had started slowing down by now. Jake had his eyes closed, testing his newly acquired ability to sense mana, when he suddenly felt something more. Within him, a change was occurring that wasn't purely the race evolution.

A vortex at his heart formed as it absorbed energy. Jake could feel the mana move and enter his body, but not where it disappeared to. It just entered a space somewhere around his heart. He felt like his heartbeat sped up, but physically it didn't. It was an inexplicable experience.

Then it all just stopped, and Jake's vision shifted as he found himself back on the bed in the dungeon once more. Not that he knew if his physical body had ever left the room, to begin with, or if it had all been some kind of out-of-body experience.

Jake did not feel any different, though. The only significant change was that he now could distinctly feel the mana in the air. It felt far less dense than up in the space-like area, but it was still easily discernible. But his body felt the same. Looking at the system prompt, it indeed did confirm the evolution, though.

> *Race Successfully Evolved*
>
> Human (F) – A newly initiated human having taken the first step up the evolutionary ladder. Your body has now become attuned to the energy of the new world. The human race is known as one of the most balanced and numerous races of the multiverse, being able to walk many different roads on their path to power. Stat bonuses per level: +1 to all stats, +5 Free Points.
>
> *'DING!' Race: [Human (F)] has reached level 10 - Stat points allocated, +5 Free Points*

The level-up bonus changes were minor, earning him just 4 more Free Points per level. He had gotten those four extra points with the level, though, meaning he now had 17 Free Points still not allocated. So that was kind of nice.

He had not gotten any skills from the evolution, but he did get one unforeseen benefit as he read the next message.

> *Bloodline Ability Evolved*

> The evolution has stirred your Bloodline, allowing it to evolve along with you.
>
> *Bloodline Ability Upgraded*: [Bloodline of the Primal Hunter (Bloodline Ability - Unique)] – Dormant power lies in the very essence of your being. A unique, innate ability awakened in the Bloodline of the newly initiated human, Jake Thayne. Enhances innate instincts. Enhances the ability to perceive your surroundings. Enhances perception of danger. +10% to Perception.

Not much of the description had changed, and focusing on his sphere did not show anything either. But then again, a big part of his Bloodline ability was either passive or only made itself known during a crisis. No, what had instead changed was the flat stat bonus to Perception. While an increase from 5 to 10% did not seem like a lot initially, it could get massive down the line.

Even more importantly, it indicated his Bloodline ability's possibility of growth. If it was 10% now with him only being F-rank, what was to stop it from getting far higher later on? It also quickly answered the question of where that extra vortex of mana came from. He was sure that was his Bloodline evolving.

With that in mind, Jake decided to simply dump all of his 17 Free Points into Perception. While it may not be the smartest choice in the short run, he believed it was the best on a long-term basis. It may also have been the euphoric feeling in his body he'd felt after the evolution messing with his head.

After he had put the points in, Perception instantly became his highest stat. Due to the immediate stat increase, he felt slight vertigo as all his senses improved, and he felt his Sphere of Perception grow both in range and quality.

It lasted for less than a second before everything was back to normal except for his improved senses. He opened his status window, happy with all the improvements.

Status
Name: Jake Thayne
Race: [Human (F) – lvl 10]
Class: [Archer – lvl 9]
Profession: [Alchemist of the Malefic Viper – lvl 11]
Health Points (HP): 660/660
Mana Points (MP): 610/610
Stamina: 300/300
Stats
Strength: 33
Agility: 36
Endurance: 30
Vitality: 66
Toughness: 31
Wisdom: 61
Intelligence: 21
Perception: 70
Willpower: 40
Free Points: 0

Titles: [Forerunner of the New World], [Bloodline Patriarch]
Class Skills: [Basic One-Handed Weapon (Inferior], [Basic Stealth (Inferior)], [Advanced Archery (Common)], [Archer's Eye (Common)]
Profession Skills: [Herbology (Common)], [Brew Potion (Common)], [Concoct Poison (Common)], [Toxicology (Uncommon)], [Malefic Viper's Poison (Rare)], [Cultivate Toxin (Uncommon), [Palate of the Malefic

> Viper (Rare)]
> **Race Skills:** [Identify (Common)], [Endless Tongues of the Myriad Races (Unique)]
> **Bloodline:** [Bloodline of the Primal Hunter (Bloodline Ability - Unique)]

Remarkable growth across the line. The only thing Jake felt bad about was Intelligence being his lowest stat by quite a bit. Not because he needed the stat for any of his skills, but more due to its sentiment. Well, at least he was a wise guy full of Vitality with exceptional eyesight.

Jake had to admit that the whole evolution felt a bit underwhelming outside of his Bloodline evolving. He imagined those without a Bloodline ability would find themselves quite disappointed by it. Or maybe he had missed something? Some hidden new power, or perhaps his evolution had gone wrong somehow?

The ability to sense mana was great. Yet that was mentioned as something one was meant to have from the beginning.

The thought kept nagging him. Luckily for him, he had a library with a wide assortment of books. While all of the books were on alchemy, many were also about random topics only tangentially related to the profession.

After going through the books for a good while, he found a couple of ones with potential. They were mainly about professions and leveling, but they did have parts on evolutions.

As he started reading, the word Records kept coming up more and more. One apparently needed to have "sufficient Records" to evolve one's race. The same went with upgrading one's class and profession.

However, what confused Jake was that it kept mentioning the first evolution for class, profession, and race were all at level 25. This was clearly not the case for him, though. He also found some interesting notes on how even the level 25 evolutions were unique, but it didn't elaborate.

He kept reading the books on the issue, and it was only after several books that he stumbled upon a side note in a chapter about the connection between mana sensitivity and race rank:

"... while evolutions and their associated level requirements have never known any credible cases of deviation, there is a rumor among some scholars that some races found in newly integrated universes have more evolutionary stages. F-stage is widely known as the lowest possible stage, but these new races start at a stage below even that if these rumors are to be believed.

It must be noted that none of these cases have ever been officially validated. However, it is hypothesized this has to do with the absence of mana in the newly integrated universe. According to the hypothesis, this stage may act as an adaptation period, allowing the new races to get used to mana. The origin of this train of thought is not known, but notable figures of the multiverse have commented on it.

This hypothesis truly gained traction when it was confirmed to be accurate by Reverend Izzshaldin of the 91st universe, one rumored to herself to be a new initiate. Many believe it to be accurate with endorsement from such a figure, despite the lack of any verifiable evidence. While a god's words are not to be doubted, it cannot be taken as the complete truth either. Especially considering the lack of comment from other prominent divines. For alas, only the divines may know the whole truth.

Once more, it must be emphasized this has never been confirmed. Many also question the possibility of a universe absent of mana ever existing. Even the most extreme cases of mana-starved areas have some remnants of mana remaining, and complete absence has only been observed in very severe cases. For an entire universe to be without it is therefore highly improbable, and honestly asinine to propose.

In conclusion, this rumor is likely to be just that—a rumor. An unfounded idea based on faulty logic and lack of understanding of mana. Mana is as essential to existence as the natural laws and the system itself, making it an insult to one's intelligence to propose a world without it."

As Jake finished the segment, he was quite amused. This researcher must have felt how scientists from Earth did when they heard someone propose that the Earth was flat. It was quite understandable that the book's researcher came off as a bit pissed for even having to address the claim.

It also explained the lack of mention in all the other books. If it only happened to the first generation of those integrated, there couldn't be many cases. Jake had a suspicion that immortality, or at least something close to immortality, was possible with a high enough level. However, he still had doubts about how many still lived from when the last universe was integrated. Heck, the book mentioned gods and divines, and if a god wasn't even immortal, it had to be a pretty sucky god.

With such a small sample size, it was apparent that it was considered a waste of time to address, according to most authors. Perhaps that would change now, with an entirely new universe being integrated into the multiverse.

Then again, there had to have been other integrations before.

Not that any grandiose thoughts of changing the mainstream evolutionary theories existed in Jake's head. For now, he had to deal with the small problems in life. Such as not dying from poisoning.

He sat up on the bed and put the books to the side. He had wasted enough time reading for today. It was alchemy time!

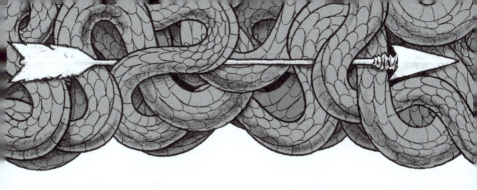

Chapter 28
Base-Building

Jake knew that he had some long days of alchemy before him. After looking at the dungeon challenge window, he exited the bedroom to the laboratory.

> Time remaining: 26 Days – 6:21:57

He had only spent a bit over three and a half days in this dungeon. He had, in his mind, plenty of time to find a cure, but not enough time to slack off. With his evolution out of the way and being completely refreshed from the process, he had no excuse not to get to it.

He had days of hard work ahead of him. No way he was going to die here. A plan was already beginning to form in his mind on how to pass the challenge. One he could only snicker at for its sheer stupidity. But sadly, the plan did not include him leaving early. He knew there was an entire tutorial going on outside, but that could wait. Jake couldn't help but think of his colleagues still outside and decided to check the tutorial panel.

> **Tutorial Panel**
> Duration: 58 days & 11:22:58
> Total Survivors Remaining: 754/1200

A bit more than a third had died by now. Jake dearly hoped that his colleagues were not among them. While he held no love for Richard, the guy seemed competent enough, and he knew that if Jacob was good at anything, it was getting in the good graces of others. He believed their chances were good unless something very unpredictable had happened.

Shaking his head, he threw the thought away. It was a waste of time to worry about others when he was already battling death. He would seek them out when he got out of there. For now, there was nothing he could do to help them in any way. The best way to help them was to help himself.

Determined, he cleaned the bowl, got the ingredients, and jumped right back into making more poisons and potions. He had a long grind ahead of him.

Jacob dragged his fingers across his chin, feeling the stubble that had now grown into a full-on beard. He hadn't had a beard for years now, always going with the clean-cut style. Not that he thought there was anything wrong with having a beard. He avoided one mainly for professional reasons as, while the company dress code did not directly prohibit beards, it strongly discouraged them. It was a silly rule, but the company directors were quite conservative and believed beards to be unprofessional for some reason.

Not that any of that mattered anymore. The world was fucked. Jacob did feel rather sour about having spent so many years climbing the corporate ladder for it to all turn out to be a massive waste of time. That time would have been better spent going to self-defense classes. Fencing or archery or pretty much any sport teaching minor combat skills would've been more useful.

He had never been a fighter. At least not in the literal sense. He had never been in a fight his entire life outside of maybe minor scuffles as a child. Instead, he'd focused on studying and excelling in academics. He'd graduated top of his class in university and become the youngest department chief the company had ever seen.

But now, in this tutorial, he was low on the ladder. As it turned out, Richard had owned a private security firm before the initiation and had come here with many of his employees. Of anyone Jacob had met so far in the tutorial, Richard excelled the most.

He was also the first one Jacob knew of that had evolved, and then afterward, to have also evolved his class. Jacob himself was only level 19 in his class still, but he had evolved his race. The entire race evolution thing was... perplexing.

When someone evolved, they would disappear for a few seconds before appearing again in the same place. The effects of evolution were also interesting. After evolving, one could vaguely feel something in the air. Some kind of energy. It didn't take long to conclude that this new energy was mana. Not that anyone knew what to do with this new mana sense.

By now, they had been in this damn place for only a bit over two weeks. Even in the beginning, Jacob had been well aware of his own lack of combat prowess, but it had only become more apparent. He wasn't the lowest level among his peers, but far from the top.

Out of the original ten, there were seven, maybe only six, left, as he had neither heard nor seen anything of Jake since he left their group.

Theodore had been the first among them to die. They had been fighting some more of those cursed badgers when he got unlucky and nearly tripped, allowing one of the beasts to bite into his neck. He had not died instantly, but they had run out of health potions. With no healer in sight... he'd bled out on their way back.

Caroline, the premier healer in the entirety of Richard's group, had not been with them at the time. In fact, they only had four healers in their entire camp, despite having already surpassed a hundred people. The highest leveled healer was Caroline, who'd upgraded her class a day or two ago.

According to all those who had, leveling got a lot slower once more after that. The first ten levels were relatively easy, then it got a bit more difficult between 10 and 25, and then even harder once more after that. Jacob had no idea what level Richard had reached, just that he was very likely still the strongest member of their camp.

The two other former colleagues that had died were Dennis and Lina. Jacob still remembered the two vibrant youths when they'd parted, both stronger than him at the time. Yet they'd died. And not by beasts either.

Another huge camp had emerged, with nearly the same amount of survivors as them. Negotiations had been going well for a while, and there were even plans of merging the two. Then Lina and Dennis' group had been ambushed by the other camp.

Afterward, everything had gone to shit for a while. Someone from Richard's camp must have taken the initiative on their own to strike back, as a group from the other camp also got wiped out, and from the state of the battlefield, it was clear that weapons had been used.

This had enraged the other faction, as they had adamantly claimed they had nothing to do with the first attack. Fights broke out daily after that.

Looking at the tutorial panel, it was depressing to see the number of total survivors falling by the day.

> **Tutorial Panel**
> **Duration: 49 days & 14:45:06**
> **Total Survivors Remaining: 599/1200**

The number of survivors dying had slowed down for a while after the first four or five days, but it still flared up on days where larger groups from the two camps encountered each other. On the worst day, twenty-one people had been killed between their two factions, and that was even excluding random deaths to beasts. Naturally, there were also other unaffiliated parties out there.

Both factions had, however, done a lot to attract survivors, such as smoke signals, casters shooting spells into the air, and more. It had worked for the most part, and was likely why their two factions were in such proximity. They had attracted one another.

Jacob was currently standing at one of the many fires spread around their camp. They had reached rather far inward at this point, and finding beasts below level 10 was borderline impossible at this point. Most in the immediate area were around level 20, but only a short walk away, one would run into plenty above level 25.

The reason for the growth was not only due to the change in geography. It was across the line that the beasts grew in level. Jacob doubted there even existed any beasts below level 10 in the entire forest at this point. While this was generally considered a positive aspect for those seeking to grow stronger, it was a clear negative for those merely wishing for survival.

Beasts once more grew immensely in strength at 25. It was manageable, as they also had people with classes above level 25, but for lower-leveled groups like his own, those beasts were formidable. Many of them had magical abilities or just incredibly powerful bodies.

The crafters, which they had come to call the ones focusing on professions, would not stand a chance if they faced any such beasts, despite many of them having decent levels.

Talking of professions, Joanna, who had been the first to get one, was still the highest-leveled crafter. While she was still a bit away from her profession upgrading at 25, she had gotten her race evolution at 10.

While many were disappointed by the evolution's effects, Joanna's case had been far from disappointing. Her leg had regrown. The wooden leg had simply been whisked away, and a newly formed leg had appeared.

She was far from the only individual with lasting damage or handicaps in their camp, and her case had given them all newfound hope, and given all those with professions vigor like never before. Even Richard had been very pleased and gone to congratulate her, offering for her to be the crafters' official leader.

Joanna had rejected it at first, but she eventually caved with the urging on from the other crafters around her. It had only been two days ago, but she held quite the political power within the entire camp by now, as professions' value had started to show. She had thrown most of her new responsibilities to Jacob, which he gladly took upon himself to be useful.

As a group, they had learned a lot about the usefulness of professions, with Jacob mainly in charge of gathering information on what people were now capable of. No one could make potions or anything like that, but some had gotten a cooking profession. The food cooked by them allowed wounds to heal faster, and many could even help the body fight off potential infections or poison. Other than that, the food tended to provide additional bonuses, like increased mana and stamina regeneration, the best of it even giving a temporary bonus to the Endurance stat.

The most noteworthy crafter of them all wasn't Joanna, though. It was one of the people who had joined their camp later on. He was a large man who had worked as a foreman in a steelworks before the tutorial, and was now a heavy warrior. As it turned out, the man even did smithing in his free time and had selected a hammer for a starting weapon, as it felt more natural in his hand.

With all those factors coming together, it was no surprise that the man had gotten the smithing profession. But more so than that, he was also a talented warrior. He had been the second person to evolve his race after Richard, and if Jacob's predictions were correct, he was currently the highest leveled when it came to race in their entire camp, despite not having upgraded his class yet. However, he was likely still above level 20 in his class. Even with professions taking longer to level, Jacob deemed him still to be around level 14 or 15 in that, if not even higher.

Jacob didn't know the man's name; he just went by The Smith. Without a doubt, he had proved himself invaluable as time went on, and many of their weapons started to require repair. Many upgrade tokens had been found, giving the equipment Self-Repair, but it only accounted for less than a fourth of their weapons and armor.

A smith could temporarily improve weapons and armor, and according to The Smith, he could also permanently increase their performance if he had the right materials. He did all of the work for free due to the experience he gained from doing so, which made Jacob consider the impact a leveling system would have had on the labor market pre-system.

Throwing the thought away, he started walking over to his cabin. The cabin had been constructed by another one of the newly discovered professions, one going by the name of "builder." As the name implied, they could build houses and even possessed landscaping skills a bit reminiscent of earth magic.

Speaking of magic, Ahmed had managed to upgrade his class a few days ago. He had chosen to be a caster attuned to frost magic. After his evolution, he packed quite the punch, throwing out sharp shards of ice. On a side note, his new abilities were also quite useful for cooling down drinks and preserving food.

Of the six survivors in their group, only Jacob and Joanna had not gained a class upgrade. Bertram, who had been at Jacob's side through everything so far, had gotten to 25 earlier that same day and a class focusing on defense. Casper had also gone through his class evolution.

Casper never got comfortable with the bow and instead ended up getting the trapping skill at level 5. He still used his bow, but now mainly to lure his enemies into traps.

The reason Casper had leveled up before himself was due to the conflict with the other faction. Night raids had started happening four days ago, and Richard had increased the number of people on watch significantly—a job that was mainly given to the archers due to their high Perception and Archer's Eye skill.

BASE-BUILDING

What Casper had done was set up a lot of traps around their camp, and yesterday, that had borne fruit. He had singlehandedly killed four attackers above level 20 and captured two others.

Neither Jacob nor Casper liked the thought of killing others. One could understand why the archer had been shocked when he was awoken in the middle of the night to system messages telling him he'd killed people. When Casper had gone through his class evolution, he had been filled with negative emotions, and that seemed to now be reflected through his traps. Jacob would be lying if he said he wasn't even more worried after his friend's evolution.

Jacob himself had yet to take someone's life, something he hoped wouldn't change before this hellhole of a tutorial was over.

After checking in with some of the builders, he arrived back at his cabin. He opened the wooden door and was greeted by Caroline, who must have just returned from another excursion with Richard and his squad.

"Hey, how was the trip?" Jacob asked as he went over and sat on the bed beside her.

Caroline, leaning on his shoulder, answered, "The same as always. Did anything happen today? Is Casper doing better?"

"Yeah, he is holding up. We all are, I guess," he said after hearing the concern in her voice.

"It's going to be fine, Jacob. We're going to be fine." She snuggled closer to him.

Feeling her intent, he wrapped his hand around her shoulder as they both fell back on the bed, cuddling.

Another significant change was their relationship. Jacob had known that Caroline liked him as more than just a colleague for a long time. As her superior, though, he had chosen to try and ignore it, as fraternizing was never a good look. He also didn't want to subject her to his family politics.

But here, no one cared. So, when Caroline made her move, he had no reason to reject her. Jacob had never even considered her before due to their professional relationship. He had to admit that she was attractive, with the evolution at 10 only making her more beautiful. Perhaps it was just the suspension bridge effect, but he didn't really care at this point.

Caroline being the "breadwinner" in the relationship hurt his vanity a bit, but he could see the humor in how their roles had completely switched compared to how it would've been before the system.

There was a lot of bad to be said about Richard, but he treated the ones he deemed important well. With Caroline at the very top of his list, she was naturally treated extremely well. The fact that they had their own cabin for just the two of them was clear evidence of this.

Her status had trickled down to Jacob also being treated better, despite his lacking abilities in combat. Jacob was not a deadweight, however. When a camp grows to the triple digits, some amount of management becomes necessary.

One could say many things about Jacob, but if he was good at anything, it was management. This led to him being in charge of constructing the camp, making shifts, and keeping track of all their members. He was a bit disappointed he had not gotten a manager profession. He had been offered a skill related to management, though, despite being a tailor, which was a bit interesting.

Their camp had grown, not just in people, but also in complexity. With individuals able to become builders, cooks, smiths, and so forth, the need for a more permanent solution became necessary. A wall had been under construction for a few days now, traps were being laid out mainly by Casper and one other archer who had to upgrade his class, and several other plans were underway.

As he pondered, he looked at Caroline. She looked back at him, staring into his eyes. He smiled as he leaned in and gave her a peck on her forehead.

"Yeah, we'll be all right."

Chapter 29
It's Just Logical

The archer ran through the woods, feeling the wind whisk by as he made his desperate escape. This entire situation was so fucked up. He had gone out hunting with his regular crew like any other day the last two weeks. While that guy Richard and his camp had been causing trouble for them, it didn't normally disrupt his particular party's daily routine.

Their leader, some ex-military guy named Hayden, had told them to avoid hunting in the area in between their two factions. An order everyone gladly followed, as no one wanted to risk fighting other humans. While fighting beasts was dangerous, other humans were just a whole different kind of danger.

Yet they had still been attacked. And not by a group, but a single person. No, a goddamn monster. He had appeared out of nowhere, not said a word, and just started killing. Daggers were flying everywhere, and what seemed like a giant freaking sawblade that cut their heavy warrior in two, shield and all.

It was mayhem with blood and body parts flying everywhere. Luckily, he had been scouting ahead, being an archer and all. With zero hesitation, he had taken off after he saw half their group die. Yet it was for naught.

A dagger hit his leg as he stumbled, followed by another, and then another. His legs got utterly destroyed as he screamed out and tried to crawl away.

"Damn, you're fast."

The casual voice came from behind him as he turned to stare at the monster that had been chasing him—a young man with blonde hair and blue eyes staring back.

"Dude, come on, you didn't have to bolt off like that," the teenager said as he walked closer, a big, sinister smile on his face. "Do you know how much mana I wasted? Ah, forget it, just give me some good info, and I promise to let you go."

The archer's eyes, however, were glued to the small red bottle in his hand. A health potion.

The archer finally saw just the tiniest glimmer of hope as he bit through the pain from his mutilated legs. He started explaining everything he thought could be of the slightest interest. Even seemingly unnecessary side notes and comments. It was a torrent of information, as the archer just hoped that the monster would decide to spare him.

After a while of desperately throwing out words, the teenager finally raised his hand, motioning for him to stop.

"Well, I guess there was some useful stuff in all that senseless yapping," the blonde teenager said as he shrugged.

"I told you everything. Please just ask me about anything. I promise I will tell you whatever you want."

"Oh, it is quite all right. I think I got everything worthwhile."

The archer breathed out a sigh of relief as the slaughterer started to walk away from him. But just as he got his hopes up, another dagger flew out from underneath the teenager's cloak and hit the archer straight in the chest, penetrating all the way to the handle.

The archer coughed up blood as he stammered: "Y... ou...»

"Oh yeah, I lied. Sorry, mate; pretty gullible to believe I was gonna leave perfectly fine experience and tutorial points alone."

The archer only heard the first part before he passed away.

The teenager, William, walked away from the corpse without looking back, leaving the dagger in the man's chest. He wanted them to know the killer was human, after all.

William was slightly disappointed in the levels of this group. Only a few of them had their class evolutions, which led to a rather dull fight. More importantly, it also meant less experience and tutorial points.

Not that he had expected much, just more than that. At least the tutorial points were worth his time. Not that he knew what they could be used for yet. He just liked to see the number go up. He especially liked to compare how many points he had to those killed—an objective measurement of how superior he was to all of them.

For William, who was already level 32 in his class, killing a bunch of humans barely gave any experience. Still, it gave more tutorial points than killing several beasts at, or above, his own level. After level 10, one had to kill around ten or so beasts at their own level, while above level 25, they had to kill even more. Coupled with beasts over level 25 getting a lot stronger, it only made human-hunting even more worth it. The notifications did say he got extra experience from killing anything above his race level, but it honestly felt negligible.

William did admit that humans were far more dangerous in a straight fight, but they were also far more easily exploited. Their intelligence was both their greatest weakness and strength simultaneously.

What he had done held the same concept as how he got rid of his first group.

Richard and his flock had met another faction of roughly similar power and numbers. Around half of the remaining survivors were in those two camps combined, and more joined by the day, which was perfect for William.

Finding humans was perhaps the only thing harder than killing them. The forest was big, the beasts plentiful, and humans customarily grouped together. Having two figurative beacons attracting more humans made it significantly easier to keep track of them.

The merging talk was not ideal, so William decided to throw a small spanner in the works by wiping out one of Richard's squads, staging the battlefield beautifully to replicate what a big fight between two groups would look like.

He had then once more spread a few small rumors that the other faction had been behind it, putting on his naïve teenager act, easily convincing some of the middle-aged women working as crafters.

Of course, Richard had been skeptical, and talks had not broken down immediately, so William wiped out a group from the other faction too. That sure as hell sparked the flames.

Now there was a full-on war with daily casualties. While groups out hunting often avoided each other, they still got into fights if they did meet, and a few choice words were thrown.

Richard's plan to split up existing groups and spread them out, coupled with the system's selection method for entering the tutorial, ended up meaning that many had lost friends or family to the war. William didn't even have to incite violence anymore; it all happened naturally.

Which also meant that he could kill others as much as he wanted. As long as no survivors remained in the party, everyone simply assumed the other camp to be behind it.

William couldn't kill the more prominent groups in the double digits, but most were only five to six people, making them easy pickings.

He was still officially a member of Richard's faction, and he had even taken credit for a few kills, of course acting all shaken up and disturbed by having been forced to kill others.

The concept of acting all messed up just for killing someone was the natural reaction, after all. Something William hadn't been particularly good at the first time he killed, but he was nothing if not a fast learner. Now he saw himself as an experienced mourner after many hours of practicing.

Not that William didn't still find the whole thing stupid. Especially here in the tutorial. Some people took days getting over having killed someone. He remembered one of the archers, who was good at traps, acting like the world was ending just because his damn traps had done their job. What the fuck did he expect them to do?

William knew that he had to act illogically to fit in with others, though. As the saying goes, when in Rome do as the Romans do, and when among idiots, act like an idiot. Richard at least took killing people rather calmly, but then again, from what William knew, the man had prior experience killing people. Speaking of Richard, he couldn't help but lick his lips.

Without a doubt, the man was the one with the highest level and tutorial points besides himself. It would be glorious when he finally got to him. When it was finally time to cash in. For now, however, the man still had work to do, acting as an excellent little shepherd gathering more prey for him. He would have to bide his time.

It wasn't like he had confidence in just straight-up killing the man, especially not if he was with his entire squad. Everyone in that squad had their class upgrades, and William knew precisely how much of a boost that gave you.

William had evolved his class to become a [Metal Savant], which was a massive boost to pretty much everything. His existing skills got stronger, his control improved massively, and he even gained a few new skills. It also granted him the metal manipulation, meaning he didn't even need the wand anymore.

He could now even conjure a steel-like metal out of mana, which he mainly practiced by conjuring daggers. Which meant he didn't have to carry around a bunch of them all the time. He still kept a couple on him, as manipulating existing ones was less mana-intensive than making them.

Conjured metal also disappeared after a while, making it harder to stage fights. On top of that, it also took a lot of time to make just a single dagger, so he had to conjure what he needed before the fight. Of course, this was outside of other skills creating metallic objects, such as the shield he could make.

It helped that one of the skills his evolution had provided allowed him to absorb metal. He could then conjure said absorbed metal, the mana cost dependent on the quality and quantity of what he made, with the skill also able to reabsorb conjured metal, regaining some of the mana.

The third powerful new skill he had gotten was one that summoned a massive spinning disc of metal that he could send flying in a straight line. This was the one he had used to kill the heavy warrior earlier, and the thing packed a massive punch.

His only real weakness was that he still lacked reliable defensive methods. While he could conjure a shield and manipulate his movements by wearing metal armor, he would have loved to be able to turn his skin steel or something. Stealth attacks were a particular concern.

Not that he had experienced being stealth-attacked yet. The funny thing was that he could often just walk straight up to people and attack them. The idiots were gullible right until their deaths.

After a good thirty minutes, he finally made it back to camp, which by now was more a full-on base. Cabins were popping up every day, a wall of stakes was slowly being built, and campfires were everywhere. William had been assigned one of the cabins, which he shared with a bunch of the crafters.

William couldn't care less for all the silly politics going on in camp. The members deemed important got stuff first, and William had never gotten anything, which was to say he was not considered important. Just like he wanted it.

Well, he was a bit important. Richard was a sharp man, after all. He knew the teenager was not weak in any way. William seriously doubted the warrior knew much about him, just that he was one of the few people able to hunt alone.

He had even been invited several times to important meetings. He liked going to those and just listening in, throwing in either a neutral or naïve comment here and there.

Even when Richard so clearly probed him to reveal more about himself, he never made his real opinions known. William did answer all his inquiries, but kept up the persona he had so carefully crafted. He deemed it too suspicious not to answer at all.

William had, for many years, gone about pretty much everything wrong. He had thought one simply had to be themselves. But he now knew that you had to be what people expected of you. What they hoped for you to be. If they have a positive impression, enforce that impression, and if they have a negative one, try to disprove that assumption.

That was precisely what he'd done. He also knew he couldn't be too dull, or it would get suspicious. He had to be shy and yet competent enough to not be ignored entirely. Attempting to be too ordinary ends up being abnormal.

He'd had a lot of time back in the center to figure all this out. That was until he'd been thrown to another center where they thought the best thing was to try and fuck him up with drugs. They just had to "rehabilitate" him a bit and throw him back into society.

Though that never came to pass, as the tutorial happened.

He was still mad at himself for getting thrown in the first center to begin with. One mistake and everything had crumbled.

Shaking his head, he smiled to himself. None of that mattered anymore. No centers, no drugs, just him and an endless universe. In this new world, his abnormality was synonymous with strength—his "defects" were an ideal.

While thinking of the beautiful future ahead of him, he dozed off into a quick nap. Even with all the levels and evolution, one still had to sleep a bit once in a while. Only a couple of hours every couple of days, but you had to. It was not exactly physical tiredness, but the exhaustion of the mind. This need for sleep was reduced by every level and was significantly reduced in one go from the evolution.

Sleeping for only a couple of hours did more or less fully restore mana and stamina, though. So it was not entirely a waste of time, as mana and stamina potions were very rare at this point, with only a few remaining, all hoarded by Richard and his elite. Even William only had a few hidden, as walking around with dozens would quickly become a bit too suspicious.

Waking up, he instantly felt fully refreshed as he jumped out of bed, ready for more hunting. It was still in the middle of the day, so none of his cabinmates had come by the cabin while he slept.

Exiting the cabin, he got his routine started. First, he went to talk to the crafters, chatting them up and making friends, and all that other social stuff. He had to keep up appearances. Also, it was beneficial when it came to getting his needs expedited.

He finished it off with a quick trip over to The Smith, by far the most interesting camp member, besides maybe Richard.

He was also the most useful besides the healers. William made no secret that he had a skill to manipulate metal, so he made it a habit to ask The Smith to improve his daggers. He had even convinced the man to help modify the armor he had, making it lighter and more suitable for him. Apparently, from what he could gather, the man had a son around William's age.

Another weird, but nevertheless useful, sentiment humans had. William wasn't exactly sure why familial relationships had such an effect on people. He only knew that it did and that humans often got illogical and, therefore, easily manipulated when it came to family matters. He had learned that the hard way.

Not that William didn't see some logic in it. He understood why his parents had helped him and propped him up. They needed a caretaker and an income for when they became unable to get one themselves, which only made their actions all the more perplexing.

Getting his daggers back, he thanked The Smith, who once again tried to convince him to pick up smithing. It wasn't that William didn't want to, but he would rather level his class for now. Once his class level got higher, he would switch to leveling a profession to boost his race levels.

Making his goodbyes, he once more ventured into the forest to hunt some more. He had gotten some useful information off the naïve archer earlier and decided to act on it. The main objective was still to hunt beasts and gain levels, but finding a small group of other survivors would sure be a welcome addition to his total number of tutorial points.

Three hours later, he was fighting a giant buffalo-thing, naturally winning. It didn't seem to possess any special magical powers despite it being above level 25. It was just big and could take one hell of a beating. Besides that, though, it was easy to fight. This had ultimately led to the buffalo being every survivor's preferred prey, as less risk was associated with the hunt.

This mighty beast was mutilated by William's spinning metal disc of death. Like a sawblade, it penetrated into the beast, whirling as blood flew everywhere. The mana consumption was insane, but it only took a few seconds before the buffalo was cut in half at its midsection.

Continuing its flight, the disc penetrated slightly into a tree, and William stopped the spinning. A few seconds later, the disc started smoking and soon disappeared into nothingness—or, rather, into pure mana that reintegrated with the atmosphere.

William was still a bit baffled by the trees' strength, as he was utterly incapable of cutting them in two, only able to penetrate the bark. Though it was only some trees; others could be cut down easily like regular pre-system trees.

His critical thoughts on trees were sadly interrupted as he heard the sound of people talking. The noise of his fight had apparently been loud enough to attract others.

Smiling, he levitated himself up to a tree by lifting his metallic armor. He hid among some leaves, eagerly awaiting the survivors coming to investigate.

He could only lick his lips as he saw five people. None of them were from Richard's group, as he did not recognize them, though he had to admit he didn't quite know everyone.

As the survivors saw the beast that had been cut in half, they all stopped dead in their tracks. Before anyone could open their mouth, a giant spinning disc of metal flew out from one of the trees, cutting into their caster.

What followed was a mad scramble to get their bearings, which was ultimately in vain as daggers started flying at them from every direction, followed by another pair of metal discs. The archer only managed to get off a couple of arrows before he too fell, all of which were easily blocked by a wall of metal protecting the tree's crown.

William, pleased with the worthwhile ambush, jumped down from the tree as he looted the corpses. All had been 25 or above, and all had plenty of points. As he looted, he thought about how it still wasn't really worth killing humans for the experience. He really hoped tutorial points were valuable.

William didn't hate humans. He just didn't really understand them most of the time. He did hate how they often acted. Their illogical approach to nearly everything. How they made asinine decisions that a million studies could tell them were stupid.

If the tutorial hadn't encouraged him to kill them, he likely wouldn't even have bothered with it. He would just have been a good little boy and made use of them for free healing and crafting. But the system rewarded him for killing them, so he would kill them. The system wanted there to be the fewest number of survivors possible.

William could do that. He would make sure the number was as low as it could be. The teenager was also nothing if not ambitious. His final goal of how many he wanted to survive reflected that.

It wasn't personal; it was only business, pure logic to further himself and his strength. So he had concluded the optimal number of survivors to be...

One.

Chapter 30
Preparations for Evolution

Jake coughed as another batch turned utterly black, and the horrendous stench of the tar-like residue invaded his nostrils. Yet this one wasn't even that bad, as this was just one of many attempts at making his very first common-rarity poison, and his first tries had gone far worse. He hadn't managed to craft anything the last two days, though he had gotten a level at one point. It turned out that you didn't need to successfully craft something to get a bit of experience.

He had eaten and acquired knowledge about the common-rarity moss and the blue mushrooms. The poison he was trying to make was relatively simple, requiring only those two ingredients along with some water. Yet it was still far more complicated than anything he had made of inferior rarity by far.

After his evolution, he had gotten better at controlling his mana—a skill that only became more and more important the further one went with alchemy.

Doing alchemy was a bit like being a surgeon doing an organ transplant crossed with a chemist trying to mix up a bunch of acids, hoping it wouldn't all explode in his face. Mana was the only real tool to help one accomplish this. The mixing bowl merely served as a medium to channel mana into. On it was engraved thousands of minuscule runes that Jake didn't understand at all; he just knew it allowed him to shape and control his mana.

With mana, one had to extract the ingredients' valuable parts, integrate it into the mixture, and create a balance of sorts. Jake found it hard to explain, as a lot of it came down to feel. There wasn't really any comparable action back on Earth, except maybe some super-complicated puzzle games.

Another issue except the increased difficulty was mana consumption. Jake's plan of dumping his Free Points into Perception became unrealistic as his crafting abilities improved. As he got better, his mana expenditure increased immensely, and even with the many levels in his profession, adding a lot of Wisdom, he still started having issues.

The common-rarity poison and its mana requirements were even more insane. More than a thousand mana was spent every attempt. This meant that without a full pool of mana, Jake had no way even to attempt it.

The reason why he was so set on making a poison of common rarity was because of all the reading he had done on Records and evolution of classes, races, and professions. Difficult achievements or performing above what was expected of his current level resulted in more experience, but it also strengthened his Records.

Having lacking Records had many negative consequences. High Records, first of all, resulted in better evolutions of one's class, profession, and even race. Having insufficient Records could even result in one being unable to evolve or level at all.

In fact, lack of experience was often not the roadblock for most powerhouses in the multiverse. It was a lack of Records. One could technically level nearly indefinitely by only taking extremely low risks or even getting carried by others. For example, if one hunted beasts with protectors removing the hunt's danger, while they would still earn experience aplenty, no Records of value would be gained.

The same concept was naturally found with professions. Jake could technically keep churning out the easy inferior-rarity potions and poisons all day, just raking in the experience and levels with little to no challenge. This, however, would give him no Records of value.

Jake had no idea about his Records. Newly initiated universes were not exactly anything that was covered in any of the books. It talked a lot about relying on your inherited Records for the first evolutions. Higher evolved beings would pass down a portion of their Records, giving their children easy progress at the beginning and removing any roadblocks.

Something he seriously doubted he had. Everyone was G-rank after all, a rank lower than any that even existed in the multiverse. There was, of course, a chance that actions before the initiation had allowed some amount of Records to be acquired, but he doubted it was anything meaningful.

He did have some things going for him, though. Challenge dungeons were not something exclusive to the tutorial, but something found throughout the multiverse. The same thing was true for regular dungeons. Clearing these would often help to gain Records and was the go-to for many races and factions.

Another thing was his Bloodline. According to what he read, Bloodline abilities were weird, and there was no consensus about how they came about or why some had them, and others didn't. It was, however, well documented that Bloodlines did influence a person's Records. This wasn't surprising, as according to what he read, literally *everything* affected one's Records.

Bloodlines were also interesting for their genetic aspect as they were directly inheritable. The only element to appear on status screens, at least. Usual things such as personality traits, talents, and other genetic details like eye color and height worked a lot like before the system. It also stated that the more powerful the parent, the more powerful the child would naturally grow to be. He interpreted that as S-rank dragons not having F-rank babies, which kind of made sense.

All of the reading about genetics and Bloodlines naturally led to Jake wondering how the hell he had a Bloodline ability. It was known that Bloodlines could be obtained through some extremely, almost impossibly, rare system-created events, but other than that, it was entirely random. A child of a layman could be born with a Bloodline out of nowhere.

It was not like Bloodline abilities were rare, though. They varied immensely and came in many types. Most Bloodlines were even completely useless and sometimes even damaging. One example of a useless one was a Bloodline merely giving a weird hair color. The negative ones also varied widely. Some led to early deaths, like ones causing cancer-like growths simply killing the holder, while others were mere annoyances, such as passively giving off a terrible stench.

After having read all that, Jake was delighted with his Bloodline. At least it didn't seem to hold any inherently bad qualities. In fact, it seemed like an excellent Bloodline. As to how good, he had no idea. The book's examples were only bad, useless, or classified as giving only insignificant benefits. Those holding strong Bloodlines often didn't share the details of their abilities, which was rather logical, as openly advertising your strengths—and possible weaknesses—did seem like a bad idea.

Despite his Bloodline, Jake was still a bit worried about the whole Records thing. The importance of them was so apparent in all the books talking of levels and evolution. The uncertainty of potentially lacking in this paramount aspect of the system led Jake to try and go above and beyond and create a common-rarity poison before his first profession upgrade. One thing he was one hundred percent sure on was that his performance now would influence that upgrade immensely.

Even if it didn't pay off right away, at least it also helped him train his concocting skills far more than just spamming out weak poisons. He still had to survive this dungeon, after all.

Taking a look at the dungeon window, he noted that nearly half his time in the dungeon was over.

> **Time remaining: 15 Days – 6:21:57**

In this time, he had made significant progress. His profession had gotten to level 22, and he was getting very close to crafting the common-rarity poison. He just needed the last part down. By then, the evolution of his profession would be imminent.

Regarding evolution, it would likely be very uninteresting. A variant profession like Jake's was something called a legacy profession, which had a rather set-in-stone progression the first couple of evolutions. It didn't mean he couldn't be offered other types of professions or even alchemist variants, but it did mean he would lose some things if he did. Alchemist of the Malefic Viper was a legacy-line passed down in the Cult of the Malefic Viper to their young alchemists.

From what he had gathered, the cult was an ancient religion of sorts following the snake-turned-dragon he had seen on the mural after the second challenge. They mainly specialized in alchemy—more accurately, poisons.

The books he read were naturally also left by them. This whole place was like a section of one of their academies or temples, ripped straight out by the system and tucked into its own little dungeon.

Jake had first thought that the system had created everything found in the dungeon, but he no longer did. Most of the books had authors, there were scribbles and drawings in many of them, and handwritten notes were found nearly everywhere. Which led him to believe that the place was either taken from somewhere or perhaps simply copied. Naturally, he had no way to know.

However, he did know that today would be the day he succeeded in making the poison. He was in the zone, and all he needed was for his mana to regenerate fully. He had already used a mana potion and was currently eating some blue mushrooms.

PREPARATIONS FOR EVOLUTION

The Bluebright Mushrooms were the main ingredient of his chosen poison, after all. They were also very dense with mana, helping his recovery speed a lot.

An hour or so later, he was back to full. The bowl was cleaned, the ingredients ready. He had even used the Alchemist's Purification he had chosen at level 20. He was unsure if it had any beneficial effects, but he did it anyway.

Looking at the skill, he at least saw nothing negative in using it.

[Alchemist's Purification (Common)] – Attempt to purify any alchemical ingredient. Purification can help remove unwanted properties from a component, making the finished mixture purer. Must have suitable ingredients. Must have suitable materials. Purification does not require any additional tools or equipment, but the skill's effect can be amplified using certain catalysts. Adds a minor increase to the effectiveness of Alchemist's Purification based on Wisdom.

No book mentioned any negative side effects either when it came to using it on the moss or mushrooms. Over the last two weeks, Jake had read a lot of books. He must have gone through more than thirty so far, and there were still hundreds left.

Speaking of skills he had gotten, at level 15, he'd picked up Sense Poison since no new attractive options had come up. He was also slightly afraid of losing access to it after his profession evolved, so he decided to take no chances.

[Sense Poison (Uncommon)] – Gives a passive ability to detect poisonous substances and their toxicity level. An

> alchemist must be able to find the materials to craft his products, after all. Adds a minor increase to the effectiveness of Sense Poison based on Perception.

Even now, Jake could feel the poisons in the garden despite being in the laboratory. The skill didn't precisely pinpoint the direction unless he got really close to it. When he was close to it, though, he could feel exactly where it was. When that close, he could even get a general feel for their toxicity level.

This had become useful even in the dungeon. Not all plants had the same strength by default despite both being identified as the same item, which meant the skill allowed Jake to pick out more suitable ingredients. As an example, mixing overly potent moss with a less potent mushroom would lead to an inevitable disaster when mixing. In the same vein, the mushroom couldn't overpower the toxicity in the moss too much.

Using this skill to pick out the ingredients for his first common-rarity poison was naturally done. It had taken some trial and error to get it down, but he was sure he had the best ingredients picked for this attempt.

The process of the mix was similar to that of the lower-rarity creations. Purified water filled the bowl as the moss was put in. Mana was injected through the engravings on it, and as the mana entered the moss and started extracting the valuable fluids found within, it gave the water a green tinge.

When around half of the juices were out, he added a third of the Bluebright Mushrooms. The process of extracting started once more, as Jake focused as hard as he possibly could. He had done this exact process many times before, but he was still nervous.

PREPARATIONS FOR EVOLUTION

Next, he added the mushrooms one by one as he slowly extracted their fluids. It was entirely possible to add all the ingredients at once, but it was easier, albeit far slower, to add them one by one. Jake did not feel like taking any risks, preferring to increase his chances of success slightly at the cost of time.

Reaching the final stages, he took a deep breath. This was where he had failed the last four times. At the very end, one had to bring it all together and finalize the concoction. This was often described as the most challenging step, and therefore often the point of failure.

Infusing the final bit of mana and focusing on bringing it together, he felt his entire body tense up. With every fiber of his being, he focused on controlling the mana.

Even his Sphere of Perception zeroed in on the small bowl before him. Slowly, the contents of the bowl started to take on a dark blue hue, giving off a faint shimmer of the familiar blue light.

> ***You have successfully crafted [Necrotic Poison (Common)] – A new kind of creation has been made. Bonus experience earned***
>
> ***'DING!' Profession: [Alchemist of the Malefic Viper] has reached level 23 - Stat points allocated, +2 Free Points***
>
> ***'DING!' Race: [Human (F)] has reached level 16 - Stat points allocated, +5 Free Points***
>
> ***'DING!' Profession: [Alchemist of the Malefic Viper] has reached level 24 - Stat points allocated, +2 Free Points***

Jake cheered out loud as the messages came in, and he smelled the aroma permeating the laboratory. It smelled like rotten beef. He didn't care, though, as he quickly started putting the concoction in one of his poison bottles.

Putting it all in, he used Identify on the bottle with the demeanor of a child opening Christmas presents.

[Necrotic Poison (Common)] – A poison with necrotic properties, infecting and killing off biological material in the affected area. Wounds caused by Necrotic Poison are extremely difficult to heal. The poison takes effect upon any contact with any biological material.

Alright, so the entire thing was a bit ominous and evil-sounding, but he was happy he had made it. The two profession levels were also more than welcome. Even more importantly, he had crafted a common-rarity poison before his first profession upgrade.

He decided to split the free stat points between Perception and Wisdom, as he had done for the most part during the last many levels. It wasn't a fifty-fifty split, but relatively close.

Opening his status window, he was once more reminded of his progress.

Status
Name: Jake Thayne
Race: [Human (F) – lvl 16]
Class: [Archer – lvl 9]
Profession: [Alchemist of the Malefic Viper – lvl 24]
Health Points (HP): 1010/1010
Mana Points (MP): 248/1250

Stamina: 287/360
Stats
Strength: 39
Agility: 42
Endurance: 36
Vitality: 101
Toughness: 50
Wisdom: 125
Intelligence: 27
Perception: 103
Willpower: 59
Free Points: 0

Titles: [Forerunner of the New World], [Bloodline Patriarch]
Class Skills: [Basic One-Handed Weapon (Inferior], [Basic Stealth (Inferior)], [Advanced Archery (Common)], [Archer's Eye (Common)]
Profession Skills: [Herbology (Common)], [Brew Potion (Common)], [Concoct Poison (Common)], [Alchemist's Purification (Common)], [Toxicology (Uncommon)], [Cultivate Toxin (Uncommon)], [Sense Poison (Uncommon], [Malefic Viper's Poison (Rare)], [Palate of the Malefic Viper (Rare)]
Race Skills: [Identify (Common)], [Endless Tongues of the Myriad Races (Unique)]
Bloodline: [Bloodline of the Primal Hunter (Bloodline Ability - Unique)]

His combat-related stats were starting to lag behind by quite a lot. Only Perception was at a pretty good level. Of course, this would likely rapidly change the second he got out of the dungeon. He had a decent backlog of poison and potions for him to use whenever he got out, and said supply was only growing by the day. He couldn't carry much of it with his satchel, but he could take quite a bit.

Exiting the laboratory, he decided to take a break from making poisons. His mana was too low, and he was mentally strained despite his delight at the successful concoction. Instead, he went to cultivate some poison in the garden. He still had plenty of ingredients remaining, but he had already started making preparations to cure himself of the poison and leave.

He had some chosen plants that he had picked out with Poison Sense, as they were the most potent. Using Cultivate Toxin, he was slowly improving them and making them grow while also increasing their toxicity.

He had decided to go with the concept of fighting poison with poison. He had come across some recipes with potential, but he was still far from settled on one. He was still searching for one that could incorporate the silver mushrooms.

Many plans had been made, and if everything went to shit, he had some recipes he would just give a shot, but for now, Jake would use all the time he had remaining. The dungeon challenge day timer had ticked from 15 to 14. Half the time was gone—half to go.

Leaving the garden, he chugged a mana potion and headed for the laboratory once more. He wanted to get a bit more work done before heading to bed. Looming death was on the horizon, but right now, only the imminent profession evolution was on his mind.

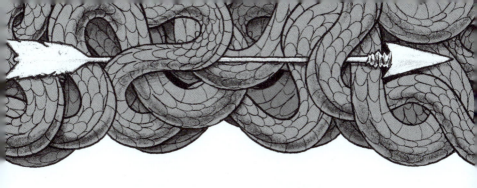

Chapter 31
Professional Evolution

Jake awoke once more after only an hour of sleep. Resources refilled, he stretched and did some light shadowboxing to get the blood flowing. The concept of tiredness and physical exhaustion being such a rarity was still not something he was used to.

His race's evolution reduced this need further, as it also did much to limit mental exhaustion. He still burned himself out nearly daily, but then again, he was always working. He either read about alchemy, did alchemy, prepared for alchemy, or thought out how to better do alchemy. His only distractions were small research trips on other topics, such as general knowledge of the system and looking for more information on Bloodlines.

The plan for today was to get another level and evolve his profession. He dearly hoped that his preparations were sufficient and that his potential upgrades would be worth it. As long as one met the required Records needed to evolve, one would have options available, but the quality of said options could vary wildly.

For now, it was time for some more alchemy. Jake had no interest in attempting to make another concoction of Necrotic Poison, as he quite honestly didn't have confidence in producing it efficiently quite yet.

Instead, he just started churning out some of the inferior-rarity poisons, mixed in with a batch of potions here and there.

The mixing itself went easy enough, the progress he had made in his endeavor to craft the Necrotic Poison showing. Jake hadn't made any lower-rarity poison for the last few days, mostly because he focused exclusively on completing his goal, but also because he feared it would level him to 25 before he managed to succeed.

The hours slowly went by as he mixed, and with little fanfare or excitement, he got the awaited notification.

> ***Profession Evolution Requirements Met***
>
> **Through struggle and perseverance, you have learned the craft of alchemy. Your path has been isolated, a lonesome journey to reach your level. Your actions have shown unparalleled raw talent and ability in the art of concocting poisons, yet also true skills when brewing potions.**
>
> **Begin Evolution now?**
> **Y/N**
>
> **WARNING: Postponing evolution for too long may have adverse effects, and no further profession experience can be earned before the evolution is completed.**

The message was a bit interesting, pointing out details of how he had operated during the dungeon. A *bit* sad to have his isolation pointed out like that, but he had always been the introverted type, so it wasn't that bad in all honesty. The last part of it, save for the obligatory warning, was especially interesting as it directly pertained to him performing well, which he very much hoped would result in something good. Also, who doesn't like positive reinforcement now and then?

Accepting the evolution, nothing happened for a few seconds. Then new notifications appeared.

> ***5 Possible Evolutions Available***

He cracked a smile as he saw that message. Five was the maximum number of available evolutions the system would ever show, according to the books, and no one complained about more options. He also knew that these options were the best ones he could get. The system had likely already filtered out lesser versions.

He decided to approach them as he did new skills and go through them one by one.

> **Experienced Alchemist of the Malefic Viper – An Experienced Alchemist of the Malefic Viper has learned the basics of Alchemy. Allows one to combine the natural treasures of the world to make potions and pills, transmute one material to another, and employ a slew of other mystical means to be discovered. This rare type of alchemist specializes in the production of poisons, contrary to the craft of potions. Your path has been ordinary so far, slowly building experience to one day reach greater heights. Have no fear, for the path to power is no sprint, but a marathon. Stat bonuses per level: +4 Vit, +3 Wis +2 Will +2 Tough, +3 Free Points.**

This option seemed to be the linear evolution of his Alchemist of the Malefic Viper profession. The stats were the same, only better, awarding 14 stat points instead of 8 every level. According to the books, an option like this was the most normal by far, hence, what the vast majority ended up with. It was relatively easy to unlock, and the Records earned through simply leveling the profession were often enough. In other words, if you unlocked the ability to evolve, an option like this would be available.

But in the end, he hoped for something better. Moving on to the next one, it got a bit more interesting... but not really.

> **Gardener of the Malefic Viper – The Gardener of the Malefic Viper has learned the art of alchemy yet prefers to find themselves tending to the gardens. The Gardener of the Malefic Viper possesses greatly improved abilities when cultivating poisons and growing herbs, helping the whole garden flourish in prosperity. While it is not the gardener's preferred path, he can still use his precious ingredients to create deadly poisons and even restorative potions if needed. Stat bonuses per level: +3 Wis, +3 Vit, +3 Tough, +3 Free Points.**

He quickly eliminated this option, as he preferred the prior one. The stats provided were only 12 total, so stat-wise, it was worse too. It did still demonstrate some of the other paths available to him. This one was another very common evolution to the profession, he theorized.

Of course, it focused on the tending of plants, mainly poisonous ones, just like the flavor text said. While Jake recognized the value of the Cultivate Toxin skill and the importance of the gardening profession, it wasn't really his cup of tea.

Moving on to the next, Jake was a bit dumbfounded.

> **Toxic Chef** – Toxic Chef seeks not to find the deadliest poison, but the one best supplementing his menu. Allows one to create dishes with toxic ingredients, providing a wide variety of benefits. This type of cook combines toxic materials not to create weapons but food. While the cook can still create regular foods, they prefer to use unusual ingredients of a toxic nature in their creation. Stat bonuses per level: +3 Vit, +3 Tough +2 Will +1 Wis, +1 Free Points. WARNING: Skills pertaining to Alchemist of the Malefic Viper may be lost or changed upon becoming a Toxic Chef.

Yeah, not going to happen, but what the hell? Jake thought as he finished reading it all. Just because he had been eating and even "cooking" poisonous mushrooms and moss as his sole source of food for the last two-plus weeks, the damn system had decided he was qualified to be a goddamn chef.

The stats did reflect his poor cooking skills with how little the profession gave. A total of 10 stat points, only two more than his Alchemist of the Malefic Viper. It also didn't seem to be a variant class of any kind, but just a regular insane poison chef profession.

Picking it would also be a complete divergence of his original profession, and as the warning mentioned, would lead him to lose skills. Unless he suffered from severe mental damage or was *really* into cooking, it would be pure stupidity to pick it. Swiftly, he moved on, still a bit grumpy by even having been given the option.

> **Hermit Alchemist** – The Hermit Alchemist is no stranger to alchemy yet has never interacted with his peers. This alchemist prefers to work in solitude and abhors interruptions, progressing their craft always on their lonesome. Allows one to combine the natural treasures of the world to make potions and pills, transmute one material to another, and employ a slew of other mystical means to be discovered. Through this isolated training of your craft, you have learned to focus on your work over everything else. Your continued path shall thus not be defined by the will of others, but the path you discover on your own. Stat bonuses per level: +5 Will, +5 Wis, +3 Int, +5 Free Points. WARNING: Skills pertaining to Alchemist of the Malefic Viper may be lost or changed upon becoming a Hermit Alchemist.

Now he was getting somewhere. The fact that it awarded 18 stat points per level was higher than everything else before it by a mile. This was another kind of variant Jake had seen mentioned in one of the books, and while relatively well known, it often had demanding requirements. It required a particular mindset and personality trait to be present in the person having it, making it impossible to gain for most.

It also often resulted in penalties to experience gain if around people for too long, and many of the crafting skills typically required one to craft alone, making all joint crafting projects impossible or heavily penalized. Hermit classes also often had a massive negative experience multiplier when hunting in parties, though that shouldn't matter much, considering it was a profession. Hermits were, in essence, very strong, but with a lot of trade-offs.

There was also the fact that there was no direct evolution in the line of the Malefic Viper. Which meant that Jake would lose or have some of his skills changed. And while he hated a lot about eating mushrooms to gain knowledge, he recognized how powerful it was. The Palate skill was just busted.

The prospects of the profession did most certainly appeal to him, though. He'd always preferred to work alone, and he doubted any of the negative side effects would really affect him much. Ultimately, it didn't matter much when he saw the last option.

> **Prodigious Alchemist of the Malefic Viper –** A Prodigious Alchemist of the Malefic Viper has come far from when first concocting his first poison. You have displayed speed and skills at the pinnacle. Allows the alchemist to combine the natural treasures of the world to make potions and pills, transmute one material to another, and employ a slew of other mystical means to be discovered. This rare type of alchemist specializes in the production of poisons, contrary to the craft of potions. Your proven talent as an artisan of death stands above all peers, signaling the coming of another harbinger of decay following in the footsteps of the Malefic Viper. Only his chosen may walk this path. Stat bonuses per level: +4 Vit, +4 Wis, +3 Will +2 Tough +2 Int, +5 Free Points.

He couldn't hold himself back from cracking a big smile as he read the entire description. It was at a massive 20 stat points per level, far above any of the other options. On top of that, it was a relatively straightforward upgrade to his profession, staying in the same lane.

If he had to point out anything negative, it was the ominous tone of the entire thing.

He firmly believed that he'd gotten this option from managing to craft the common-rarity poison before his evolution. Getting a return on your hard work was always satisfying. He wasn't quite sure about the whole prodigy thing, but recognition was kind of cool.

He hadn't seen this type of upgrade mentioned in any of the books, but then again, the more powerful it was, the rarer. In fact, Jake had a suspicion that most who got this profession just claimed to be an Experienced Alchemist of the Malefic Viper or another more common variant instead. He assumed other "steps" between Experienced and Prodigious existed depending on how good the system judged one to be.

With this clearly being the best option in his mind, he picked it. Hermit Alchemist did seem kind of up his alley, but he didn't want to lose any of his current skills.

As he confirmed his choice, he prepared himself for an influx of information, but instead, he felt his vision shift. The surroundings started to blend together as if he was entering some Picasso painting, and everything went murky and indiscernible. Even his Sphere of Perception got thrown all off, telling him that everything was moving all at once.

Everything finally started to calm down, and the first thing he noticed was how dark it suddenly was. Due to his vastly improved Perception, he could still see a bit, though. And what he saw was just a vast plane of nothingness. He stood on what seemed like black rocks, and kneeling down to feel them, he found their texture smooth, like polished granite.

Another thing he quickly noticed was the light mist or fog in his surroundings. Oddly enough, the mist stopped a few millimeters from his skin, and when he breathed in, he felt nothing different.

Just as he was starting to wonder why the system had brought him here, he felt something. Turning to the side, he knew something was observing him. Before he could try to Identify what it was, a man appeared before him.

Though calling him a man was a hard sell. Extremely fine black scales with a slight dark green tinge lined his entire body. At first glance, it looked like skin, but it clearly wasn't. He didn't seem to wear anything except a tattered black robe. Yet the very first thing Jake noticed was the eyes. They shone with dim green light, a pair of piercing vertical slits reminiscent of a snake gazing back at him, only slightly obstructed by his long, unkempt black hair.

"Now, what do we have here?" the scaled man said with a raspy voice.

Jake didn't know who or what this being was, but he didn't have the slightest tinge of threat or fear. That didn't mean his instincts were silent, though. Every fiber of his being told him that whatever this being was... it wasn't something he could even consider fighting.

Based on the method in which the figure had appeared, Jake had no doubt that the scaled man was unimaginably stronger than himself. The only reason he kept his cool was how silent his danger sense was. In fact, he had never felt safer in his life than this very moment.

"Your guess is as good as mine," Jake answered. "One moment, I was evolving my profession; the next, I appeared here." He tried to Identify the man.

[?]

"Oh... That is... interesting," the man said, his eyes shining an even brighter color as he observed Jake. "Ah, I see..."

He then nodded, seemingly not interested in sharing his thoughts.

«So...» Jake started, prompting the scaled man to explain.

"Just the system doing what it does," he answered with a shrug. "It transported you here, right?"

"It did," Jake said, seeing no reason to hide anything. Furthermore, he suspected that the being in front of him already knew.

"And you have obtained a profession related to the Malefic Viper?"

Jake nodded once more.

"Well, I am the Malefic Viper... Nice to meet you and all that crap," he said, waving dismissively. "Now fuck off."

Chapter 32
A Very Weird Encounter

The scaled man's words momentarily dumbfounded Jake. No, if he was to be believed, the *Malefic Viper's* words.

Unsure what to say, Jake just stared back at the man. After what felt like an eternity, the scaled man's face turned to one of confusion as he observed Jake closely with apparent puzzlement.

"I told you to fuck off," he said as he scratched the back of his head. "You must know who I am, right? So do as I say and leave me alone."

"Well, yeah, I heard you. But I thought the Malefic Viper was a snake-turned-dragon?"

"Oh, that?" The man laughed as an explosion of green mist burst out of him, with Jake standing completely unaffected.

The scaled man was still there, but behind him was a giant projection nearly identical to the dragon he had seen on the mural. "See? It *is* me. Can you leave now?"

"Yeah, I see it," Jake answered, still utterly lost as to what the hell was happening. Why had the system brought him to meet the namesake of his profession?

"Gotta be honest, I have no clue why I am here or how to leave again."

Dispelling the projection, the Malefic Viper continued to look confused back at him. "Seriously, you're a member of the Order, right?"

"No—I don't think so, at least?" Jake said truthfully.

Would he be considered a member of the Order, considering that everything he knew came from what seemed like an old sanctuary? He hadn't formally signed up for anything. Also, wasn't it a cult?

"Then how in the hell did you acquire my legacy? And why did it bring—wait." As if suddenly enlightened, the Malefic Viper chuckled a bit to himself. "You are a newly integrated human to the system, right? In one of those tutorials." He had an amused smile on his face.

"Yeah, I got the profession through a Challenge Dungeon," Jake answered, confused as to the apparent mood-swing the other man was showing. What was so amusing about him more or less appropriating a legacy?

Laughing even louder, he put his hand on Jake's shoulder, though his hand didn't actually make any physical contact. It appeared that touching one another was stopped by the system somehow.

"You have no idea, kid. This brings back some memories. Oh man, I can't believe you actually got through all that bullshit." He tried to pat Jake's shoulder again in vain.

"I don't get it," Jake said, his confusion growing by the second. Had he unintentionally gotten himself involved with some unstable ancient being?

"No, I assume you wouldn't. It would be damn weird if ya did. But it is funny, so I'm gonna tell you."

"Okay?" He actually kind of wanted to just leave now...

"Back in my younger days, I was very much into all of these events made by the system. You know what Records are?"

"Partly."

"Eh, just look up Akashic Records or something. Pretty much all pre-system cultures had some myth related to it. Just know that having sufficient Records is quite crucial for everyone. Mortals and gods alike. Which brings me to the next part.

"Newly integrated universes aren't just for the newly integrated races themselves. Many beings throughout the multiverse can obtain countless benefits from it. Most notably, a huge amount of Records can be earned. One such way of earning more Records is by investing in the tutorials and getting rewards from the system. It's essentially just glorified gambling making such investments."

Jake was finally starting to understand why he was so happy.

"Well, you being here means that I very likely already earned back that investment," the Viper continued. "Geez, you must have done well to come here."

"Yeah, I…" Jake wanted to explain what had happened in the dungeon, but the Malefic Viper raised his hand to interrupt.

"Don't bother. I quite frankly don't give a fuck. Besides, the system tends not to like oversharing. It's a bit overprotective when it comes to new universes after some gods accidentally ruined a lesser universe back in the fifth era." He plopped down on the ground, sitting with his legs crossed. "Totally wasn't me, by the way."

Jake was about to ask some questions, but was once more interrupted.

"No, I am not going to answer anything. Again, the system wouldn't like that either. Shit, you being alive should be proof enough. Never heard of anything below S-rank able to survive in this part of my realm."

As the Viper finished those words, with a movement Jake couldn't even see, an explosion sounded out. It threw up dust and broken stone everywhere.

With a whisk of the Malefic Viper's hand, the dust dispersed, and Jake found himself standing on a small, floating stone platform, utterly untouched by even a single speck of dust. Around him, nothing remained as far as his eyes could see. Everything had simply been disintegrated into nothingness.

"See? Overprotective. Could collapse the entire damn realm on you without leaving a scratch. Ya couldn't even kill yourself if you wanted to right now."

With another wave of his hand, the whole place was restored back to exactly how it had been before he shattered it, leaving it as if nothing had ever happened.

"Back to the story. You see, long ago, I made a certain Challenge Dungeon during a time where we gods had quite a bit more free rein on designing them. I am both incredibly proud and a bit embarrassed about how I made it, but at the time, it was super amusing." The Viper gave a cheeky smile.

"Honestly, I more or less made it as a joke. The requirements were bullshit made up on the spot to make the challenger feel special, going like, 'Oh my god, I barely fit these, this must be destiny!' And then, just after entering the first room, I would have them get impaled by a poisoned spike."

"That does sound very familiar," Jake said, nodding. He had found the design of the first part of the dungeon a bit suspect. Though he was embarrassed to admit it, he hadn't really caught on to how suspicious the requirements were. Thinking back, it was a bit weird.

"It was a bit funny, right? The only sad part is that you don't actually die in a Challenge Dungeon. At least, not normally. Quite proud of myself for gaming the system on the last part of the challenge where ya have to cure yourself. Took quite a few workarounds to make that work and have the lethality stick." He laughed, clearly proud.

"So, Challenge Dungeons aren't normally lethal, but you somehow found a way to make it so, and now you're bragging to the person who is suffering the consequences?" Jake asked pointedly.

"Yep."

"Well, aren't you a massive dick," Jake said, but he couldn't help snickering a bit himself.

"Guilty as charged. How was the part forcing you to feed me stuff not to die while on a timer? Forced to study my history, only to be rewarded with a mural of me being awesome?"

"Very narcissistic."

"I take that as a compliment," the Viper said with a huge smile. "You are surprisingly un-angry."

"Wouldn't it be a bit boring if you couldn't even die from the challenge?" Jake asked. "Makes it all a bit more exciting."

The scaled man looked at him a bit to discern if Jake was serious. He was. "That's some fucked-up logic right there. I like it!"

"Anyway, why am I here?" Jake finally asked. Funnily enough, he didn't really feel like leaving anymore. As weird as it sounded, he found talking to the snake-god in front of him relatively easy. It was... relaxing. Maybe because he hadn't spoken to anyone for a few days, or because his conversation partner wasn't human. Or maybe they just vibed.

"Now that's an excellent question," the Viper answered, nodding his head slowly. After several moments of looking like he was deep in thought, he finally turned to Jake, staring him straight in the eyes. "No idea. Well, some idea, but it's more fun if you figure it out yourself."

Jake was once more floored by the flippant attitude of the Malefic Viper. How the hell had the revered and worshipped dragon he had seen challenge the heavens themselves and ascend, turned into... this?

"Can you at least tell me where exactly we are?" Jake answered, hoping to get *something* tangible out of the eccentric snake-turned-dragon.

"Oh, that's an easy one—we're in my realm!" he shouted loudly, spreading out his hands in a comical way. Noticing Jake still staring at him, confused, he elaborated. "That means it is kind of my world. I made it. Don't worry about it; it is a god-thing. So, what do you think? My realm is pretty darn awesome, right?"

Looking around at the flat, desolate surroundings in all directions, Jake wasn't particularly amazed.

"It sure is something," he answered, dodging an answer. "You mentioned something about being a god?"

Jake had run into the mention of gods in some of the books he had read, but nothing concrete. It would make sense for the Malefic Viper to be considered a god, having a cult and all. He just wasn't sure exactly what it meant by "god."

"Totally am," the Viper said, keeping a jovial smile on his lips. "Just keep doing stuff, gain levels, evolutions, all that jazz, and you'll get there eventually. It's hard work, but it's worth it just for the immortality alone."

Jake just nodded along, pondering what the hell was wrong with the so-called god in front of him.

"My turn to ask something!" the Malefic Viper said. "How come you're so casual despite how fucked up this entire situation is?"

Momentarily taken aback, Jake did wonder how he was so calm. His Willpower stat had most certainly increased a lot. But more importantly, he hadn't felt anything negative from his instincts since he came here, not a single shred of danger at any point, not even at the Viper's show of power.

"I guess my Willpower stat has grown a lot," Jake answered truthfully.

"Yeah, that isn't how Willpower works, mate. You don't suddenly become a bastion of calmness from a stat." As the Viper explained this, he turned uncharacteristically serious. "Stats may change some parts of you, but your mind remains untouched. You become able to think faster, process everything far more efficiently, and remember every single detail, but changes to who you are fundamentally will never happen. It has never happened. Many beings of unimaginable power, having a Willpower stat at an incredible height, have fallen to the plagues of the mind."

Jake turned solemn at the Malefic Viper's words, sensing a faint trace of sadness.

"Willpower will allow you to endure the endlessness of immortality, help you resist attacks on your mind, and keep you calm in situations of great danger. However, for those to be possible, you have to possess the ability to do those things to begin with. Some never learn to endure... and time doesn't heal all wounds."

The Viper's look was very downtrodden as he stared out into the vast, desolate wasteland that was his realm. Turning back to Jake, he continued once more.

"The path to power is a long and lonesome one, but you will meet many along the way. Friends, comrades, subordinates, and superiors, an endless web of karmic threads will be left in your wake. But the march of time is ruthless, the need for constant progress endless. Those friends will be left behind, your comrades abandoned as they fail to keep up, your subordinates lost, superiors surpassed. Families... taken from you."

The last few words were barely audible. Jake wasn't quite sure what exactly to say or do.

"Sorry, I'm rambling again," the Viper apologized. "Haven't spoken a word to anyone for a very, *very* long time."

Jake looked back at him for a few seconds, unsure of how to reply. If he should even reply at all. As the silence continued, however, he collected his thoughts and spoke honestly.

"You sound like you've gone through some shit. I am not going to stand here and pretend to understand what someone like you struggles with, but I am pretty sure doing nothing isn't the solution."

"And what makes you think I haven't tried to do *everything* already?" he asked back, a formless aura spreading out from him.

Jake felt like he suddenly stood before an incarnation of death and destruction. Yet he didn't back down. He pushed back, his Bloodline fully awoken, refusing to be inferior. The aura failed to affect him as he stood unmoving.

"Just sounds like a challenge you haven't been able to beat yet. And if it isn't that kind of issue..." Jake's voice grew a bit softer. "Then, sometimes, moving on can be the best."

The Malefic Viper looked back at Jake, clearly a bit surprised at how he still stood unaffected.

"When you lose everything, what is there to do but try to regain it?" he asked pointedly.

"If what you've done so far hasn't worked, then shift up your strategy or the rules of the games, but... sometimes victory is found by just walking away." Jake sighed. "I didn't know them... but I have never met anyone who doesn't want their loved ones to be happy, even after their own end. Maybe your victory is found not through fixing what you can't, but by creating something new. It doesn't have to be better... just good enough."

Jake didn't exactly know where his words came from. In some ways, he was trying to channel his inner Jacob, and in others, he was borrowing from something his father had once told him. When he'd gotten injured and had to give up going pro with his archery, he'd been broken... but those words had helped him find a new goal.

The Viper just stared back at Jake for what felt like an eternity. He finally chuckled a bit as he smiled—his first genuine smile for a long time.

"Look at you, going full-on philosopher on my ass," he said as his chuckle turned to a laugh. "Oh man, this shit is absurd. A mortal comforting a god—what has the world come to?"

Thinking about it, Jake had to agree. He was a bit embarrassed to admit that he had kind of forgotten the scaled man in front of him was a god for a second. In his defense, he didn't exactly act like one.

What followed was a sight rarely seen. A mortal and a god sitting on the ground, just chatting. The Viper was throwing out advice on minor things, with Jake just telling random anecdotes from his own world. Perhaps even Jake, with his ordinarily introverted personality, had missed talking to anyone during his isolation. The Viper having missed conversations was even more evident.

Jake had no idea how long they talked, but he thoroughly enjoyed their time together. He heard stories about the multiverse, about how the Viper had met a fellow god and fallen in love. It was never spoken, but Jake knew that it was she he had talked about earlier, as he always had a glint of sadness in his eyes whenever he mentioned her.

Just two lonely people, caring neither for status nor power.

It was no secret that Jake came away with the most knowledge. The Viper knew far more than Jake on pretty much every subject. Yet he held back on giving direct advice on anything related to the system. He did provide a bit of general knowledge, but nothing major. According to the Viper, there was more value in Jake discovering those secrets by himself.

After a few hours, the Malefic Viper finally got up and motioned for Jake to do the same.

"It seems like it is your time to return soon," the Malefic Viper said as Jake got to his feet.

"We still haven't found out why I came here," Jake added. They had managed to somehow not talk about that.

"Oh yeah, that. When I made the dungeon back in the day, I didn't have anyone else around with permission to approve the better evolutions, so the responsibility naturally fell to me. One could call it a happy little accident that you came here." The Viper laughed.

"Ah! Now I remember! The description did say something about being chosen. Does that mean I passed the job interview?"

"You got lucky, young man," the Viper joked back before turning a bit more serious once again. "I won't give you anything concrete, but I can give you a tip. Focus on the mana. You can feel it all around you. Feel it more. The earlier you do so, the better. It will help you in more ways than you can imagine."

Extending his hand toward him, the Viper motioned for a handshake.

Without hesitating, Jake took his hand, knowing physical contact couldn't be made. Yet to his surprise, his hand met with scaly textures. Before he could question anything, he felt a warm flow encompass his body as he shook the hand.

"Something for your journey... A small string of karma, if you may," the Malefic Viper said as he let go of Jake's hand.

Feeling his vision blur and spin once more, Jake knew that his time here was over. The last thing he saw was the green eyes staring back at him as he heard the Viper speak one last time.

"And thank you once more, Jake. See ya later!"

With those words, he disappeared, and the Malefic Viper was alone once more.

The scaled man didn't take off back to the decrepit old cave. He couldn't even remember the last time he spoke with anyone. Met anyone, to be honest.

Looking at his hand, he still felt the aura of his little visitor. Compared to him, it was so small, so insignificant. And yet it felt strong. Limited, but powerful still. Deep within the Records, he felt a power that gave even him pause.

"What a powerful Bloodline..." he whispered to himself. It wasn't just powerful; it was intimidating. Even the Record's mere remnants carried the charms of something that refused to back away from his probing gaze. It was primal, like a wild beast, one refusing to surrender to even *him*.

Many might see this foolhardiness as a weakness, but the Viper felt only strength. One would never achieve true power from avoiding danger. It might lead to a short life, but without said determination, one would never reach the pinnacle either.

Smiling, he thought that he might just have made a good investment. It didn't come cheap, as he still felt a faint trace of weakness, unlike anything he had felt in countless eons. Despite this, he felt no regret. More than just an investment in a powerful initiate, he may have made something even more valuable.

The smile quickly disappeared, however, as he thought back to their conversation. The calmness and straightforwardness of a mortal had truly impressed him. But the fact that he was so genuinely straightforward also meant that the words carried more weight. Being spoken to directly was not something he had ever been used to.

Taking a step, he appeared in a valley. This valley, compared to everything else surrounding it, was not desolate but brimming with life everywhere. Small animals ran in the shrubbery, birds chirped, and a calm wind blew throughout.

In the center of this valley, two obelisks stood. One of them had countless runes with unimaginable power, covering every speck of its surface. Each rune held more information than a mortal mind could comprehend in a lifetime.

The other obelisk only had a single rune even though they were the same size. This solitary rune did not exude any power and was only a single word:

> Hope

The Malefic Viper stood there for a while before moving forward and putting a hand on each of them.

"Perhaps I have wallowed enough. You always told me to smile and never doubt myself," he spoke, gently caressing the runes on the filled obelisk while only having his palm rest on the other's lone rune.

"Perhaps it's time for the Malefic Viper to make his return."

Chapter 33
True Blessing of the Malefic Viper

As Jake's vision started to return, the only feeling in his body that remained was a constant searing pain in his hand, extending up his arm and into his entire body. It didn't feel malicious, just far more powerful than Jake's body was capable of handling.

The moment his feet hit the ground, he also collapsed down on his knees, heaving for air while clutching his chest. The pain gradually faded away and was instead replaced by a strong feeling of power. It was unlike any level-ups he had felt before, and certainly far more than when he'd evolved his race.

He basked in the feeling for a while before everything finally calmed down. Raising his hand, he could feel that he had gotten stronger. The Viper had done something. Given him something.

Opening his status screen, he was met with a slew of messages, but the first one alone gave him great pause.

> *Blessing received*: [True Blessing of the Malefic Viper (Blessing - True)] – An alchemist recognized by the Malefic Viper himself. Few throughout the ages have found themselves blessed by the Primordial, despite their desire to be so. Through your direct karmic connection, the Wisdom and Willpower of the Malefic Viper empower you. +10% Willpower, +10% Wisdom. Grants access to many new paths. Only one blessing can be held at a time.

Jake was confused as he read it, before finally getting a bit annoyed. "Could have at least asked first," he muttered to himself.

> Renounce the Malefic Viper as Patron? All faith-based skills, titles, and Blessing will be lost.

"What? No, no, no, it's fine. Jeez," Jake quickly said as the prompt disappeared. While he was a bit annoyed, it wasn't like he wanted to throw away free stat points like that.

Wisdom had been his highest stat before his evolution and would likely remain that way for quite a while, so getting 10% extra was already giving him bonus stat points in the double digits. Willpower was also a great stat to increase.

Jake had believed that Willpower was what had allowed him to stay so calm and controlled throughout the tutorial, but he would have to reconsider that.

However, reading the description, he was confused. The blessing described him not as a god but a Primordial. Perhaps they were the same thing? Though he doubted it was just semantics, as he added something else to hit the books on. Nevertheless, the Willpower bonus was nice, and if nothing else, it increased his mana regeneration, which was always welcome. Besides that, he didn't really see much use for it currently.

Moving on down the list, he noted how he had apparently unlocked his profession upgrade after he got the blessing.

Congratulations, you have successfully evolved your profession

Prodigious Alchemist of the Malefic Viper – A Prodigious Alchemist of the Malefic Viper has come far from when first concocting his first poison. You have displayed speed and skills at the pinnacle. Allows the alchemist to combine the natural treasures of the world to make potions and pills, transmute one material to another, and employ a slew of other mystical means to be discovered. This rare type of alchemist specializes in the production of poisons, contrary to the craft of potions. Your proven talent as an artisan of death stands above all peers, signaling the coming of another harbinger of decay following in the footsteps of the Malefic Viper. Only his chosen may walk this path. Stat bonuses per level: +4 Vit, +4 Wis, +3 Will +2 Tough +2 Int, +5 Free Points.

'DING!' Profession: [Prodigious Alchemist of the Malefic Viper] has reached level 25 - Stat points allocated, +5 Free Points

'DING!' Race: [Human (F)] has reached level 17 - Stat points allocated, +5 Free Points

Not anything was out of expectations there, besides perhaps the massive influx of stats from the profession and race leveling up.

With the profession evolution, he had naturally also gotten some skills. But contrary to when he'd gotten the profession, the upgrade only gave two new skills.

Gained skill: [Alchemical Flame (Common)] – The flame of an alchemist is one of the most critical aspects of the crafting process. The flame itself is affinity-less and not polluted by the impurities of burning a catalyst. The path to refining one's alchemical flame is a long and arduous one for all alchemists seeking the pinnacle. Allows the alchemist to create a small alchemical flame, emitting heat. Adds a minor increase to the effectiveness of Alchemical Flame based on Wisdom.

Gained skill: [Touch of the Malefic Viper (Rare)] – With a single touch, the Malefic Viper has slain countless foes. Attempt to inject poison into a being through physical contact. The nature of the poison is determined by the user. The alchemist can only use toxic effects he has concocted or created prior. Some toxins cannot be used. Adds a minor increase to the effectiveness of Touch of the Malefic Viper based on Intelligence and Wisdom.

According to the books, the first one was a fundamental skill that all alchemists got at level 25. The next one, however, was more interesting. This could easily be construed as the first combat-related skill he had acquired from his profession. A rarity, but not an impossibility if the excellent books were to be believed.

It wasn't immediately useful, still being stuck in a dungeon and all, but he could see it being a valuable skill outside. It was also great to make use of his high Wisdom and growing Intelligence stats.

As he moved on down the list, the last two notifications were... *What the hell?*

> *Gained Title*: [Holder of a Primordial's True Blessing] – Obtain the True Blessing of a Primordial. Many have claimed divinity in the vast multiverse, and numerous pantheons rule, but the Primordials are few. Even fewer still, those truly blessed by a Primordial. May you bring glory to your Patron. Grants the skill: [Shroud of the Primordial]. +5 all stats, +10% all stats.

That title was just straight-up ridiculous and explained where the feeling of power he felt came from. 10% to all stats was just insane. Even now, it gave him so much, and he couldn't imagine its value down the line as his stats grew.

Then again, he was unsure as to how common percentage multipliers were for stats. He currently had four already, after all. One from his Bloodline Patriarch title, one from his Bloodline ability itself, and two from the blessing and title he had just gotten. Which meant that he had technically only obtained them from two sources – the blessing and his Bloodline.

Though he was sure there had to be more out there.

Moving on to the last skill, the surprises only continued.

> *Gained skill*: [Shroud of the Primordial (Divine)] – A shroud surrounds your very being, your Records masked, your status inaccessible. Scryers weep at the thought of tracking a single of your steps, as you remain an enigma to their sight. Using Identify on you is but a futile effort. The karmic threads in your wake form an endless web impossible to unravel. One does not merely peek behind the Shroud of the Primordial. Hides your Records and Status from all but the most powerful of prying eyes. Hiding ability increases based on Willpower.

He had little clue what most of the skill did, but it seemed to hold some kind of obscuration effect on people trying to use magic to locate him, and it could block people using Identify on him. This also finally confirmed that the Identify skill could be used on other people. Perhaps his could now that it had been upgraded to common rarity, but he would have to wait with testing that.

Besides that, he felt like most of what this skill did was something he would never be aware of it doing.

The final point was the rarity. Divine. As in god-tier. Which was kind of insane to imagine. His second-highest skill rarity was rare, and even those skills, he felt, were damn strong. How many ranks above rare was divine?

The only sad thing was perhaps the fact that the skill had such a peculiar nature. If it were a defensive or offensive skill, it would likely be an unimaginably powerful trump card. The passive shroud was nice, but the grass is greener on the other side and all that. He could see several advantages in being harder to track with magic, and of course, with Identify being blocked.

After going through all his new skills and titles, he finally opened his status screen to see the final result.

Status
Name: Jake Thayne
Race: [Human (F) – lvl 17]
Class: [Archer – lvl 9]
Profession: [Prodigious Alchemist of the Malefic Viper – lvl 25]
Health Points (HP): 1220/1220
Mana Points (MP): 1560/1560
Stamina: 459/460
Stats
Strength: 49
Agility: 52
Endurance: 46
Vitality: 122
Toughness: 63
Wisdom: 156
Intelligence: 38
Perception: 120
Willpower: 81
Free Points: 10

Titles: [Forerunner of the New World], [Bloodline Patriarch], [Holder of a Primordial's True Blessing]
Class Skills: [Basic One-Handed Weapon (Inferior)], [Basic Stealth (Inferior)], [Advanced Archery (Common)], [Archer's Eye (Common)]
Profession Skills: [Herbology (Common)], [Brew Potion (Common)], [Concoct Poison (Common)], [Alchemists Purification (Common)], [Alchemical Flame (Common)], [Toxicology (Uncommon)], [Cultivate Toxin (Uncommon)], [Poison Sense (Uncommon], [Malefic Viper's Poison (Rare)], [Palate of the Malefic Viper (Rare)], [Touch of the Malefic

Viper (Rare)]
Blessing: [True Blessing of the Malefic Viper (Blessing - True)]
Race Skills: [Endless Tongues of the Myriad Races (Unique)], [Identify (Common)], [Shroud of the Primordial (Divine)]
Bloodline: [Bloodline of the Primal Hunter (Bloodline Ability - Unique)]

The stat increases were massive across the line. A bit of quick math also confirmed that stat percentage bonuses were additive and not multiplicative. Which still resulted in a 20% increase to his Wisdom and Willpower stats from the titles gained today alone. And that was beside the bonuses from the levels and the 5 in all stats.

Not bad... not bad at all. I should go meet snake-gods more often, Jake thought jokingly to himself, smiling at the ridiculous nature by which he had gotten all of these massive gains. *Imagine what he would have given me if I had brought along a gift... note to self: bring blue mushroom next time.*

Richard sighed loudly as the man finished his report. The former archer, now upgraded to a class called scout, had brought more bad news. A daily occurrence at this point.

"Sir, that kid is way too volatile," the scout said. "We should just put him down already. He is too stuck in his own world to notice anything around him. He believes himself some kind of god. Just say the word, and I will have an arrow in the back of his head within the hour."

Richard shook his head. "No, just keep shadowing him and keep track of his movements. I have seen plenty of his type before. He is an arrogant whelp, but his skills are the real deal. Someone like him is useful if controlled."

The scout sighed as he turned to the door. "I hope you know what you're doing, boss."

"I do too, honestly," Richard said, returning the sigh.

He had to admit that he was beginning to regret his decision to let William run wild. The kid was *too* self-confident, to the level of pure ignorance. For god's sake, if his rampant killing hadn't made him stick out, the fact that everyone in the damn camp could see his way-too-high level with Identify did. The young man had held back on learning a profession, not upgrading the Identify skill. He appeared to not even know it got upgraded, despite it being common knowledge around the camp. And now, after having gotten a profession, he still hadn't put two and two together.

No, he had just utterly ignored everything. Instead, he'd focused on his own foolish mission. Drumming up war. And as much as Richard hated to admit it, the kid's actions were effective. *Too* effective.

For a while, the conflict had escalated, and all hell had finally broken loose a week ago when the other faction leader's son was killed. And not just killed. William had sent his head flying into their base with a dagger stuck in his head.

To make matters even worse, he had written, "Richard says hi" on his forehead. Needless to say, Hayden, the other leader, was royally pissed. He had personally gone out and slaughtered an entire group from Richard's faction. From the looks of the battle, he hadn't just killed them but tortured them to death, likely attempting to find the culprit behind his son's murder.

After that, it had only gotten worse. Lines that should never be crossed had been. Now the fights were no longer simply killing each other. Killing, Richard could handle. He had done plenty of that while overseas. But what was happening now was just wrong.

It had reached a point where anyone not from your faction was automatically designated an enemy. The unaffiliated ones, the ones merely trying to survive on their own, had also become victims. There had even been a single occurrence where two people from the same faction ended up fighting out of pure paranoia, one of them even dying.

Hearing the door to the cabin open, Richard looked up to see Jacob and Caroline entering. Perhaps a small bright spot in this entire nightmare was two people finally finding love through adversity. Richard was genuinely happy for them. Jacob had also proven himself to be invaluable in managing the camp.

"I heard about your friend. I am sorry for your loss," Richard said as they took their seats in some wooden chairs across his desk.

Ahmed, one of the base casters, had been one of the people who fell today. Not by William, but by a group from the other faction. *A necessary sacrifice.*

"Thanks," Jacob said, looking dejected at the other man. "You know, today marks half of my colleagues either dying or going missing."

Hearing that, Richard smiled internally at the unexpected cue. "Speaking of that archer, what are his whereabouts?"

Taken aback, Jacob looked at the man in bewilderment. He hadn't seen or heard from Jake since the day they parted, and quite honestly, despite his early confidence in him, he was beginning to doubt he still lived. While Jacob hadn't expected him to actually come back and check on the regular, he had expected some kind of contact for what was now nearly a month.

"I have no idea where he is or if he even lives," Jacob answered honestly. "But if he does live, I would expect him to have perhaps made his way through the barrier somehow."

The barrier was something they had encountered as they went further into the forest, right in the middle of the entire dome that was the tutorial. They had yet to figure out how to enter it, but at least nothing had exited it either.

"Perhaps," Richard said. He didn't actually think the archer was involved, but he was a potential red herring. "I have a feeling someone is pulling strings. I have felt it since the very first of their groups got killed. No one ever took credit for the first kills. I have heard no chatter or rumors as to who did it. I fear that a third party may somehow be involved." Richard leaned back on the wooden chair.

"You think that could be Jake?" Caroline asked, turning the attention of the two men to her.

"It is entirely possible," Richard said. "It may also just be Hayden and his men behind it all."

"I really doubt Jake is involved," Jacob said. "I have known him for a while; he isn't a homicidal maniac. You have seen what people do out there. That isn't Jake."

"I am not accusing anyone. Let's just not ignore a potential threat. Now, what is the progress around the camp?"

Jacob sighed but complied as he went over the newest key numbers.

More and more combatants had started learning professions to gain more stats and race levels. One of the primary reasons was the general lack of high-level beasts providing experience in the forest. Another reason was the hugely increased danger with the faction war going on.

Levels got harder and harder as one progressed, but this difficulty applied to professions and classes separately. Those with high-level classes even had an easier time leveling professions than those focusing solely on professions due to their higher stats.

A balanced approach between the two was deemed the most efficient. Getting a profession to 10 could quickly be done in a couple of days, including unlocking the profession itself.

Even Richard had leveled smithing, as that profession gave the best stats for him. The current "meta" was getting level 25 in one's class and then focusing a bit on one's profession.

Jacob reported that Joanna was the first to get her profession evolution. She had gone from Novice Tailor to Experienced Seamstress. The stat gain had doubled from 4 to 10 per level and had, of course, come with some valuable skills.

The second part was that despite the brutality of the conflict escalating, the number of actual deaths had not. It wasn't exactly a surprise, considering the vastly reduced number of survivors. They checked the numbers briefly.

> **Tutorial Panel**
> **Duration: 33 days & 23:45:06**
> **Total Survivors Remaining: 423/1200**

They were close to two hundred people by now in their faction, and they needed some way to Identify each other out in the forest, as simply remembering everyone wasn't plausible. To fix that, they had codewords for all those going out to hunt.

Finishing the conversation, they said their goodbyes, and the two left the building.

Richard leaned back in his chair, closing his eyes. He had made a lot of gambles in this tutorial. Far more than he liked. Hayden and his faction had proven a challenge. William was a useful tool to spur on action. It was also good to have a scapegoat in case too many caught on.

Opening his quest window, he squinted at the progress. Soon he would have half of the entire tutorial in his grasp. After getting rid of Hayden, it should be possible to throw William under the bus as the instigator of the war and try to lessen the resentment between the two factions. It was a plan filled with flaws, but it should be workable.

William had finally picked up a profession, but it didn't appear to him at all how stupid he had been in the past to not pick one up earlier just for the easy levels. He also made a mental note to make William go after the trapper, Casper. The trapper had begun to get suspicious of Richard and William, but more than that... he was becoming unstable. William was at least predictable, but Casper was just pure emotion. Richard couldn't help but shiver at the traps he made.

This tutorial was to be the foundation for what he would build in the new world. Sadly, Casper didn't fit into that.

Chapter 34
Manipulation

As he closed his status window, Jake was momentarily a bit lost. He had been in the zone for two weeks, doing alchemy at every waking hour. His first interaction with another living being for over two weeks had been with an ancient being of immense power that had ended up giving him quite an overpowered blessing, along with a several-hour-long pleasant conversation.

Now, however, he would have to get back into it. It would frankly be a bit embarrassing if he ended up dying to a poison weeks after receiving the blessing of a snake-god. On that note, they hadn't at any point spoken about how to cure it. Jake hadn't asked, and the Viper hadn't offered up any information. They had an unspoken agreement that it would be... well, boring.

But the Viper did give something, as he thought back to the one solid piece of advice the snake-god had given. To focus on mana. He knew mana was necessary for all the concocting and brewing he had done; it was easily the most crucial aspect of the crafting process.

Yet the Viper hadn't mentioned anything about alchemy necessarily. He'd spoken of feeling it around him...

Closing his eyes, Jake could still feel the ever-present mana in his surroundings. He never thought much of it, much like how one would stop smelling it if one lived with a particular smell for long. The same was valid with mana. Something that was there, but unnoticed. Perhaps that had been a mistake.

Feeling the mana was easy, his Sphere of Perception making it even easier. Jake just wasn't sure exactly what he was supposed to do with that feeling. Moving his hands around, he could vaguely feel the mana being dislocated from where his hand was, but otherwise wholly unaffected.

Did the Viper just mean for him to try and feel it more? No, that couldn't be it. Did he then suggest to somehow manipulate or control it? But Jake didn't have a skill for that. He did have some skills to manipulate mana through his alchemy, but those were very specific.

When doing alchemy, he made use of the small runes in the mixing bowl. He had to control the mana in the bowl through those. One could say that the bowl itself functioned as a joystick, his mana the hand controlling it.

Jake saw no way to manipulate the mana in the mix without these runes.

Jake proceeded to try the whole "believe hard enough" tactic, but it had yielded nothing after an hour of trying. Still, he refused to give up. The Viper may have been slightly unstable in many ways, but he didn't strike Jake as a liar. A bit of a jokester, maybe, but he'd had a serious look in his eyes when he gave the advice.

Instead of attempting futility, he decided to quickly test out his new Alchemical Flame. Like with all other skills, it came with instinctive knowledge of how to use it. When he raised his hand and opened it, a small flame appeared, swaying back and forth on his palm.

The heat was low, but so was the mana expenditure. The most surprising was the color of the flame. It was nearly entirely colorless. If Jake poured more mana into it, the intensity and heat increased in turn.

While playing with fire, he discovered that it could cause him injuries, but only when he poured in the maximum mana he could while holding his hand over the flame for a long time. In other words, the offensive capabilities, at least in its current stage, were nearly nonexistent. Not that it was the purpose of the flame to begin with.

As he kept experimenting, he noticed something through his sphere. When he poured more mana into the flame than it could contain, it seeped out the side of his hands, slightly affecting the surrounding mana. A lightbulb went off in his head as he had a revelation.

He couldn't move the surrounding mana, but he had many ways of moving his own. When he used Cultivate Toxin, he always poured mana straight out of his hands into the plants, and when using his crafting skills, he naturally poured mana into the bowl.

So, what if he moved the mana not according to the pattern of a skill, but simply as an attempt to affect his surroundings? It was weird that the thought hadn't occurred to him earlier, but in his defense, the concept of moving an invisible force was not exactly a natural thing to him.

Hours later, he hadn't found much progress, but he did have some. It was early days, but he felt like he could slightly move the atmospheric mana by using his own as a catalyst. It was currently hugely inefficient, the mana literally pouring out of him. But he did slowly learn and improve.

His huge mana pool was naturally a great help, and his Willpower increased his regeneration up to a level where he could keep the practice up for quite a while. Chugging a mana potion, he decided that he couldn't practice using mana all day. He had to keep the alchemy up, after all.

He was starting to run low on mana potions, so he decided to start out with those.

The preparation stages were the usual, but he began to feel some faint differences when he started the mana injection part. Despite his brief practice, he could already feel that his control had improved slightly, though it may also have had something to do with his increased stats and new profession.

The fact that he was making the most accessible type of potion that was also the closest to pure mana manipulation played a part too.

He had evolved his profession and gained massive bonuses all around, and he finally felt like it was time to make a final push to clear this dungeon. His theory on how to cure the poison was still in its early iterations, but it was coming along.

Ahead of him were days of grinding and practice. If this plan worked, he wouldn't leave early, which gave him two weeks of intense leveling.

Hard work in front of him, and with his life on the line, Jake could only smile in satisfaction. This new world might be a bit fucked up in many places, but it sure as hell was more interesting.

Making their way through the camp, the two newfound lovers made some small talk. Heading toward the forge, they greeted The Smith, who was currently working

MANIPULATION 133

hard toward his own profession evolution. The man had achieved his class upgrade already. Jacob and Caroline both agreed that he would likely be the first with both an upgraded class and profession from how he was doing.

"Hey, Smith, how is work going?" Jacob asked as he got close. "Any progress on the spearheads for Casper?"

The bearded smith raised his head from the forge as he grumbled, "Didn't bother. Had the kid make 'em. Ask him."

Brief as ever, Jacob thought, as he turned to "the kid" who worked the forge beside the man. He had kind of turned into a half-apprentice of The Smith over the last week or so. A caster who specialized in metal-magic. Jacob knew he had also gotten his class upgrade but wasn't exactly sure when, or what the evolution's specifics entailed. All he knew was that the young man had a high level.

Going over to the teenager, Jacob asked once more, "Hey, Will, Smith told me that he had you make some spearheads for the trappers?"

With a big smile, the kid looked up from the forge with his soot-covered face. He lifted ten or so spearheads off the ground with his manipulation skill and levitated them in front of Jacob with some difficulty.

"Here they are, Chief!" he replied, seemingly proud of his levitating trick. "Made them just like Mr. Smith asked!"

Jacob grabbed them out of the air and put them in a small sack he had been carrying. Jacob had never quite liked the kid. He just felt... off. For some reason, he reminded Jacob of several of the more ruthless CEOs he had encountered when he went to meetings with his father while young.

While Jacob stored away the spearheads, Caroline went forward and started wiping the kid's face with a handkerchief. A gift from Joanna. The kid stood still as she wiped his face clean and healed his slightly injured hands from the small cuts and bruises he got during his crafting. As a caster, his defensive stats were quite a bit weaker than The Smith's heavy warrior class, after all.

"I told you to watch out when working at the forge," she said with slight concern. "I still don't get why you didn't just do tailoring with Joanna, Jacob, and me, or maybe even leatherworking like many of the other casters."

The teenager just stared back, his features once more revealed with the soot removed.

Jacob hated to admit it, but the kid was maybe even more handsome than he was. Blonde hair, clear blue eyes, and a bright personality. Not that Jacob felt any threat to his love-life. All the women in the camp treated William with partiality, like how you treated a little brother or son.

Saying his goodbyes to the two smiths, he left with Caroline to deliver the spearheads to Casper. Casper was working nearly every day on his traps, having also picked up the builder profession. The synergy between those two was... frightening.

He constructed most of his traps alone. He had to in order to get his class bonuses, and the construction itself also yielded experience to his builder profession. However, he couldn't do everything himself, as he often needed help from the smiths to make weapons.

Casper had thoroughly gotten past his trauma of taking another human's life. He had gotten close with another archer, a woman, and they had spent a lot of time together. That was until four days ago, when her headless corpse had been found just outside their base. To make it worse, Casper had been the one who found her as he was out setting traps.

His mercy to the other side had died that day. Before, he'd mainly tried to make traps to capture. Now he only made them to kill. Jacob tried to make conversation but was met with no response, as usual.

The first day after she died, Casper had spent the entire day crying and mourning. The second, he had started making traps like a madman. He had even tried to leave and fight the other side directly, but luckily, they had managed to stop him. His hatred, however, seemed to only grow by the day.

Jacob barely managed to get a small grunt out of him when he mentioned Ahmed dying. Jacob was lost as to what he could do. He cursed this tutorial, he cursed the system, and he cursed whatever sick fuck had started this entire fucked-up war he now found himself in the middle of.

Caroline, seemingly noticing his mood as they left the trapper, grabbed his hand in an attempt to cheer him up a bit. It helped a little as they made their way over to the tailors and sat down. It was a good distraction from the madness. Sadly, Caroline couldn't stay as she had forgotten to tell Casper something from Richard, so she left Jacob there.

Back at the smithy, William was working hard as he did every day. The stats didn't do much for him, but he got the ability to craft more specialized weapons for himself. Daggers were all fine and good, but he knew that he could make something better.

The teenager hadn't initially planned on doing the whole profession crap, but had to admit that the race levels and stats were worth it. On top of that, leveling his class was just a waste of time at this point. Even killing other humans for tutorial points seemed like a waste of time, considering the difficulty of finding them.

He had tried to piss off the other guy Hayden by killing his son, but somehow it had ended up just making it worse. The number of people fighting hadn't increased much; instead, everyone had gone full-on psycho. He couldn't even do the "innocent teenager" act anymore without getting attacked on sight.

William found the entire thing baffling. He thought he had a good grasp on human emotions, but the fact that everyone would turn absolutely insane like that was unexpected. He didn't get the point of torturing people. Sure, a bit of torture could get information, but it had been well proven through several studies that information gained through torture was unreliable.

Trying to find more lockboxes was also a waste of time as they had undoubtedly been found by now. Beasts were also way too damn scarce. William could find a lot below level 25 if he went back toward the forest's outer perimeter, but the experience from those sucked.

So William made the best of the situation. He had ingratiated himself with The Smith and gotten some awesome training in. This meant that William got a lot of useful guidance early on and leveled his profession faster than he had expected.

He had also managed to improve his social position within the camp. The premier healer, Caroline, clearly approved of him, all the women leading the blossoming tailoring industry liked him, and now he even had The Smith, who looked out for him.

By now, pretty much everyone was in the two bases, a fortunate side effect of his little escalating attempt, which made his plan of being the sole survivor far more probable. Sure, Caroline, The Smith, and many of the tailors were friendly enough, but sadly, their existences were detrimental to whatever reward he would get at the tutorial's completion.

As long as nothing unexpected happened, he felt somewhat confident in his plan succeeding. Something he seriously doubted, as he had yet to learn of anyone who posed a serious threat to his goals.

His thoughts were interrupted as Caroline returned. William looked a bit confused, as she came alone. She was usually with that boytoy of hers all the time.

"Hey, William, I just came to warn you not to go anywhere close to the enemy camp for now," she said. "Richard said it is okay to go out, just avoid going in their direction too much."

William gave an affirming nod.

She sighed as she smiled at him. "I knew you were trustworthy. Sadly, Casper is dead set on going out there alone to set up some traps between our two camps... Oh geez, how many tutorial points do you think he has gathered already? He is sure getting high level too, so I hope he makes it back safely."

"Okay, I promise to stay away from there if I head out," William answered with a big smile. He had a small glint in his eye, as he'd just made a mental note of his next prey.

Richard waited for Caroline to return as he went over some notes. He saw her enter with a bitter look on her face. Once she was inside, he spread out her hands and covered the two of them with a transparent barrier.

"It's done—William will go after Casper," she said as she tried to keep a stoic look.

"Good job, Caroline," Richard said in a comforting tone. "I know you don't like this, but it has to be done. Casper knows too much and is getting both too strong and too unstable. None of us want to risk entering our cabin at night only to be impaled on a cursed spike."

"It's just too cruel..." She sighed.

"You and Jacob tried. If he didn't insist on heading out there alone, but instead listened to the two of you, we wouldn't have to do this. But now we do." Richard got up from his chair and went over to her. "This tutorial may be cruel, but it will soon be over. Once we're back on Earth, we can find time to rest. To rebuild. You and Jacob can get your happy ending, and I swear I will support you as long as you support me. And don't worry, Jacob doesn't need to know anything about this... unsavory business."

Caroline looked at him a bit before turning around to leave. "Let's just get out of this hellhole and be done with this stupid war already."

With those words, she exited the cabin, dispelling her barrier in the process. Richard watched her leave as he smiled. *Oh, what the young and foolish won't do for love.*

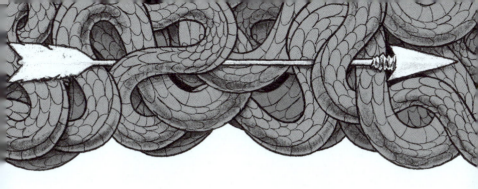

Chapter 35
Blood of the Malefic Viper

A scrap of paper floated in the air as if a small string were attached to it. It was slow as it weaved out the door, evading obstacles in the way. It finally floated into another room before it landed in the palm of Jake's hand, to the sound of a small cheer.

Jake could barely contain his laughter from finally succeeding in his exercise. He had made it a habit to do this kind of practice daily, following the advice of the Malefic Viper.

Through mana alone, he had managed to lift and manipulate a physical object. It didn't seem like much, but for Jake, it was huge. Through sheer mana manipulation, he had managed to create a small tether or string that he had then attached to the paper. It was incredibly weak, no more durable than a thread of spider silk. But it was something.

He had hit the books hard on this aspect of mana and how to use it, and he'd found a lot.

Mana was, after all, a natural force found throughout the entire multiverse. It was known as one of the big three prime energy sources. Health points were also known as the vital energy, and stamina the inner energy, similar to martial artists in legends.

Mana, on the other hand, was the worldly energy. It is the energy used to shape the elements, the laws of the universe itself.

One might be led to believe that one of these energies was superior, but that assumption would be wrong. In many ways, mana was simply another form of stamina, stamina another state of health, and so on and so forth. One type of energy was able to transform into another.

Potions were perhaps the most straightforward example of this happening. In crafting a health potion, only mana was spent, yet it directly restored health points upon consumption, which isn't to say that health potions were liquified energy of life. While the ingredients did contain some life-energy, most of the potion was still the original crafter's mana. That mana would be transformed, with the entire potion held together by system-fuckery.

In addition, some beings only possessed stamina, some only mana, and some didn't even have health points. An example of this was a race known as the automatons. According to the books, the automatons were a powerful race of mechanical beings who only possessed mana to keep their bodies running.

Another example of peculiar races was the very plants he so often practiced alchemy with. Some plants had the power to evolve and gain levels and sentience, the most powerful even achieving sapience and reaching human-like intelligence. These plant-like lifeforms very often didn't have stamina, only health and mana.

Stats naturally also changed according to race. These stats' names varied and often had similar functions as the ones humans had, but some also changed significantly. Having nine different stats like Jake also wasn't a necessity. Some had less, and some had more.

But the point was that all the resources one had available could, through specific methods, achieve most of what all the others could. None of the books detailed any such methods, keeping it very vague.

Through the two weeks since the meeting with his new snake pal, he'd gotten a better grasp on why the Malefic Viper had told him to focus on mana. It had helped immensely with his concocting, and his practice was very close to reaching fruition.

Looking at the timer, he took a deep breath.

Cured yourself of poison 0/1

Time remaining: 23:58:42

Less than a day remaining. The thought that he could be dead in less than a day was a bit weird. For nearly a month, he hadn't felt anything from the poison whatsoever.

But his progress had been impressive. Actually, impressive was an understatement. Around two weeks had allowed him to grind more alchemy than ever before. He had leveled, and leveled a lot, which had even ended up netting him his first "true" race evolution at 25.

The evolution was as he had expected. It had come with a prompt telling him, "Yay, you made it to 25. This is just the first step. Keep it up, pal!"

There had been little fanfare during the evolution itself. Nothing special had happened; he had just appeared in the weird middle-of-the-universe place again. There he'd waited, marveling at the absolutely insane density of mana, before being returned back to his bed.

Not that he was complaining about the evolution and what it came with. The first of which was the improved stat gains.

> Human (E) – A human confidently climbing the evolutionary ladder. The human race is known as one of the most balanced and numerous races of the multiverse, being able to walk many different roads on their path to power. Stat bonuses per level: +2 to all stats, +5 Free Points.

What was a bit different was that the evolution had actually come with a skill.

> [Meditate (Common)] – Enter a state of meditation, cutting off the outside world. While in meditation, regenerate stamina and mana significantly faster. While meditating, no other actions can be taken, and your perception of the external world is reduced immensely.

Meditate was very similar to sleeping. Once one entered it, all one's senses would be muted to nothingness. One couldn't smell anything, hear anything, or see anything. Only the feeling of touch remained... for most people.

Jake, however, was a bit different. All his senses were pretty much completely cut off like everyone else... but his Sphere of Perception remained, completely unaffected. This meant that he could meditate without being completely defenseless. But more importantly, it meant he could keep practicing mana manipulation within his sphere.

Oh, and speaking of his Bloodline, it too had evolved with him.

> [Bloodline of the Primal Hunter (Bloodline Ability - Unique)] – Dormant power lies in the very essence of your being. A unique, innate ability awakened in the Bloodline of the newly initiated human, Jake Thayne. Enhances innate instincts. Enhances the ability to perceive your surroundings. Enhances perception of danger. +15% to Perception.

Another 5% added. Jake couldn't detect anything besides that. Not that he was complaining.

On the profession-leveling side, he, of course, had gotten a lot also. His grind had allowed him to reach level 43, getting a bit more than a level a day on average. It didn't seem like much, considering that he'd grinded out the first twenty-five in less than two weeks, and that was also including way more research through books and him learning the basics of alchemy.

But one had to remember that leveling got more challenging with every level gained. So for him to keep up such a good pace was, in Jake's own opinion, quite... prodigious.

Horrible jokes aside, through the progress of the levels, he had naturally gotten some more skills too. Sadly, the rate at which he earned them had decreased. Now it was only every tenth level.

At least the first skill came at level 30, though. Jake had been offered five new skills, and they were all... well... a bit fanatical?

Just checking out one of the skills sent a shiver down his spine.

> [Preach (Uncommon)] – As a humble servant, the will of your Patron is your privilege to spread. Allows the alchemist to spread the sacred words of the Malefic Viper. Makes the alchemist appear more trustworthy when speaking to others about the Malefic Viper. May his word be law. Adds a minor increase to the effectiveness of Preach based on Willpower.

Yeah, fuck that, was his first thought after checking it out. The four others weren't any better either. One of them was quite literally related to sacrificing people.

Luckily for him, though, he had learned something valuable from the Viper he could apply at this moment. It was common knowledge that two closely related skills could fuse... so he picked Sense Herb.

> [Sense Herb (Common)] – Gives a passive ability to detect herbs and a rough feeling of their properties. An alchemist must be able to find the materials to craft his products, after all. Adds a minor increase to the effectiveness of Sense Herb based on Perception.

After picking it, nothing happened right away. Jake felt the instinctive knowledge begin to enter his mind, the thought of the Malefic Viper having possibly trolled him occurring to him for only a moment before another notification had come. This message told him about the two intended skills fusing.

> [Sense of the Malefic Viper (Rare)] – Fusing the skills of Sense Herb and Sense Poison, the Prodigious Alchemist of the Malefic Viper has earned Sense of the Malefic Viper. The Malefic Viper sought out many natural treasures on its path to power; it is only natural to learn to sense them. Gives a passive ability to detect herbs and poisons in different forms and a rough feeling of their properties. Allows you to far better sense the poison you have inflicted on others. Adds a small increase to the effectiveness of Sense of the Malefic Viper based on Perception.

With the two skills fused, he had gotten an even more useful one. He wasn't exactly sure if it could sense herbs and poisons equally well, and his testing had been inconclusive so far. However, the fact that it now allowed him to sense poison he had inflicted on others was likely going to be very useful.

Jake was a bit surprised the fusion wasn't mentioned in any of the books, though. It was two fundamental skills for Alchemists of the Malefic Viper, so it being noted wouldn't be out of place. Jake had a sneaking suspicion that the system had somehow removed this information, or maybe the skill just hadn't fused like that back in the day?

It wasn't as if the books didn't have any actual examples of skills, items, and even ways of unlocking new evolutions. It had to be said that the information wasn't that plentiful on skills and evolutions, as it could all just be boiled down to one word: Records.

But his skill gains didn't end there. Ten levels later, at 40, he got this second chance to get one. He half-expected to once more be disappointed by choices trying to make him into a cultist, but was pleasantly surprised instead. *Very* pleasantly surprised.

[Blood of the Malefic Viper (Epic)] – The blood of the Malefic Viper is a toxin more deadly than most poisons. Allows the Prodigious Alchemist of the Malefic Viper to turn their blood poisonous, imitating their Patron. The blood can be used as an ingredient in alchemy and as a deadly weapon against your foes. The nature of the poison is determined based on the Records of the Alchemist. The blood's toxicity level is based primarily on Vitality and Wisdom but receives an increase from all physical stats.

It was his very first epic-rarity skill, and a juicy one at that. He predicted epic to be a tier above rare mainly due to videogames.

The skill itself was great. A bit disturbing to think about your blood turning into a deadly poison, but Jake was kind of relieved to find out that it wasn't a passive ability. He had to actively channel mana according to the skill into his blood, and with that, it would turn toxic.

Using Identify on the poisoned blood didn't yield any results, but he could clearly feel it was different. His new Sense of the Malefic Viper gave him a good idea of how different it was from regular blood. The toxin was somewhere in between high-end inferior-grade poisons he had made and the weaker common-grade ones.

He hadn't had the chance to test the nature of the toxin yet, so he saved that for later. Of course, the blood couldn't only be used as a weapon, but also in alchemy.

At first, he hadn't thought that his blood as an ingredient would have any usefulness. It turned out he was wrong on that one. His blood was an excellent catalyst, especially in concert with the blue mushrooms. Just adding a bit to the mix also made the mana injection far more comfortable, as he was literally adding a bit of himself.

This had given Jake newfound confidence in his plan for completing the Challenge Dungeon, and he had been working tirelessly for the last two, nearly three days since he got the skill.

He had found recipes for potions and even toxins that could cure poisons and had even crafted a couple at inferior rarity to practice. Still, he was unsure as to their effectiveness on whatever had infected him.

His plan wouldn't have worked weeks ago, but he had confidence with his newly improved status. Speaking of his status, it had indeed gone through a metamorphosis along with him, especially in the stats department.

Status
Name: Jake Thayne
Race: [Human (E) – lvl 26]
Class: [Archer – lvl 9]
Profession: [Prodigious Alchemist of the Malefic Viper – lvl 43]
Health Points (HP): 2460/2460
Mana Points (MP): 2890/3150
Stamina: 528/580
Stats
Strength: 61
Agility: 64
Endurance: 58
Vitality: 246
Toughness: 139

Wisdom: 315
Intelligence: 90
Perception: 205
Willpower: 159
Free Points: 0

Titles: [Bloodline Patriarch], [Forerunner of the New World], [Holder of a Primordial's True Blessing]
Class Skills: [Basic One-Handed Weapon (Inferior], [Basic Stealth (Inferior)], [Advanced Archery (Common)], [Archer's Eye (Common)]
Profession Skills: [Herbology (Common)], [Brew Potion (Common)], [Concoct Poison (Common)], [Alchemist's Purification (Common)], [Alchemical Flame (Common)], [Toxicology (Uncommon)], [Cultivate Toxin (Uncommon)], [Malefic Viper's Poison (Rare)], [Palate of the Malefic Viper (Rare)], [Touch of the Malefic Viper (Rare)], [Sense of the Malefic Viper (Rare)], [Blood of the Malefic Viper (Epic)]
Blessing: [True Blessing of the Malefic Viper (Blessing - True)]
Race Skills: [Endless Tongues of the Myriad Races (Unique)], [Identify (Common)], [Meditate (Common)], [Shroud of the Primordial (Divine)]
Bloodline: [Bloodline of the Primal Hunter (Bloodline Ability - Unique)]

His stats had naturally had a meteoric rise with the levels, primarily his Vitality and Wisdom. As for Free Points, he had mainly chosen to distribute them between Perception and Wisdom, but had recently also put some into Vitality and Toughness. His way of curing himself of the poison would likely require him to be quite durable, after all. He had even found out that his exploration of the status had been insufficient.

For example, Jake found that he could bring up how he had distributed his Free Points if he wanted to.

> **Free point distribution:**
> Strength: 1
> Agility: 1
> Endurance: 1
> Vitality: 21
> Toughness: 22
> Wisdom: 100
> Intelligence: 0
> Perception: 100
> Willpower: 0
> **Total Distributed: 246**

Some perfectionist part of him couldn't help but bring Wisdom and Perception to 100 each. The percentage increases had also truly begun to show their worth.

Expanded Status

Stats:	Base stat:	Amplifier:	Final value:
Strength:	53	10%	61 (58)
Agility:	54	10%	64 (59)
Endurance:	53	10%	58
Vitality:	205	20%	246
Toughness:	127	10%	139
Wisdom:	263	20%	315
Intelligence:	82	10%	90

Perception:	164	25%	205
Willpower:	133	20%	159
Total:	1,134	15%	1,337

The most noteworthy thing on this entire screen was, for some reason, the parentheses. Looking down at his forearms, he had kind of forgotten that he was wearing the bracers at all times. They had kind of become a part of him by now, and he only took them off when he showered, even keeping them on while he slept. That +3 Strength and +5 Agility sure were handy.

This screen also demonstrated the power of the percentage amplifiers. Jake got a total of 195 stat points from the percentages. His Wisdom alone had increased by 52.

He also discovered that, sadly, the items weren't affected by percentage amplifiers.

Closing all the various windows, he went straight back to work, having finished his mana-control training. He doubted he would have time to train that further before he got out of here... if he got out of here.

His plan to cure himself was relatively simple, honestly. Concoct a poison to kill the other poison.

Over the last day or so, he had finally started to be able to feel what was infecting him. With every second moving him closer, he could feel it more and more. It felt powerful yet subtle. But more importantly, it felt far more magical than physical. Narrowing down what type of poison it was should be possible if he had more time, but sadly, he didn't.

With Blood of the Malefic Viper, his plan had changed slightly. The goal was still the killing poison with poison approach, but now he would actively use his own blood and align the "cure" with his own body.

On the herbal side, the main ingredient would be the silver mushrooms from the first challenge room.

> [Argentum Vitae Mushroom (Rare)] – A silver mushroom only grown in places with extremely high mana density. The mushroom has a solid exterior that, if broken, reveals the actual mushroom within. This type of mushroom's juices usually are highly poisonous, but this mushroom has evolved to bring life instead. +1 Vitality upon consumption.

His highly toxic blood would be used in place of water. Aged Moss of common rarity, on which he had used the Cultivate Toxin skill daily for the last two weeks, would be coupled with the concentrated juices of the blue mushrooms, which he had also been cultivating.

The Argentum Vitae Mushroom would then be the final ingredient. The vitality in those was overpowering and would add powerful energy of life to the concoction. The creation would be volatile and would need to be consumed shortly after being finished, based on all his deliberations.

He would consume the creation just before the poison flared up. Two extreme bursts of toxicity would then ravage through his body, one of immense death-attuned mana, and the other poison containing overpowering life-energy.

If everything worked as he hoped, these two would cancel each other out while his powerful body kept it all together.

Which was also the reason he had invested some points into Toughness and Vitality. He had severe concerns regarding whether his body could handle the sudden influx of energy.

The plan was a bit stupid and extremely reckless, for sure, but despite the dangers, Jake was looking forward to it. There was also a part of him that was a bit greedy… If he consumed the ten mushrooms as they were, he would get 10 Vitality. But if he could achieve some kind of synergy, he should be able to get even more.

Jake believed it would work, and if it didn't, well, Jake would go out on his own foolhardy terms.

Chapter 36
A Battle of Life & Death

Jake knew that before an important exam or test, there were many approaches to prepare oneself. Some studied intensely up to the very last second, in a desperate attempt to obtain as much knowledge as humanly possible.

This approach often led to overload and stress, and during the actual examination, one could not perform their very best.

Another way was to seek approval that one's preparations were adequate. Asking fellow students or colleagues, hoping that perhaps they too felt as underprepared as you, could indicate if it was merely your own mind tricking you into thinking you were behind the curve. These people would be found camping outside the examination room for hours before it was their time, trying to probe for any and all useful information from those just tested.

A third way was the path of denial. Shutting down in panic, unable to act. The actual performance from these people, however, varied wildly. Some even performed with incredible confidence despite their panic beforehand. These were also the ones who felt the most relieved after the fact.

Some looked for a way to either get out of the exam entirely or avoid a fair examination. Cheating was the go-to for these, obtaining the answers beforehand or even during the test. Perhaps even attempting to take high risks to peek at the ones beside you, searching their sheet for the correct answers. Performance-enhancing drugs were not even off the table for these. The most nervous and panicked perhaps belonged to this group.

The final ones were the relaxed ones—the ones who simply rested, trying to get their brain in top shape before the test. Perhaps faux confidence led them to this, or maybe said confidence was well-founded. One could only know after the test was over, after all.

Jake had, throughout his life, fallen into all these four categories at one point or another. He had studied until he had headaches and sat outside the exam room for hours, asking anyone for tips. He'd been nerve-wracked the night before an exam, not getting a wink of sleep. Once, he had even tried to cheat by sneaking in notes not allowed. He hadn't ended up needing them, and he felt like shit afterward, but he had still tried.

But the approach with the most success for him was the last. He would just relax the day before. Read a good book or even play some videogames, perhaps even a trip to the movies. And then finally go to bed early to wake up well rested for the exam.

This had worked out for him very well. Jake was the kind of person to have high expectations of himself, often leading to panic. During his years of pursuing professional archery, perfection was the only option. He'd been competing with the best, so he had to be the very best he possibly could.

University had been very different. In archery, one could quickly come to feel like they had all the knowledge required to perform their best. That the only thing he had left to do was perform his best in the moment.

When one studied theory on strategic business management, as an example, things weren't as straightforward. There was always more to know, more knowledge to seek. If you felt like you knew everything, it meant you simply weren't aware of how much you didn't know. It was complicated, with endless theories formulated and expanded upon for hundreds of years.

The knowledge on alchemy in the small library, albeit still containing around a thousand books, was already far more than Jake could go through during the month he had been here. Even if he had spent every second reading, it wouldn't have been enough. Yet he knew what was in the library was only a drop in the bucket.

The knowledge gained only made him more aware as to how complex alchemy was. Ultimately, all professions were a valid path to power in the system and contained near-limitless possibilities. Even a path to godhood, according to the Malefic Viper.

So, with that in mind, Jake just had to accept that he couldn't perfectly prepare. He had done what he could, and it would have to be enough.

The hours of the day ticked by as Jake relaxed. He read books he had set aside prior, most containing historical tales that read more like a fantasy novel than actual history. Jake thought of his colleagues surviving outside but quickly tried to purge the matter from his mind. He had followed the number of survivors dropping by the day, and with only around a third remaining, he knew it wasn't looking good. Some of them were very likely dead, and he wasn't in any way looking forward to discovering who.

But he did have some time to reflect on his own feelings. The solitude had allowed him a lot of time to think if he liked it or not. He had made some realizations. His crush on Caroline had always been just that, a crush. He didn't actually know her at all, and only found her physically attractive.

His impression of Jacob hadn't changed in the least. In his mind, he was still the same beacon of positivity and hope he had always been. He was also the one Jake hoped was fine most of all. *It doesn't help thinking about it,* he reminded himself. He needed to get in the right mindset for the final push.

For the last eight hours, he slept and meditated. Cultivating the plants he had prepared for the concoction was the only thing that could be called work. That concoction would determine his life or death, after all.

Time passed, and it was finally time to begin. With only four hours to his potential death, Jake felt oddly serene. He felt prepared.

He began by collecting the moss and mushrooms, carefully plucking them according to the methods he had studied. Using the techniques he had become oh so familiar with over the last month, he carried them to the mixing bowl.

Taking out the Bloodletting Dagger, he made a small cut on the palm of his hand and focused on Blood of the Malefic Viper. He saw the now green-tinged blood slowly drip into the bowl. After a couple of minutes, it was filled enough. He had to cut his hand twice more during that time, despite the enchantment making the wounds harder to heal. A testament to his high Vitality and a good sign for what was to come.

His health and mana slowly regenerated as he started extracting the toxic juices from the Bluebright Mushrooms, carefully adding the slightly shiny blue liquid to the concoction. Meanwhile, with extreme caution, he guided the process using his mana.

Letting it soak for a while, and hearing the small crackling that sounded like electricity as the blood and mushrooms combined, he started grinding up the Aged Green Moss into a fine powder with a mortar. When he heard the sizzling and the cracking calm down, he added the moss powder, once more seeing a reaction as the entire thing seemed to boil slightly.

Throughout it all, he carefully injected mana. This part was why he had needed so long, as he had to carefully balance the concoction and guide it to where he wanted it. The necrotic properties were slowly eliminated from the mix as he focused his mana, thus allowing the vital energy found within his blood to prosper.

He could have done it the other way around, amplifying the necrotic properties, since his blood acted as a catalyst that strengthened that property. But now, however, the necrotic energy served as fuel for the vital energy, so he had to be careful.

The reason he had extracted the highly condensed juices from the mushrooms and not just added the entire mushroom was because he only needed a small, highly concentrated amount of necrotic energy to remain. That condensed ball of energy would become the catalyst for the Argentum Vitae Mushrooms, the final ingredient.

He had added a total of twenty-eight mushrooms' worth of extracted liquid. He had tested and probed, and based on his Sense of the Malefic Viper, the condensed energy found within should be enough to help empower the vital energy in the silver mushrooms.

The time he injected mana was long, tiring, and, most importantly, very mana intensive. His pool of 3,150 was quickly being drained. He knew this would happen, of course, as he had invested plenty in Wisdom to make this possible.

Perception had also shown its value, especially in complicated crafting processes such as this. Small changes in mana flow were unavoidable, but with sufficiently high Perception, Jake could detect them before they became an issue. His senses were tense, focused to the limit.

With only twenty minutes remaining, the arduous process was completed. Jake had technically finished the concoction now and would come out with a potent common-rarity poison. Without a doubt, his most powerful yet. But he wasn't done.

Taking out the ten Argentum Vitae Mushrooms, he hesitated a little before simply throwing them all into the bowl. Nothing happened for the first few seconds, he carefully observed with both hands on the bowl. But soon, the silvery layer on the mushrooms got eroded, and as soon as a small hole appeared in the first one, their ridiculous vital energy rushed out like a riptide.

After he quickly chugged his most powerful mana potion, Jake still had around half his mana remaining before he threw in the silver-shrooms. He had considered not putting the potion use on cooldown and instead using a healing potion during the consumption, but honestly, if his plan didn't work, a healing potion would do jack shit.

His remaining mana pool was liberally spent as he contained the vital energy rushing out. Very soon, the energy of all ten mushrooms had started affecting the concoction, and this was precisely the moment he had been waiting for. With a small suggestion through his injected mana, he released the condensed ball of necrotic energy. It clashed with the vital energy.

Or perhaps clashed was not the right word. The vital energy absolutely devoured it, and with his guidance, it assimilated the Necrotic Poison to fuel itself. The minutes ticked by, one by one, as he pushed his mana into the bowl.

When he only had a measly 300 mana remaining, he felt like he was about done. With a final push, spending over 200 mana, he finally heard a small *ding* as he saw the system messages.

*DING! *: [Malefic Viper's Poison] has been activated! The transcendent power of the Malefic Viper has forcefully increased the rarity of your creation to Rare, increasing all effects substantially.

You have successfully crafted [Unstable Amalgamation of Malefic Vitau (Rare)] – A new kind of creation has been made. Bonus experience earned

'DING!' Profession: [Prodigious Alchemist of the Malefic Viper] has reached level 44 - Stat points allocated, +5 Free Points

Quickly inspecting the sludge left in the bowl, he couldn't help but make a weird compromise between grimacing and a smile.

> [Unstable Amalgamation of Malefic Vitau (Rare)] – An unstable creation, made by mixing opposing energies, achieving something more potent than the sum of their parts. It contains an immense power of vitality, powerful enough for it to turn into a poison. Not fit for consumption. Incredibly Unstable: Unable to maintain current form in 9:57.

It was what he had hoped for. Perhaps more than he had hoped for. He had gotten a whole level from it, as he had also just leveled up from the last batch of poisons he made. He quickly threw the Free Points into Vitality. He would need everything he could get.

He hadn't expected Malefic Viper's Poison to trigger. Truthfully, he wished it hadn't. It had thrown all of his prior calculations off course... He feared what he had made was too strong. Sadly, he didn't have time to attempt anything else.

Looking at the timer, he prepared himself.

> Cured yourself of poison 0/1
>
> Time remaining: 2:38

Two and a half minutes, and the poison would flare up to take his life. At that moment, he would drink the sludge in front of him. He didn't dare touch it, but would simply drink it straight from the bowl.

A BATTLE OF LIFE & DEATH

As he just sat there, looking at the timer tick down, he did something he couldn't remember ever doing before. He prayed.

He had never been the religious sort. He never went to church, not even during Christmas. But today, he prayed. Not to the gods of earth, but to the one god he had met.

The Malefic Viper may not have been the most stable being he had ever met, but he was powerful. He had blessed him, allowing him to complete the miracle he had created today. He was the one behind his profession. At least it was based on who he was, or his Records to be more exact.

So, he prayed. His prayer was as humble as can be.

"I fucking swear, you stupid snake, if I end up dying from drinking mushroom juice, I am going to return from the dead and hunt you down."

To his surprise, he felt a response. Just a vague emotion from beyond. A faint encouragement, coupled with a barrage of mockery.

He smiled to himself. He had done what he could, and now it was up to his own willpower and determination.

The timer mercilessly ticked down.

> 0:28

He looked at the sludge as he put his hands on the side of the bowl.

> 0:17

He took a deep breath and thought back to his days here in this dungeon.

> 0:13

Serenity overtook him as his body relaxed.

> **0:11**

With a quick peek, he confirmed his health pool was full. *Good*.

> **0:07**

He lifted the bowl and prepared to drink.

> **0:05**

"Here goes nothing," he said as he lifted up the sludge and gulped it all down.

The taste was a bit sweet, but he barely had time to notice it because of what came next. His entire body and mind were consumed by a wave of pain from everywhere the sludge touched. A source of pain that only a moment later was joined by another.

From somewhere around his heart, a massive amount of energy suddenly manifested—one seeking only to destroy every trace of vitality in his body.

His instincts screamed at him, making him fully aware that if the deathly energy spread to his brain, it would mean game over. He would be unable to mobilize his will and energy control to fight.

Luckily, the energy couldn't easily spread, meeting significant resistance from his powerful physique. But it was far from enough. He felt himself literally rotting from the inside, not unlike what had happened during the second trial and the toxic liquid.

A BATTLE OF LIFE & DEATH

But as the energy crept upwards, it met a force it couldn't conquer. His mouth and the upper part of his body had already started growing red as the vital energy overpowered his being, also slowly killing him. Tumors began growing at a visible speed, as the vital energy had nowhere to go, nothing to regenerate.

The vital energy was not entirely pure either but mixed with the necrotic properties of the Bluebright Mushrooms. Jake's thoughts were jumbled and thinking straight was borderline impossible as he simply lay collapsed on the laboratory floor. Every sliver of his focus was on the battle within him.

The two energies sought to destroy each other. Two mighty armies, one of death, and one of life. Jake's body was the battlefield in which they fought.

If Jake had not consumed his concoction, the poison that flared up would have been significantly weaker than it currently was, as the two both sought to destroy, yet also empowered, one another.

With what little will he could muster, with it mainly being his instincts taking charge, he mobilized all the energy he could to protect his head. This was the most dangerous stage, as both energies were at maximum capability, and all he could do was hide away and hunker down.

This didn't mean he only hid away. The two energies fought, but both had failed to recognize the powers already present on the battlefield. Another army rode in from the same place the energy of death had initially come from.

The third source of energy was another source of vitality. But unlike the others, this one was controlled and with purpose. It was Jake's original health points, a massive squadron of vital energy stemming from his second-highest stat, Vitality.

It entered the fight not as a contender, but as a force to control the battlefield. A mediator to make the armies of life and death battle on equal terms, slowly canceling each other out. At the right moment, it would then enter the fray, strike down the vulnerable energy remaining, and seize victory.

His body was rotting, yet, shortly after, regenerating the decaying flesh once more. Other parts grew red as tumor-like growths appeared; however, they quickly got squashed by the energy of death.

Jake couldn't even scream, as his airways also alternated between life and death. At all times, death was a moment away, but it was always crushed by overpowering vitality before it could take hold.

If his Vitality or Toughness had only been just a few tens of points lower, he would have died by now. But he didn't die. He suffered, he screamed internally, but never once did he wish for the embrace of death. He fought with every fiber of his being to live.

For in the end... what is death, but just another challenge to overcome?

Chapter 37
Leave Nothing Behind

The Malefic Viper stood in the desolate middle of nowhere, surrounded by the ever-present white mist. He had stood here for days now, unmoving. The decision to leave had been made, but the last step still stumped him. It wasn't that he couldn't or that he didn't want to go. A single thought would bring him away. But he still felt doubt. It had been a long time since he last left... A very long time.

Suddenly, he felt a small trickle of faith come to him, for the first time in many eras. Of course, he knew from where it came. He had only one being in the entire multiverse who held his blessing, after all. The prayer was simple, if a little insulting.

The Malefic Viper couldn't help but chuckle to himself as he peered through the void into the Challenge Dungeon, observing Jake drink his concoction.

"Crazy bastard," he muttered to himself, smirking. "And entirely pointless. Should I tell him that his body would be powerful enough to survive the poison already and how he is unnecessarily putting his life at risk? Nah, gonna save that one."

Looking at Jake drink down the sludge, his own hesitation seemed like a joke in comparison. He feared the unknown, while his one blessed mortal faced death with courage and a bit of foolhardiness.

"I guess I should stop stalling."

With those words, he disappeared from the desolate realm.

A ripple went through the multiverse as he passed the veil. An aura that hadn't appeared for eras washed across existence, only detectable to the most powerful of gods. Some had already felt the movements of karma when he granted his True Blessing, but now there was no doubt.

The Malefic Viper had returned.

Two mighty giants stood on the metaphorical battlefield, one representing life, the other death, equally matched as they each tried to fell the other. Their fight had allowed them both to grow, but at the same time, had whittled away their strength. The end was near.

Yet, at that very moment, the third, forgotten, entity struck. A mighty arrow of life surged forward, utterly destroying the avatar of death. The giant of life took this chance to leap on the fallen avatar but was only met by the consuming grasp of the hunter. It had no recourse, as it was too weak from the long battle.

The war of life and death had finally come to a close. It had only been a bit less than an hour; however, the pain had been utterly consuming, and Jake felt delirious despite his body now slowly healing. Yet he felt triumphant. He had won, all the poison now either firmly nestled harmlessly away in his body or wholly eliminated.

Jake suddenly heaved in a breath as his throat finally finished healing, and he could once more draw in air. The experience had also inadvertently taught him that he didn't really need to breathe much anymore. Not that it made the inability to breathe any less hard to get used to.

He stayed on the ground for several minutes as he became aware of his surroundings, noticing he was still in the dungeon. His head was a mess, and he couldn't move a single finger. The pain had subsided significantly, but it still hurt as his body kept healing. Whatever vestige of poison remained in his system was pretty much gone by now, and his natural resistance would handle the rest.

His mind started clearing up, and as it did, he couldn't help laughing. Or at least he tried, but ended up just gurgling out blood instead. After spitting out a lungful of blood and grime, his attempted laughter did go through, though.

He had lived. His foolish gambit had worked. Honestly, he did feel a bit like an idiot currently. Based on the power of the poison, a single well-made, inferior-rarity antidote would likely have cured him or at least suppressed the effects enough for his body to handle the rest. Maybe his body could have taken it even without any external help.

THE PRIMAL HUNTER

His own little concoction had only amplified the flareup and turned it into the nightmarishly potent poison that nearly took his life. Not that any of it mattered now. He had won, after all. And with his victory came a slew of system messages.

> **You have assimilated a potent source of vitality.**
> **+1 Vitality**
>
> **You have assimilated a potent source of vitality.**
> **+2 Vitality**
>
> **You have assimilated a potent source of vitality.**
> **+1 Vitality**
>
> **You have assimilated a potent source of vitality.**
> **+1 Vitality**
>
> **...**

It went on for a bit, and Jake could see that it had periodically given him stats after the initial intense burst.

In the end, he had ended up getting a total of 31 Vitality. The energy naturally came from the Argentum Vitae mushrooms, which would have granted him 10 Vitality if he'd just eaten them straight up. Fewer stats, but it wouldn't have required him to nearly die.

With the poison cured, he had naturally also passed the trial.

> **Dungeon Challenge:**
>
> **Cured yourself of poison 1/1**
>
> **Congratulations! You have successfully cleared the tutorial Challenge Dungeon!**
>
> **Rewards given are based on performance during all trials.**
>
> **Dungeon shutting down in 3:57:11**

Looking through the message logs, he found he had completed the dungeon a bit over two hours ago. It had taken him only a couple of hours for his body to heal enough for him to regain proper consciousness. Not that he was entirely healed yet, as he couldn't really move his body. Like, at all.

As for rewards, he had gotten not just one but two titles. However, these were more in line with his initial Forerunner of the New World, compared to Bloodline Patriarch, or his quite overpowered Holder of a True Primordial's Blessing.

> **[Dungeoneer I] – Successfully clear a Dungeon suitable for your level. +1 all stats.**
>
> **[Dungeon Pioneer I] – Be the first to clear a dungeon suitable for your level. +3 all stats.**

The stat points were fine and all, but most important was the number 1 in both of them, in his honest opinion. This clearly indicated that these titles were not just one-offs but would likely grow for every dungeon he did.

Finding nothing else of note in his notification window, he closed it and just lay there. His Sphere of Perception made him aware of his surroundings, and he noted the bottles of health potions inside one of the cabinets. With nothing better to do, he began weaving a small string of mana to try and drag one of them to him like he had been practicing.

So far, the heaviest he had lifted using only pure mana was a pen. So a bottle, even a tiny bottle, still took quite the effort. First, he had to open the cabinet to get the potion, cursing himself for even closing it to begin with. Why did he need to close cabinets? Or doors, for that matter? Not like anyone else was going to wander in and scold his lack of etiquette.

The process of opening the cabinet was a real struggle, not that Jake in any way minded it. He was alive. And he was feeling great. Well, aside from the whole body-being-paralyzed part. Looking at his health points, they were at a measly 700 out of nearly 3000, and this was after they had regenerated quite a bit. He had likely been below 200, perhaps even below 100.

Health points, also known as vital energy, functioned as the fuel that healed the body and kept a living being alive. Undead creatures famously didn't possess any health points but instead had an energy of death that kept them un-dead.

This meant that the natural healing of the body consumed health points. When one took damage, an initial portion of health was consumed, with another part used to heal the wound afterward. As long as health points remained, so did the life of the being who possessed it.

But being "alive" is a rather broad term. If the poison had consumed Jake's brain, it didn't mean that all his health points would've instantly disappeared. He would've remained alive, and his health points would've kept healing his brain. If the poison was then cured, his vitality winning the bout and his brain healed, no permanent damage would be sustained.

The problem was that the brain was still the organ that served as the director of consciousness. The mind existed within the soul, but it couldn't do anything or even be aware of itself without the brain. Memories, personality, and what makes you *you*, existed disjointed from the physical body. Many beings in the multiverse didn't even necessarily possess a brain or a set physical form; some only had an intangible spirit form. At least that was what all the books Jake had read on the topic said.

For humans, at least at his current rank, losing the brain would mean losing all semblance of control and consciousness until it regenerated once more. If Jake had lost access to this control, he would no longer be able to affect the two opposing forces at all. He would be unable to fight on the metaphorical battlefield, which was why he'd struggled so hard to defend his brain during the assault.

Jake had no idea if this weakness was amendable, but guessed that there were skills that allowed a human to still act despite having no brain. Perhaps it would naturally happen with an evolution in the future.

And speaking of health, Jake's epic quest for acquiring a health potion had reached a critical stage. He had managed to budge the cabinet's door slightly, a major win in his book.

After a few more minutes, as he was finally getting close to fully opening the cabinet, he felt a bit of his mobility return. At first he could move his fingers, then his hand, then arm, and soon he managed to sit himself up.

It turned out, the whole quest for the health potions had been a waste of time. Dragging himself off the floor, Jake still felt weak throughout. With difficulty, he opened the cabinet and took out a healing potion.

He felt a bit better after drinking it, but getting back to top shape would still take a while. Overdrawn vitality was not so easily overcome. From what he had read, the weakness typically disappeared when the health pool was once more maxed out, and he still had about half to go for that.

As he walked out of the laboratory, his Sphere of Perception picked up something new.

He had spent thirty days in the dungeon, and with his sphere always active, he had every single minute detail memorized. But in the room where he had initially gotten his profession, two lockboxes now sat on the shrine within.

He didn't hesitate to enter the room and check them out. One of the boxes was rather large, while the other one small. Both were jeweled, and as he approached them to use Identify, he was pleasantly surprised.

[Challenge Dungeon Lockbox (Rare)] – A system-created magical lockbox enchanted with the ability to block off all types of

> attempts to peek inside before opening.
> Awarded for passing the Challenge Dungeon.

The bigger box had a rare rarity. Opening it, Jake saw a pair of boots.

They looked old and well worn. Both looked to be made of leather that had once been brown but was now a dull gray color. Small scratches and minor imperfections marred their surface, and the soles looked like they had accompanied their last wearer for countless steps. In all honesty, they looked far worse than his slick leather bracers.

Using Identify on the old boots, however, he was not disappointed.

> [Boots of the Wandering Alchemist (Rare)] – Boots once offered to an alchemist before setting out on a journey to experience the world outside. Despite being made of simple leather, the Records of the alchemist have left a deep mark on this item, allowing it to transcend many ranks. Enchantments: +20 Endurance, +15 Agility. Reduces stamina expenditure from all movement-related skills by a small amount. Increases sensitivity toward earthbound plants.
>
> Requirements: Lvl 25+ in any humanoid race.

They rewarded 35 total stat points and two passive effects. The reduced stamina expenditure was useless to Jake currently as he didn't have any movement-related skills, but he was sure it would show its worth down the line. It would be bizarre if he didn't get any movement skills from his Archer class.

The increased sensitivity would likely also be useful, he assumed. Without any hesitation, he put on the boots. He hadn't been wearing anything beforehand, since his old shoes had been entirely devoured by acid around a month ago. It felt great to finally have something on his feet, and the boots themselves felt amazingly comfortable.

The comfortable feeling only increased as he injected mana into them and felt the familiar feeling of his stats improving.

Feeling great in his new boots, he turned to the other, smaller lockbox and was once more pleasantly surprised.

> [Challenge Dungeon Lockbox (Epic)] – A system-created magical lockbox enchanted with the ability to block off all types of attempts to peek inside before opening. Awarded for passing the Challenge Dungeon with excellent performance.

He'd had his doubts if the system would reward him for taking a more difficult path than necessary to succeed, and it turned out it did. Barely able to hold himself back, he opened the lockbox and looked inside.

A very expensive-looking necklace lay within. The entire thing was made of what seemed like silver or perhaps even platinum. A green gem beautifully adorned the chain. With great anticipation, he used Identify on the stunning work of art before him.

> [Prodigious Alchemist's Necklace of Holding (Epic)] – An amulet awarded to a prodigious young alchemist upon completion of a trial. An ornate creation of high craftsmanship

> made of metal attuned to the space affinity, holding a spacegem in place. Allows the user to store items in a small pocket dimension found within the gem. Due to the nature of the gemstone used, living, non-sentient entities can be stored without harmful side effects in temporal suspension. Enchantments: Alchemist's Spatial Storage. +25 Wisdom.
>
> **Requirements: Soulbound**

Jake cracked a big smile as he read it. The good old trope of the item box. And his item box was even the type that could store living items. The 25 Wisdom was also more than welcome. The bonus of storing living entities was naturally to allow plants to be stored, and a lot of plant life went bad not long after being picked, so keeping them alive through temporal suspension seemed almost like a must-have.

He was a bit worried about the Soulbound requirement, as he wasn't quite sure what that meant. Though he doubted he would be unable to use it unless this was a massive prank by the system. If he had to guess, he would say it just meant that it was bound to him.

Picking up the necklace, he put it around his neck before injecting mana into it. With it came the feeling of his Wisdom increasing, but it was accompanied by something else—knowledge of how to operate the spatial storage.

In his mind, he had a mental image of a room. The room had no source of light but was pretty extensive. How big exactly, he couldn't quite comprehend. The lack of any point of reference made it even more difficult, as the room was completely empty.

Looking at the timer for the Challenge Dungeon shutting down, he still had two and a half hours left. Quickly, he went to the library and started storing books. At first, he did it individually, but soon he was scooping up bookshelves at a time. After keeping all the bookshelves, he even grabbed the desk, chair, pens, and pretty much everything he could get his hands on.

In the spatial storage, he found that the items had barely taken up any space. Quickly, he went to the bedroom and threw it all into the spatial storage too. Bed, dresser, another small table—everything went in.

Next, he stopped by the laboratory, but here he met his first difficulty. A lot of the instruments were fastened to the wall and floor. Luckily, the mixing bowl, the most essential tool, was able to be brought along. The small burner, however, was fixed. It seemed like he had to either find a new one or use his Alchemical Flame skill instead.

A bunch of the other instruments, like the mortar and pestle, he also brought along. Next, he started storing the potions and poisons he had made over the last month. In reality, most of them had been created only over the last week, as he had to empty out a lot of the bottles periodically to recycle them.

Luckily, the cabinets storing the bottles were freestanding, allowing him to grab them whole and toss them into the storage. Looking at the barrels of purified water, he kept the full one and picked up the other as he headed toward the garden.

Carrying it to the garden, he filled it with purified water before he threw it too into the storage. Looking at all the plants, he cracked his knuckles. *Leave nothing behind.*

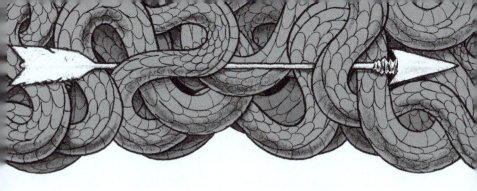

Chapter 38
Broken

Many herbs were still in the garden and cave. After all, Jake had never made anything above inferior rarity in potions and still had all the common-rarity ingredients left entirely untouched. With the spatial storage able to store plants, he needed a way to get them into it.

He quickly discovered he couldn't just will them to enter it. Sadly, the spatial storage couldn't just tear them out of the ground.

So the next one and a half hours went by as he dug them up by hand. He also went by the cave afterward and collected all of the mushrooms and moss.

It didn't take him long to gather everything—his improved physical stats were finally being used constructively.

With less than half an hour left in the dungeon, he did the only logical thing he could think of and took a shower. He didn't know when he would next get access to a nice bathroom, something to be made use of as much as possible while he still could.

After cleaning up and putting on his clothes once more, he went to the garden and waited for the time to end. Looking at his reflection in the pond, he saw the minor changes the evolutions had brought about.

It had made him a bit more handsome, if he had to say so himself. His features were all a bit sharper. He'd initially been a bit on the short side but had grown a couple of centimeters too, from the looks of it. His fashion sense did ruin his improved looks a bit, though. The brown cloak, leather bracers, and old worn boots were standing out like a sore thumb.

He looked a bit funny, admittedly. If one looked below the cloak, they would find some old linen clothes he had found in the bedroom dresser. His old clothes had been wholly ruined a long time ago.

As his thoughts wandered, time ticked on, and with a final look at his reflection, he disappeared from the dungeon.

Caroline exited the cabin with Richard after reporting what she had just learned. Casper had made himself known once more.

Two weeks ago, he had wandered out of the camp in the middle of the night. Their expectations had been broken, as he'd just vanished without a trace. No one had heard or seen anything from him before today, making them believe that he was actually dead.

He wasn't. He had contacted them through a stake outside their base... addressed to William.

Casper hadn't headed toward the enemy camp... Instead, he had gone back. Back to where they had entered the tutorial initially. And now, she and Richard were thinking of what to do.

A small sphere was around them, blocking out all sound as they walked through the camp.

"Just send William..." Caroline said. "Wouldn't it be better just to kill him already?"

"Casper or William?" Richard asked.

"William, of course. Casper hasn't done anything for two weeks... We can have him return." She spoke almost pleadingly. Jacob had been in a slump emotionally ever since Casper disappeared... and guilt had been gnawing at her too.

«... Fine," Richard conceded. *Even if William dies, I can figure something else out.* The only positive thing one could say about William was how little he had done for the last two weeks. He had only been hunting beasts, really, and spent the majority of his time with The Smith.

However, despite all that Richard tried, people had begun to question too many things. He was also relatively sure Jacob knew that the kid was way off. He had wanted to get rid of William and Hayden already, but sadly, no opportunity had presented itself.

Now, with Casper calling out William directly, too many had begun connecting the dots. Richard was unsure of what to do. If he acted like he didn't know anything, he would appear incompetent. So he went with the most straightforward solution of hopefully just having the two kill each other.

Can I still use this to lure Hayden out? he thought as he began to gather his hunting party with Caroline. Not to go after William... They had to keep leveling themselves too.

Casper sat on the ground, meditating.

He knew *he* was coming. The narcissistic bastard wouldn't be able to resist.

For the last day, he had prepared the clearing. Everything was ready for the ritual. He just needed that one final piece.

His last two weeks had been... eventful. It had all started when she died.

Her name had been Lyra. His shining star in this hellhole. He had fallen head over heels for her instantly. They had begun a relationship that never had time to truly flourish. He had been too cowardly, and their time too short. She had been murdered.

Hatred overtook him. He didn't care about some war; he didn't care about the other faction leader, claiming that his son had died. He was past caring.

So he made traps, traps to slay the beasts in human skin roaming through the forest. It was his personal mission to thin out the herd as much as possible before he joined her. Casper had no naïve hope of surviving the forest. He knew it would be his final resting place, and he would lie down here gladly to rest eternally beside Lyra.

Yet, at that moment, as he was weeping alone, he heard a whisper—a call from the forest. One he followed.

There he found a door leading to a Challenge Dungeon. The dungeon hadn't contained any challenge. It was just an island with a single tower on it, surrounded by a black sea. Not of water, but a black sludge that Casper hadn't dared to touch.

Within the tower, he'd met *him*. Or at least a part of him. And that being had offered him a deal, one he couldn't refuse. It had helped prepare him, evolve as his race reached level 25. A level he still sat at now. He couldn't progress further quite yet.

Throughout the clearing in which he sat, hundreds of spikes of dark metal were embedded, each impaling the corpse of a beast. Runes ran down their surfaces.

Casper felt a jolt as he opened his eyes, aware once more. He looked up and saw the blue-eyed, blonde teenager of his former camp staring back at him. William.

"Hello, oh master of traps and deceit," the teenager said as he did an exaggerated bow toward Casper. He had a playful look in his eyes and a friendly smile on his lips. Yet he was staying pretty far away, not daring to enter the clearing entirely.

"You actually came," Casper said, a part of him a bit surprised despite *his* words.

"It is a free tutorial, mate; ain't nobody telling me where I can and can't go," William answered with a laugh, clearly mocking Casper.

"No, but you follow their whims nevertheless," Casper mocked back. "So, why have you come, William?"

William completely ignored the first part and responded to the second. "I am just curious why you asked for me; I don't recall us having any beef?"

"Stop being willfully ignorant already," Casper said, a bit annoyed. "Your attempt at starting a war is clear as day to anyone not constantly stuck inside the camp. Richard knows. Half of his men know. So just stop this silly farce and speak as your true self for once."

The young teenager's demeanor changed as he looked back, his smile remaining, but his eyes going cold. "Fine. Let's talk. But I go first... What the hell is your plan out here? Your plan with recklessly trying to hunt down Hayden and his men for days and then just disappearing in the middle of it?"

"I wanted revenge, you bloody moron, for what they did to her. I know you didn't directly kill her, but you still fucking caused it!" Casper yelled before taking a deep breath to calm himself down once more.

William looked at him, obviously a bit bewildered at the outburst.

"Gonna be honest, I don't get why they go so much overboard when killing, and I think torture is quite dumb. But isn't it equally illogical to react to it like you are? You risked your life needlessly by going closer and closer to their base instead of just going for the easier beasts. Don't you care about tutorial points or experience at all?"

William didn't ask to provoke. He was honestly curious. He didn't understand it. He had been lost on why the reaction had been so violent from Hayden to begin

BROKEN 185

with. He had lost his son, an essential asset for sure, but why the response?

Casper looked a bit at the youth before he answered with a question of his own, one he already knew the answer to. "Have you ever lost someone you loved?"

«Let's say I have. Why would that make me seek revenge to the level of forsaking all logic like you?" William was a bit confused by the question. He had quite honestly always been a bit stumped when it came to the term "love." It seemed like a somewhat undefined emotion, and he was very unsure how exactly it worked.

"If you love someone, they become important parts of your world. If you love someone enough, they become your entire world. Then, if someone takes away that world, wouldn't you want to take theirs in return?" Casper was unable to hide his emotions. He hated himself for not realizing how much Lyra had meant to him. They had only spent a week together... He knew it wasn't logical, but he couldn't let it go.

"But will taking their world away give yours back? If it doesn't... Wouldn't it be better to try and construct a new world? Though it does seem a bit stupid to invest so much in something that you lose everything by losing it." William could kind of understand the analogy, but he still wasn't entirely sure.

"You wouldn't understand, William. Love is an emotion far too complex for one such as you to comprehend." He was purposely trying to rile the young man up. Petty revenge, if you will.

"Define love?" the youth asked, a bit annoyed.

"You won't ever get it, William. You won't ever understand the feeling of losing someone. Truly losing someone." Casper smiled at the youth. "And that is your biggest weakness."

"What the fuck are you on about?" William sneered. A weakness? What was this moron on about?

"You are broken—even more than I am. You believe emotions are a weakness... when your inability to feel is the true weakness." Casper stood up.

"If they are so important, then why don't you explain them?" the young caster said, preparing to strike. "Make them *actually* make sense for once? Because from what I've seen, the only thing emotions bring with them is stupidity."

"I am not going to waste my time engaging in futility." Casper chuckled.

William, now well and truly pissed off, went back to a tried and tested method. Threats.

"If you do as I say, I promise not to kill you. You know what I am capable of."

Shaking his head, Casper could only sigh. "William, that threat only works if the person you are threatening cares about living. Oh, also... I'm stronger."

As the words left his mouth, they both made their move. Daggers flew out from William as he simultaneously summoned his wall to protect himself against any attacks. Internally, he'd already summoned up the energy to create his disc.

Casper, on the other hand, just spread out his hands... and the forest hummed. All of the spikes around him began to glow with a ghastly light as tendrils of shadows extended from each of them, gathering in a giant sphere of darkness floating above his head.

The daggers didn't even get halfway before they fell to the ground harmlessly, the mana within gone, his control of them lost. William's wall also disintegrated as the mana holding it together was overwhelmed. The energy he was building up to summon his disc was utterly suppressed by the mighty aura of the dark sphere.

"Wha—" William yelled out as he froze up.

"Resentment, William. The resentment of the fallen. Pure emotion turned to power, a curse left by beasts and men alike." Casper looked up at the sphere.

He wasn't controlling it. He couldn't. It was power far above what he could wield... the result of the magic circle taught to him.

"This is what you call weakness," he went on. "Look at you. How weak and insignificant you are. Observe the kind of power you are too broken to even attempt to grasp."

William could only stand there, wide-eyed, his mouth quivering. "Pl... Don't kill me! I didn't kill—I won—»

"Oh, I am not going to kill you. It would be pointless anyway. Another has already claimed you. Neither my teacher nor I have an interest in attracting unnecessary conflict. No, you are a witness." Casper smiled.

From below his cloak, he took out a spike. The same kind he had made countless traps with and used to kill dozens of humans. On it was a script more complex than any of the ones around him.

"Goodbye, William. I shall take my leave from this accursed place first. May we never meet again." Then he impaled his own heart. The dark runes spread from the spike into his own body.

The sphere above reacted to his death, finally finding something to inhabit. The energy of resentment dove down and bore into his body through every orifice as he slowly began decaying. William just looked on, horrified and confused.

Moments later, with all the energy now within the dead archer, the runes transferred from the spike lit up. The mana of death began spreading from the body—which was when the final part activated.

An amulet, formerly hidden, activated. And with that, Casper disappeared from the tutorial.

"He did well," the being said as he nodded in satisfaction.

"Adequate," a female voice concurred.

"Our Patron gave express orders, after all," a third chimed in.

They had been observing a seer-stone moments earlier as they saw Casper disappear. A powerful magic circle before them had activated at the same time. Immense amounts of mana were mobilized as a figure appeared standing in the middle of the circle.

"It's done," the newcomer spoke as he walked forward, bowing to the three of them.

He had done everything as told. He didn't necessarily know *why* he had to do all the things he had done. It was just a part of the pact he had made. William had been led to the intended spot, and he had witnessed what he had to witness.

"Well done, Casper—the Patron is satisfied with your performance," the first figure said with unabated envy in his voice as he motioned with his skeletal hand for the young undead to rise. "And welcome to your afterlife."

Chapter 39
Powershot

Jake cursed under his breath as he walked through the narrow cave. He had totally forgotten the shitty location of the Challenge Dungeon. At least he could walk out a lot faster than he had gotten in.

He was also happy to finally get his weapons back. He had missed his bow. It would have been a great stress-reliever in the dungeon to do some target practice. The quiver had naturally also come back with the bow.

One of the two daggers he had was now redundant after having gotten the Dagger of Bloodletting. It was common rarity, and despite being made of bone, it was far sharper and far more durable than his steel knives. And that was ignoring the enchantment to make things bleed more.

Another absolute positive was how damn comfortable his new boots were. It was utterly illogical how some old, worn leather boots could feel like walking on clouds while simultaneously getting your feet massaged. He feared that he would never be able to go back to regular footwear.

The winding tunnel took him only half an hour to go through this time, though he purposely ignored all the blue mushrooms in his path. He had had enough of those for now, and with his bow in hand, he felt himself become slightly restless. He hadn't fought anything for thirty days after just getting a taste of it.

He had briefly considered seeking out his colleagues. But he was afraid that he was not powerful enough. He had minimal information and no idea what kind of growth all the other survivors had gone through.

Professions were inherently not combat-focused, while classes were. Jake's class being at only level 9 meant that he had fewer combat skills. His Strength, Agility, and Endurance—the stats that also happened to be the most important, along with Perception, for archers—were his three lowest stats by quite a bit too.

Reaching the end of the cavern, he once more found himself at the foot of the hill. He couldn't help but take a deep breath as he looked around and took in everything within his Sphere of Perception. He had been confined for a month, either in small halls or the cave and garden. While the garden was spacious, it was nothing compared to the vast forest.

His sphere instantly picked up something that put a smile on his face. A small group of deer was on the hill above him. They were a bit larger than he remembered, but based on the one evolved stag among them, it seemed like the same group he had chosen to avoid before entering the dungeon. *Must be fate*, he joked to himself.

There were five of them: one stag and four deer.

Making his way up the hill, he could only describe his feelings as childish anticipation. He had grown stronger in so many ways, his stats increasing manifold, and yet he had no outlet in the dungeon. He had nothing to test himself against.

He was more powerful than he had ever been now, and he had far more methods than ever before. At the top of the hill, he finally saw the beasts. The stag's antlers were glowing a faint white light, while both the deer and stag had rune-like motifs covering their hides. They weren't even trying to hide that the beasts were magical in some way or another.

Using Identify on the stag, he was happy that the now upgraded skill showed the beast's name and level.

[Lucenti Stag – lvl 24]

Identifying the other ones, he found them all in the low 20s, the weakest only 19.

[Lucenti Deer – lvl 19]

Despite their levels being literally twice that of his class, he felt not a shred of threat from them. This meant that he, with no hesitation, took out his bow while at the same time taking out a hemotoxin of inferior quality that he had stored in the necklace.

He dipped five arrows in the concoction, one for each beast. He had absolute confidence in winning, but not in killing them quickly without the use of poison. He still remembered his rather horrible damage output from

before he entered, and even with the overall stat growth, it likely still sucked.

But a poison would make up for that. The hemotoxin would increase the bleeding from any wounds Jake made and, of course, deal damage in general. Toxins were most commonly cured by merely having your vital energy overpower and wash it out.

This naturally consumed health points. Some intelligent beings would simply allow a poison like a hemotoxin to remain in their system until it naturally dissipated, as its effect was relatively harmless as long as you didn't take any hits.

The beasts, however, had proven themselves to be anything but intelligent. They seemed to function off pure aggression and instinct. And trying to get rid of the poison in your system seemed like a somewhat instinctual thing to Jake. He would know; his instincts were quite something, if his Bloodline ability was to be believed.

The only slight annoyance with using poisons was the fact that the poison had to stay in its bottle or it would lose its potency fast. Unlike normal pre-system poisons, the mana within concocted poisons would become ineffective within ten minutes or so of leaving the bottle. His Malefic Viper's Poison did extend that duration, allowing it to stay toxic for up to half an hour, so that did help quite a lot.

He also couldn't just soak an arrow in poison and then put it in his storage. As the arrows were conjured, they couldn't be stored, or they would just turn to mana whenever he tried. Not that it would have helped anyway, as the "duration" of the poison still decreased despite the temporal suspension in the necklace. He tried it with a dagger by coating it in poison, but when he took it out an hour later, all the potency in the poison was gone.

Having his arrows prepared, he nocked the first poisoned one and aimed at the stag. The arrow was loosed with great speed and power as it flew true and hit the stag in the neck, only penetrating with the arrowhead—more than enough to deliver the poison, though.

Momentarily stumbling, the stag, and the rest of its group, for that matter, were obviously taken by surprise. None of the deer had any chance to react before another arrow hit one of them, followed by another and then another.

Jake shot faster and more accurately than ever before; he hit the last deer just as they had located him and started charging. Deep trails of blood were left after every beast, and Jake was happy to continue peppering them with wounds as they approached.

Only three beasts managed to reach him as Jake had successfully hit the stag in one of its legs, nearly severing it. A second deer was stuck in the eye and was now lying and spasming on the ground, likely only waiting to bleed out. Which left Jake with only three beasts to deal with in melee, since the stag very probably wasn't getting back up.

The other three beasts finally made it into melee range, all dropping buckets of blood from their wounds. Jake took out two daggers, one of bone and one of steel. Just as they got close, they all exploded with light, burning Jake's skin and blinding him. Not that it mattered much, as he didn't really need his eyesight that much.

Dodging the initial charge, he swiped the bloodletting dagger across one of the deer, leaving a long gash that spilled blood like a waterfall. The second deer was not much luckier; it was granted several stabs with his other dagger. The third one, he simply allowed to ram into him as he wrestled it to the ground.

His danger perception had barely reacted, making him willingly take the risk of fighting it in close combat. With the four others down for the count, he didn't see much threat from a logical standpoint. Something that was a mistake, as he failed to dodge a beam fired as a last-ditch effort by the stag in its dying moments.

The beam left a nasty burn wound, almost like a high-powered laser. Yet despite Jake assessing the wound as "nasty," it didn't affect much and already started healing itself mere moments after it was inflicted.

As for the beast pinning him down, he raised his hand and placed it on the neck of the creature, digging his fingers into its hide, then used Touch of the Malefic Viper on full power, throwing away all subtlety the skill allowed. Instantly the effects were made clear. The flesh his hand touched started rotting, showing clear signs of necrosis, as the deer let out a whimper before it collapsed.

Jake got back up and noticed the rest of the beasts either dead or in their final moments. Taking the dagger, he made a quick round and finished the rest of them off.

He had felt the levels more than once throughout the battle and knew it had been a fruitful hunt. Quite honestly, him being level 9 at the beginning was just sad in a way. His stats were clearly not that of a level 9 Archer at all.

Opening his status window, he saw the kill notifications for the first time in a month. It felt incredibly satisfying. One could argue it was a bit sad that the first living things he met he had killed. Discounting the Malefic Viper himself, of course. Snake-gods didn't count.

You have slain [Lucenti Stag – lvl 24] – Experience earned. 4000 TP earned

You have slain [Lucenti Deer – lvl 20] – Experience earned. 3000 TP earned

You have slain [Lucenti Deer – lvl 19] – Experience earned. 2750 TP earned

You have slain [Lucenti Deer – lvl 21] – Experience earned. 3250 TP earned

You have slain [Lucenti Deer – lvl 22] – Experience earned. 3500 TP earned

And as for levels, he had gotten quite a bit in that department too.

'DING!' Class: [Archer] has reached level 10 – Stat points allocated, +1 Free Point
...
'DING!' Class: [Archer] has reached level 13 – Stat points allocated, +1 Free Point

'DING!' Race: [Human (E)] has reached level 27 - Stat points allocated, +5 Free Points

'DING!' Race: [Human (E)] has reached level 28 - Stat points allocated, +5 Free Points

Four levels from a single fight lasting only a few minutes. The bonus experience from killing higher-leveled enemies sure did its work. While the kill notifications didn't explicitly state that he got any bonus experience, he clearly did. If he had to guess, then classes and professions had separate experience meters?

The race levels were, however, where the real value lay. Whenever Jake got a level in his class, he got a measly 5 stat points and 1 Free Point. On the other hand, his race levels gave 2 in all stats, or 18 in total, and 5 Free Points. So, a total difference of 6 and 23 stat points per level. Nearly four times.

Of course, his profession was also quite ridiculous, with it providing 15 stat points and 5 Free Points, or 20 in total. But one had to remember that was evolved and a variant. Plus, it took two levels in either profession or class to get a single race level. It had at least been consistently that way so far.

Passing level 10 in his class naturally also meant something else.

Archer class skills available

Jake knew he had to mentally prepare himself after getting skills from his profession. He couldn't expect a random rare or even epic skill from a basic starting class, after all. So, with little expectations, he went through the list, the first one being about as basic as he expected.

[Twin Arrow (Common)] – The Archer's arrows are never-ending; a single arrow becomes two. Allows the Archer to shoot an arrow that splits into two during its flight. Adds a minor bonus to the effect of Agility and Strength when using Twin Arrow.

This one was very fantasy-esque. It had several useful applications; the sneak attack component alone would be great. Oh, you thought one arrow was heading your way? Sorry, it was two. But the thing he was most concerned about was how exactly a splitting arrow would work with his poisons. Would both have it? None of them have it? Or only the "original" one? Or did the skill just conjure new arrows entirely? He just felt there were so many unknowns. If it didn't work with his poisons, he didn't care.

If it merely divided the poison between the two split arrows, it would be worse than not splitting at all. It was far better to deliver one strong dose to one area than two weaker doses in two regions. The former was far harder to heal and get rid of.

With him having more concerns than excitement for the skill, he moved on.

> [Bow Bash (Common)] – Who says the bow can only be used at range? Allows the Archer to bash with his bow, knocking back the target. Increases the bow's durability and gives a minor bonus to the effect of Strength when using Bow Bash.

This skill was way more straightforward. Just a skill that allowed him to hit people with his bow better. The purpose of the skill seemed to be keeping his enemies at a distance. The skill would indeed be useful, but Jake wasn't exactly getting excited over reading it. Moving on, he hoped for something better.

> **[Bouncing Arrow (Common)]** – The Archer has many tricks hidden in their quiver. Allows the Archer to shoot an arrow that bounces off the first object it hits. Adds a minor bonus to the effect of Agility and Strength when using Bouncing Arrow.

This one was just gimmicky as hell. It seemed fun and interesting, but he had some serious questions as to the usefulness. He reckoned it was the kind of trick that would work once against an enemy and then be utterly ineffective from that point onwards. And if one had already seen the trick before, they wouldn't be tricked by it as easily the next time. Again, another disappointing skill in his honest opinion.

> **[Active Camouflage (Uncommon)]** – Sometimes, mere stealth is not enough, but one must hide their very being. Focus your mana and attune your presence to your surroundings, allowing you to stay hidden far more effectively when standing completely still. Adds a small bonus to the effect of Wisdom when successfully remaining hidden.

This skill was a bit more exciting. Jake assumed it would allow him to hide from methods of detection other than the five senses, likely even allowing him to avoid detection from magical perception skills. *Would it work against my Sphere of Perception?* he couldn't help but wonder.

Another interesting point was that it used mana and scaled with Wisdom. All his other skills in the archery class scaled with Strength, Agility, and sometimes

Perception. The resource used when activating the skills—or well, skill, as he only had Archer's Eye so far—had been stamina and not mana. This one was also of a higher rarity, so was certainly a contender. As for the last skill, it too was of uncommon rarity.

[Powershot (Uncommon)] – An Archer with time to line up the perfect shot can be the deadliest foe. Allows the Archer to charge up a shot, increasing the power based on time charged. The longer the shot is held, the greater the stamina expenditure. Adds a small bonus to the effect of Agility and Strength when using Powershot.

This skill was relatively simple—channel and charge up a devastating shot. Jake thought of the application of the skill, as he had done with all the others. It would sure be useful as an opener since he would have plenty of time to charge up the shot.

One thing he had contemplated was also the possibility of the power behind his arrows not being high enough to penetrate the outer skin, or perhaps even natural armor of an enemy. For example, the big boars had a rough hide protecting them, and Jake remembered barely being able to penetrate it.

Beasts such as reptiles often had natural armor too. Heck, the Malefic Viper was a snake, and even his current form had scales covering the entire body. Jake would be incredibly surprised if said scales didn't offer a lot of defense.

If he thought of other humans, it would also be useful. The prior skills seemed to revolve around trickery and hiding, two things beneficial against humans but not very useful against beasts currently. Beasts, at the moment, had horrible perception of enemies in their surroundings and were far too easy to sneak up on. Trickery was also wholly unnecessary as the beasts did little more than just charge and use whatever innate abilities they possessed.

Powershot, on the other hand, would allow him to possibly take down one beast far quicker, hence making the fight easier.

On the negative side, the skill was channeled and likely took time to use properly. Chances were, Jake would only ever get one good shot off in a fight, possibly two if he somehow managed to open a lot of distance between him and his foe.

Overall, he was a bit disappointed by the skills offered. Then again, he had been a bit spoiled by the Malefic Viper skills.

Jake had no intention of going after humans at that moment. Never, if he could avoid it. Jake didn't like fighting people, and the challenges he sought after could as easily be found against beasts. So he picked the skill he deemed the most effective against those: Powershot.

Ultimately, the skill would allow him to take down powerful foes easier, and currently, he saw it as the most useful.

New skill gained:

[Powershot (Uncommon)] – An Archer with time to line up the perfect shot can be the deadliest foe. Allows the Archer to charge up a shot, increasing the power based on time charged. The longer the shot is held, the greater the stamina expenditure. Adds a small bonus to the effect of Agility and Strength when using Powershot.

And with that settled, it was time to get some more levels under his belt.

As he was preparing to move, he felt something not that far away from him. It was still a few kilometers, but the feeling was... powerful. He couldn't quite describe it, but it felt like a huge mass of energy had gathered there, drained from where he was and everywhere around him. Maybe... maybe even from the entire tutorial area.

No matter the case, he had to investigate. Hopefully, he could find something worth fighting there.

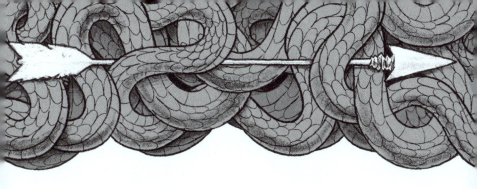

Chapter 40
Defect & Meeting

William looked at the now pitch-black clearing where Casper had disappeared from earlier. He had been standing there for minutes now. William didn't get it. But more infuriating than that was that he didn't understand why he didn't get it.

That power was something William wanted... He *needed* it. But he couldn't even begin to understand what it was. No clue remained either, as all of the spikes and the corpses of the beasts they'd impaled were gone.

Casper had claimed it was some kind of emotional power... resentment. William understood being mad at someone, but how could that possibly be so tangible? His claim of doing everything and reaching the power he had due to love was also... ridiculous. Illogical.

He had never gotten it. Love was a weird, ethereal word not commonly found in his internal dictionary. He knew that his parents had claimed to love him. But if love was such an all-consuming feeling as the trapper claimed, why had the parents who claimed to love him chosen to abandon him?

Why did people think he was broken?

William had always thought himself a smart kid. He had been quiet, controlled, and done as he was told. His schoolyears had been straightforward and easy. He'd never had any friends, and he did recall seeing "specialists" who'd concluded that he just had a hard time understanding empathy. Putting him on some spectrum, something that allowed him to avoid much suspicion later on in life.

At only eleven years old, he had found an old book, looked up the word "love," and tried to do as it said. Do to others as you want them to do unto you, which meant that the next many years were fine. He was a well-behaved child and never did any wrong. The problems only started arriving when his brother was born.

He remembered his parents being happy, having fulfilled their biological quota of two children to carry on the bloodline. He also remembered them being sad when they discovered that the child had a defect. A product that Darwinism would have claimed if nature was to run its course without the interference of society.

William was twelve when the kid was born, and he would never forget the difficulties it brought. His mother had to quit working, and all semblance of free time and family outings stopped. William may have had his issues, but he still enjoyed what other children did and sorely missed going to amusement parks and the zoo.

As the years passed, the problems continued, and William tried just to do his own thing. His parents had forgotten their otherwise "troubled" teenager, being far too busy with his little brother, who required constant care.

Then, and even now, William never understood why they'd kept the child. They'd known even before the birth that it wouldn't come out whole. It would never amount to anything; it was a failed attempt. In all other areas, you were told that if a product turned out terribly, you just throw it out and start over or move on to more important matters. But his parents had used the ever-ethereal argument of love to bring the child into the world.

Once more, William didn't care. As long as he did nothing illegal, his parents didn't care either. Back then, William had big plans. He'd enjoyed studying, he'd liked to learn, and he'd found great pleasure in learning about other humans, most of all. He'd learned how they worked and how he was supposed to act around them. But more importantly, how to make them act as you wanted.

His plans were grand. He still remembered the day he found out he had gotten into the best university in his area. He remembered the genuine joy he had felt. But he also remembered his parents' slightly reluctant attitude to his happiness.

It turned out that having a child requiring a person to care for it every hour of the day, combined with a lot of medicine, is expensive. They never told William, but he discovered it himself as he heard his parents whisper in the middle of the night. They were about to go into debt. William would have to move to go to the university... He would need money—money they didn't have.

William did not take the news well that his plans for the future wouldn't become a reality. The child, his so-called brother, was making that impossible. So William did as he had read in that book so many years ago. He did unto others what he wished they would do to him. He helped them.

He knew the law. He knew that the child, now five years old, was still wheelchair-bound, and quite frankly, at risk of dying to any unexpected danger. It wouldn't be suspicious if it happened.

A device was used to allow the child to breathe during the night. The thing they called his brother was so defective, it couldn't even do that without help. The night was also the only time the child was left alone for just a bit of time. Still regular check-ins every hour, but alone in between.

William snuck in that night. Having just turned eighteen, he got to work. He considered bringing it up to his parents, but he knew no legal defense was better than not having done anything illegal. With that in mind, he decided to do it alone.

Switching off the alarm was easy enough. Guides to those devices were on the internet if one looked hard enough. Next, he did the most straightforward thing and simply twisted one of the tubes delivering oxygen, stopping the flow. And with that, he went back to bed and slept like a baby. He had done a good deed, after all.

It was a pure win-win situation. His parents would be freed from a burden, their economic situation would improve, and with that, his plans of higher education made possible. He saw nothing getting in the way but a possible legal investigation, but he had made sure to make the twisted tube look like it happened by accident. So, if anything, it would be some unrelated caretaker getting in trouble, as she had been the last one to operate the machine and was responsible for keeping watch.

He was awoken an hour later by shouting and screaming as the caretaker panicked, and his mother was even worse off. His father had been at work, as he was working nearly every waking moment to make ends meet.

William had succeeded. His brother had slept in, never having even woken up. And now he would never wake up ever again. William was proud of himself. After the panic and mourning, an investigation was made, and it was ultimately deemed an accident.

Throughout the entire process, he had never once been suspected. He had only been questioned once, and he'd just claimed that he was sleeping the whole time.

But to William's surprise, things didn't immediately improve. Despite having removed the burden, his parents didn't get newfound freedom, and the focus of their family didn't go to making sure his university plans were fulfilled. Instead, it became endless mourning, and his mother even deliriously wanting to sue both the caretaker and the company that made the machine due to the alarm failing.

William didn't get why they were so reluctant just to move on. Why they had to act as they did. When the movements to sue got closer and William discovered that the legal proceedings would put the family even further in debt, for what even he could see was a pointless legal battle, he decided to finally come clean. There was a bit of a risk that an investigation would get reopened, but the risk was worth it.

Their response had been far from what he expected. He knew they would be angry—lying and acting deceitful was not okay, after all—but the reaction was way out of proportion. He tried to explain; he tried to reason; his logic had been flawless. He had acted entirely rational throughout it all.

His father yelled more than ever; his mother broke down crying. After that, he had been sent to his grandparents' place. He was forced to talk to shrinks, therapists, and many other so-called "experts."

He was sent into programs, homes, and in the end, a fucking closed facility. His parents never told anyone what he had done, and yet they locked him up like he had been the one to ruin their lives. Like he had been the burden.

He was pumped full of drugs, his logic dying, and from then, it all turned into a blur with only moments of clearness. One and a half years he spent living like that. Even now, his memories of the time were shrouded, like a cloud of mist was obstructing his mind.

He only had a single one with a clear head of those many months as he managed to fool some new hire that he was getting. That he understood what they wanted. That he understood the emotions that they all found oh so important. But he could only fake it for so long until a more experienced employee caught on, and he had no peace after that.

The system saved him. It freed him. Not just physically. It freed his mind.

Here, in the tutorial, he had time to think. He had time to do as he'd always wanted. He would manipulate, exploit, and do everything possible to win. He had viewed his inability to understand these emotions as a perk for the past month, not a fault.

But today, Casper had made a small crack in that belief. Was he missing something? Was he... broken? *No, impossible.*

There wasn't anything to fix. It was a strength, his strength. He had been called "mentally ill" before; it wasn't new. Casper was just an outlier. William had brilliantly fooled Richard, Caroline, Jacob, everyone! Not a soul suspected him. He was perfect.

William only saw the world as consisting of two kinds of people. Those useful to him reaching his goals, and those not. If someone didn't hold value for him, there was only the value he would get from harvesting their tutorial points and the experience they offered.

The system itself agreed with his reasoning. It only confirmed his thoughts. He was rewarded for every kill. Not punished like the old world. Rules didn't apply to the strong. And William... William was strong.

He firmly believed that. He was finally untethered. No laws, no parents, no vague moral obligations to anything. The only one he had to please was himself. His only limiter was the extent of his own power. So he would do anything to obtain more power.

William, lost in thought, found that he had wandered quite a distance. A bit closer to the camp, but not in a straight line. He did see some beasts, but all were below 25, so he was still in the outer area for sure.

As he turned to the camp's direction, he spotted something out of the corner of his eye—a single individual walking through the shrubbery. It was a man, judging from the build, and he was wearing an upgraded common-rank archer cloak, but he saw no bow in sight. Nothing else about him was of interest, as the cloak concealed his entire body.

William considered attacking, but something made him pause. There was a presence to the man. He couldn't put his finger on it, but through all the evolutions and levels, a certain innate sense had been unlocked. And that sense was currently making him aware that the man wasn't simple.

William used Identify on the man. He knew he was terrible at remembering to use it, as he hadn't even bothered to use it on Casper before. Or anyone really. *Something to improve*, he told himself. But when he got the response, his eyes widened.

[?]

It was just... nothing. No feedback at all. A single question mark was all William got. After he had gotten the Identify skill to common rarity, it had told him the race and level of everyone... but now it didn't work.

One would typically take that as a sign to avoid combat, but William saw it as the exact opposite. This was a perfect opportunity. *Casper was an anomaly*, he reminded himself. This lone person in front of him appeared strong. He was alone. William would make him the case study of why he wasn't wrong.

"Hello there!" he said with a huge smile, completely back in his faux persona. "Haven't seen anyone else for a while out here. What you up to all alone with how things are?"

William tried hard to make the man let down his guard. The man he presumed to be an archer took off his hood too, and William got a good look at the man. Brown hair, forgettable face, utterly dull. The only thing that made him stand out was his eyes. His gaze was sharp, focused.

The teenager had met a lot of people out in the wild. He had seen a wide range of emotions: fear, curiosity, caution, anger, and even happiness and relief at some points. But the eyes of the man held none of those. He couldn't quite place his finger on what his gaze held, but William didn't like it.

He had never tried that before, and it put him slightly off his game. As he was wondering how to proceed, the man answered.

"Good question. Just got here myself. Been a bit busy in an oversized cave for a while. Or would calling it an ancient temple be more accurate?" He shrugged before asking, "You heard of any gatherings of survivors around here? A camp or something like that?"

William looked a bit bewildered at the man. The first part was nonsense. He had been in a temple? The young caster had been many places, and he hadn't seen even the shadow of something that one could describe as a temple. The latter part was also confusing. How could he not know of *any* gatherings of survivors? The two bases hadn't exactly been subtle with their hardcore recruitment.

"Eh, yeah, we got some bases," William answered, seeing an opportunity. "I am a part of one of them myself, actually. I can bring you to it, if you like? It is a bit far, and it is easy to get lost in the forest, after all."

«Hm... what's the name of the leader of the camp? Or notable people? And you mentioned bases, as in more than one? Just take me as someone absolutely clueless to the situation currently in the tutorial. Because I am." He'd dodged the offer of the escort with his own questions.

"Sure thing! We got two bases, one run by a dude named Hayden and another run by another bloke named Richard. Both are a bit bonkers, and a big war is kinda going on. As for notable people... we got a good smith named Mr. Smith? Or well, some call him The Smith. Anyway, he is excellent, and I am sure he could help fix up your stuff."

He was trying hard to sell his camp—not that he had any intention of the archer ever making it there in one piece. But if they traveled there together, there were bound to be opportunities.

The archer stood a while, contemplating. William's brain was working at high speed, trying to see every possible scenario. He wanted to avoid a straight-up fight if possible, as a direct confrontation with an enemy of unknown power seemed like a bad idea.

Finally, the archer responded, "Sure, I guess you can take me there. Meanwhile, tell me of the other members of your camp. Perhaps I know some of them."

With delight, William smiled and cheered internally. The sucker seemed oblivious to his intentions, on the surface at least. He hadn't spotted any openings yet, but the teenager seriously doubted that anyone could stay completely vigilant at all times. The way back to base was far. Especially far, considering William wasn't going to take him in the direction of the camp at all.

"Of course! My name is William, by the way. A caster, as you can likely see by the robe. It's a bit far, and my physical stats are a bit bad with my class and all, so it may take a while. But I will have plenty of time to answer any and all questions you may have."

William put on the attitude of a true used-car salesman. He also used the age-old trick of downplaying yourself, inevitably making the other party feel superior, making them more likely to relax.

"Well, nice to meet you, William. Now, on to the other members of your camp...»

A bit annoyed that the other party refused to even give his own name, William simply endured as he happily started yapping away about his base's outstanding members.

It was going to be a long trip back.

Chapter 41
Clash

Jake walked beside the teenage caster as he happily chatted away. Jake had been taken aback by learning about two massive camps that, combined, held nearly all the remaining survivors in them. He had come here looking for the source of mana before, but instead, he'd found a caster, and from his aura, it didn't feel like it was him. *Oh well, this is fine too.*

The archer was able to remain relatively relaxed as he walked. He had naturally inspected the young man when they first met.

[Human – lvl 24]

He was happy to see that it now finally worked on humans. It only showed race level, giving Jake no idea about the teenager's class or profession details. He knew he was a caster based solely on his clothes.

Jake didn't feel like sharing any personal information either, despite the other party's subtle, and not so subtle, probes. The caster called himself William, or Will for short. He had stressed the last part quite a bit. Being friendly was all well and good, but Jake seriously didn't like the guy. He was far too chippy and animated to appear genuine.

All of that was naturally ignoring the fact that William was likely going to try something. He wasn't sure what, but he had a feeling. If he had to make a guess, Jake would guess a classic ambush, or maybe he would just try to backstab him at some random point?

Jake wasn't afraid, though. He was low-key looking forward to it. With the kid being a well of information, he saw no reason not to travel together for a bit. It would also allow him to better understand the level of power other survivors possessed. Even if Jake couldn't win, he was confident in escaping with his high Vitality and Toughness.

They walked a while, the teenager still talking and Jake giving brief answers. His Sphere of Perception, as always, made him passively aware of his surroundings. He was still half-expecting an ambush to be somewhere, but no matter how long they walked, he saw nothing.

Suddenly, William stopped and knelt, motioning Jake to do the same. Perfectly aware that nothing was in the area, Jake nevertheless played along. *This is silly.*

"Did you spot that?" the teenager said as he pointed down the small hill they were approaching. "I have a skill that allows me to see hidden concentrations of mana, and there is a big ambush just up ahead. They haven't spotted us yet, but I am unsure how many there are."

"What do you want me to do?" Jake asked, trying to act as seriously as he could. His sphere still didn't pick up quack. While he wasn't going to rule out people being able to hide from it, there sure as hell wasn't anyone close.

"You are an archer, right? Can you maybe go up that hill we passed earlier and try and see if you can spot anything from up there? I know you guys got, like, super high Perception, right?" William motioned with his hands once more. "Don't worry, I will keep watch here and help in case they try anything!"

Jake nodded along as he listened. *Cool story*. Yet he followed the directions. Was he really going with that?

Jake started slowly walking up the hill, going backward, trying to act as if he was still actually looking for an ambush. William had turned his back to Jake, as he seemingly focused hard to keep an eye on things.

After a few meters, Jake turned his back to William, and the moment he did, a barrage of daggers flew soundlessly out from beneath the caster's robe. Jake couldn't help but smirk internally as the expected attack came, but he quickly furrowed his brows a bit at the power and number of attacks.

Fourteen daggers were coming. Without any hesitation, he jumped to the side, all the blades missing their initial attempt to skewer him. As he barely got a footing, the daggers turned in the air and swiftly came his way once more. When a bow appeared in Jake's hand with a quick motion, he dodged once more and returned an arrow toward the caster.

William had turned toward Jake at this point, surprised that the archer had dodged his sneak attack. Even as he dodged the second and third blow, the archer seemed to have eyes on his back. The counterattack was quickly blocked by William, as he was once again surprised.

What surprised him this time was not the power, but the lack of it. The arrow had been weak. He doubted the attack was from someone with even 100 Strength, something pretty much all physical fighters had—especially one an even higher level than himself.

The arrow thus easily got blocked by his iron wall as he continued to manipulate the daggers. This was by far the most slippery foe William had ever faced. He wasn't as fast as others he had met, but he seemed to be perfectly aware of all the attacks aimed at him.

The arrows continued as he blocked again and again. It felt like a waste of time, but the archer just kept shooting. Not wanting to lose momentum, William started deploying walls of iron to try and trap the archer, but he kept weaving in and out, never having more than one side blocked at a time.

He wanted to throw a disc, but the arrows made it hard to focus. He couldn't lessen his control too much on the daggers or the walls either. It was beginning to annoy William, and he was starting to get impatient.

Jake was, in his own mind, relatively relaxed throughout all this. He felt in control, and he felt the kinetic energy of the daggers lower than expected. The walls were a bit of a problem, but he reckoned the other party was draining mana fast.

Another thing he quickly noticed was the control of the daggers worsening as he moved further away. With a plan in mind, Jake kept retreating more and more as the caster started chasing him. The wall of iron always floated in front of him, making Jake only able to see that. With his eyes, that is.

As he managed to jump a reasonable distance back, he felt the caster somehow slide himself forward, almost as if he was flying. No, he was controlling his own body like he controlled the daggers.

Jake took this chance to stop retreating, deposit the bow in the necklace, and charge toward the caster. Dagger of Bloodletting in hand, he managed to close half the distance as the daggers caught up to him from behind.

Taking a gamble, he chose to betray expectations as he allowed five daggers to hit him in the back, penetrating into his flesh. However, his movements were unaffected as he vaulted over the wall of iron, swiping down with his dagger.

William was surprised by Jake's gamble. He scrambled to activate mana barrier, one of his starting skills. The barrier barely did anything as the dagger came down. William did manage to slide himself backward slightly, only taking a minor cut to his forearm.

Smirking, he had the daggers resume their assault at full power, forcing the archer on the defensive once more. In William's eyes, Jake had taken far more damage from the daggers in his back than the minor cut he had inflicted. Of course, he didn't know about Jake's ridiculous Vitality. And he hadn't noticed the blood already on the dagger before it cut him.

He only noticed as he started getting slightly dizzy, losing control for a moment and allowing the archer to close in a bit more. William, in panic, looked to his arm and saw the wound, now black and festering.

What the fuck? he yelled in his mind, now genuinely panicking. He had experienced poisoning from the evolved badgers before, but this felt way worse. To make matters even more horrifying, the archer was nearly upon him once more.

When the archer was only a couple of meters away, William made his final gambit. No longer aiming to necessarily kill his enemy anymore, all he thought of was to escape. Even if he won, the poison would simply consume him anyway.

The final card William had up his sleeve was called Flashing Steel—the newest skill in his repertoire. His entire body lit up with a bright light reminiscent of a flashbang as small pieces of scrap metals exploded out of him. The whole area around him exploded and formed a small crater.

Jake was already too close, and even with his danger sense, he was taken entirely by surprise. He managed only to raise his hands as the metal hit him. The metal's momentum shot him backward tens of meters before he finally hit a tree, unfortunately only pushing the daggers in his back further in. It was like he had just been hit by a super-powerful frag grenade at close range.

The final thing he saw before the caster left his sphere was William himself flying backward, manipulating his own body once more. Jake quickly lost track as he saw the caster disappear into the trees.

Pushing himself off the tree he had smashed into, he groaned and tried to reach for the daggers sticking out of his back. They hurt like hell, but his bodily strength was not comparable to an average human's anymore. Ripping the daggers out took a while because some of them were tricky to reach, but he got it done in a few minutes.

His frontside was perhaps even worse than his back. The scrap metal that William had blasted him with at the end had quite the power behind it. Luckily, his cloak had absorbed a lot of the impact, leaving it in tatters. He really hoped the Self-Repair enchantment still worked despite the extensive damage.

Sitting on the ground and breathing heavily, Jake meditated as he thought back on the fight. He had underestimated the other party. He had seemed carefree and inexperienced during their walk, but the caster had been ruthless and calculating in the battle. The control of his abilities had been impressive.

Jake had only met one survivor so far, but his plans of approaching his colleagues just yet were already questionable. He didn't have any clue as to William's relative power compared to everyone else. He knew that the teenager was a part of Richard's base, which led Jake to believe that Richard had to at least be stronger.

Lack of information was a great weakness for him currently. What if William was just an example of a regular member of Richard's base? He had confidence in facing one caster of that level, maybe even two if he got the jump, but anything more and he would surely be on the losing side. Even then... he had only won because of his poison. If the caster had known about it already, Jake wasn't one hundred percent sure things would have gone as well as they did.

William had, during their conversation, been very careful to reveal nothing about the powers of others. He had, however, mentioned that both bases combined had numbers in the hundreds. If facing just one other survivor had ended up with him losing nearly a third of his health, facing any random small squad would likely be fatal.

Worst of all, while Jake had won, he had likely failed to kill the opponent. He used the word *likely* as there was still a chance the caster wouldn't make it. Before his charge, Jake had used Blood of the Malefic Viper to soak his dagger in his toxic blood, effectively poisoning the enemy. He would need a healer for sure, as Jake doubted the kid had high enough defensive stats to battle it himself. That, or he would need a potion.

Which was another thing Jake didn't know about. Did they have any alchemists? If they did, could they make any detoxification potions? Smiths, tailors, and builders had all been mentioned, so them having professions was indisputable. It was also very believable that they would keep any knowledge of alchemy hidden from outside sources, along with other powerful profession types.

All of this ultimately led to Jake being very hesitant in trying to seek out his former colleagues. He had parted with Richard by killing a bunch of his men, so he had serious doubts that the guy would just welcome him with open arms.

No, for now, he needed power. Power to be able to seek them out with his head held high, and at least the confidence to escape if things went sideways. So he decided to hunt. His class was only level 13, and he could efficiently kill level 20+ beasts for some quick levels. His colleagues would have to wait for now.

After meditating a while, he took out a health potion and drank it. It filled his pool back up quite a bit, his body visibly healing. *I need to get stronger.*

Turning toward the depths of the forest once more, he started searching for new prey. It was power-leveling time!

Caroline looked at the gloves in her hand as she smiled proudly at her creations. They were only inferior rarity and didn't offer any stats or anything. But it did give her plenty of experience to her profession.

"Oh, those are nice. Made for a certain someone, eh?"

Turning her head, she saw Joanna taking a seat, the premier tailor and the one who had taught her a lot of the techniques she currently used.

Caroline jokingly hit Joanna on the shoulder, reprimanding her. "Stop it... I just thought he needed some gloves, you know?"

She laughed. "Don't get me wrong, I am supporting you one hundred percent! You and Jacob are so cute together; it reminds me of when I first met Mike..." Her bright smile dropped toward the end.

"Joanna, we don't know what happened to everyone else," Caroline said, laying a hand on her friend's shoulder. "I am sure he is just in another tutorial, and I am just as sure that he is fine. Mike was always a tough guy; he can take care of himself."

Smiling, Joanna snuggled up to her young former colleague. "You are such a sweetheart. No wonder Jacob couldn't keep his hands off you. Speaking of Jacob, have you guys talked to—»

But before she could answer, an archer stormed over to them, yelling loudly, "Is Caroline here!? Come quickly, we got an emergency! Richard is asking for you ASAP!"

Without any hesitation, Caroline got up and ran after the archer. Around the gate to enter their camp, she saw dozens standing around, a few of Richard's men keeping them away.

As she got to the gate, she saw one of the other healers sweating as he tried to heal a caster on the ground. When she saw that the wounded person was William, she was taken aback. One of his arms was entirely black, and protruding veins were visible, extending from his shoulder onto his chest. Instantly, she knew that he had been poisoned by something powerful.

Richard stood at the side, throwing her a glance. She looked questioningly back at him. When he nodded, she got to work.

Focusing, she started casting a curing spell, as she allowed the other healer to continue trying to keep the young man stable. The poison was strong. Very strong. And to make it worse, it even had magical properties, making it only harder to cure.

But Caroline was not the strongest healer in their base, possibly the entire tutorial, for nothing. She flooded the teenager with a pulse of mana, washing away some of the toxins. A couple of powerful pulses later, the black color had started fading slightly. With a final push, she managed to dispel every trace of poison within the teenager.

William himself was unconscious as she and the other healer managed to finally fully heal him. Caroline felt that he only had one wound on his body, a small cut on his arm. If they hadn't healed him, he would have died without a doubt. A significant weakness of casters was not getting any defensive stats from their classes, and from the looks of it, William really had terrible physical stats.

From her assessment, a warrior like Richard, especially with his class evolution, would be able to fight the poison himself, solely due to his higher Toughness and health pool.

William, now healed, still hadn't woken up. From what Caroline felt as she flooded his body, both his health pool and mana pool were pretty much empty. She didn't know their values, but she could get a rough estimate that he was low.

After making sure William was fine, the next task was to find out what exactly had happened. She put up the barrier around them with a wave of her hand, only her, the archer, and Richard within.

"What happened?" she asked.

The archer, who was, in fact, the scout who had been following William, shook his head.

"I don't know. I was following the little psycho as always when I failed to notice a trap. I don't know what the hell it was, but I was stuck there for hours. It didn't even do anything; I was just stuck... until suddenly I saw him fly over me, and the second he did, the magic binding me was dispelled too... It was fucking weird."

"So, it's Casper?" Richard said, frowning.

"No." Caroline shook her head. "This isn't the same type of attack as his at all. He is focused on curses, dark mana. This was poison. Moreover, the cut on his arm was made with a weapon for sure. This isn't a beast either."

"An accomplice, then... or an entirely new player. This isn't Hayden. Casper would never work with him, and if Hayden had poison this strong, he would have used it before. Shit, this is all getting needlessly complicated." Richard sighed with annoyance.

"What's the plan?" the scout asked. "Make the kid wake up, get info, and finish him off?"

"We could, but I have a better idea," the former heavy warrior said. "For now, get him in one of the cabins."

The entire situation was a shitshow, and everyone was aware of it.

Someone or something had potent poison, and Caroline was the only healer who could cure it. The other healer could heal through it, perhaps giving the person a chance to rely on their own stats to survive before they ran out of mana. But it wasn't a reliable method at all.

The matter of William nearly dying spread throughout the camp like a wildfire. William was viewed favorably by most in their base, especially the crafters. The Smith, without a doubt, favored him the most of everyone

None of them really knew about the kid, from Richard's understanding. They only knew the persona he had cultivated while within the camp. Which meant a lot of people had gathered around his cabin, asking worried questions. Even if they wanted the teenager dead, it would be incredibly difficult. *Plan C, then*, he thought.

Jacob had also gathered outside with the others. While he was undoubtedly worried about William, he was more concerned with Casper. It wasn't a secret that the trapper had called William out, and now the caster was nearly dead... He could only fear the worst. Either he had tried to kill William, or he was a victim himself... *Damn it.*

Taking a deep breath, he looked toward the sky, the artificial sun hanging above. Even if everything was bad... he couldn't be the one to break. He knew others relied on him. Jacob had a responsibility. He refused to let others lose hope, so he would grasp for anything he could. Because at times, he felt like hope was all he had going for him.

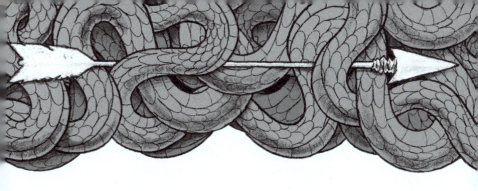

Chapter 42
Twin-Fang Style

Jake held the bowstring as he felt his stamina slowly drain. When he finally let go, the arrow literally exploded forth from the bow and smashed into the ostrich. The arrow itself broke into splinters upon impact due to the massive power behind it. Not that the ostrich fared any better.

The arrow had hit it on its neck, effectively blowing its head off. Jake could only smile at the tremendous power of his new Powershot skill. The stamina drain was quite insane when he made shots like he just did, but it was still oh so satisfying to do.

The skill had many drawbacks, though. First of all, you had to stand nearly entirely still while channeling the shot. You could make minor movements by turning your upper body, but taking a step would "drain" a bit of the charged-up energy and force you to sometimes start over entirely, which wouldn't be so bad if it wasn't for the second big drawback.

It was a very slow skill to use. It took several seconds to charge a shot that did just half-decent damage, while it could easily take close to ten seconds to fire a shot like

Jake just had. The skill's power increased exponentially as he charged, but so did the stamina drain and the general drain on his body.

Funnily enough, his high defensive stats turned out to be very useful with the skill. He could imagine if he'd tried to use the skill after simply leveling to 10 in his class a month ago. He wouldn't even be able to charge the shot for five seconds without his arm giving out.

Earlier in the day, he had tried to do the maximum charge he could. He'd held it for twelve seconds before his arm simply gave out, its veins bursting and half his arm getting covered in blood. It had also given him a very sore shoulder and upper body. However, this did show the skill's potential, as the arrow hit a tree and carved a fist-sized hole into it. The wooden arrow was borderline disintegrated upon impact, completely splintered in all directions.

If he had been able to use that skill against the metal-manipulating caster, he would have been able to pierce straight through that wall of iron, or at least have the kinetic force behind the impact be strong enough to send the wall smashing back into him. Too bad the guy didn't allow him to stand still and charge a shot for over ten seconds. Quite rude, actually.

Checking his notifications, he noted that he had put another level under his belt.

*You have slain [Velocta Ostrich – lvl 24] –
Experience Earned. 4000 TP earned*

*'DING!' Class: [Archer] has reached level 19 –
Stat points allocated, +1 Free Point*

The leveling was getting quite a bit slower now, and that was disregarding the difficulty in finding beasts. He had yet to see a single one above level 25 so far, but he had also purposely avoided heading further into the forest.

It had been around two days since he met the caster who called himself William. He knew the caster still had to be alive, as he had never gotten any notification for the kill. He wanted to avoid other people for now, since he still deemed it too risky to meet others. A squad of Williams would very likely result in certain death.

So he leveled. His plan currently was to get to at least level 25 before making contact. It all depended on how long his leveling would take, but for now, he had time. Looking at the tutorial panel, he noted that less than a month was remaining.

> **Tutorial Panel**
> **Duration: 29 days & 23:17:03**
> **Total Survivors Remaining: 389/1200**

He said less than a month, but it was still nearly an entire month—plenty of time for a lot to happen. A month in the dungeon had resulted in him getting a profession, leveling it 44 times, evolving it once, and even evolving his race twice. Oh yeah, and he'd met a god.

Jake was still worried about his colleagues, but if they had lived to now, he saw no reason to rush to their side. If they hadn't survived... he would process that if the time came.

The levels had naturally also come with a skill at level 15. Jake had honestly been expecting nothing, and had thought of going with the basic tracking skill he passed up at level 5 over a month ago, the logic behind it being to try and use it to locate his colleagues when the time came.

He also considered getting basic dual-wielding briefly. Jake preferred using a weapon in each hand a lot more than just a single dagger. So when he finally leveled and saw the choices, he went with a new option that was a welcome addition for sure.

> [Basic Twin-Fang Style (Uncommon)] – The Twin-Fang Style is an ancient dual-wielding fighting technique. Fighters of this style prefer shorter weapons and do not shy away from using afflictions to take down their foe. Unlocks basic proficiency in the Twin-Fang Style and adds a minuscule bonus to the effect of Agility and Strength when using a fitting melee weapon. Grants an increased bonus while wielding melee weapons of bone.

It was essentially a kind of dual-wielding specialization. How Jake had unlocked it, he didn't know. Maybe it had something to do with the Dagger of Bloodletting being made of bone, but it also mentioned the use of afflictions, which was very closely aligned with his profession.

Of course, there also was the whole Malefic Viper angle to consider, fangs being easily associated with vipers and all. Not that it mattered much in the end; he was just happy with the skill.

As with other skills of its nature, it came with a lot of instinctive knowledge. But compared to an inferior-rarity skill, this one also came with more "true" knowledge. Like he had been thrown a guidebook into his memory, but he still had to learn and practice it himself, which he had spent a while doing whenever he had time. Yet he found that he barely used what it taught. He only used it to improve his existent style, if you could even call it that. Currently, he just acted based on instinct when fighting, relying on making split-second decisions over anything else.

Speaking of other skills he'd been offered, they were all rather basic. One of them even gave a small passive danger sense, which he found kind of funny, considering he already had one through his Bloodline. He did consider picking it up to see what would happen, but skipped over it.

Having obtained another skill requiring practice did give him more to do while not hunting. He was already practicing his mana techniques whenever possible, so having a physical exercise was actually pretty nice.

His mana manipulation was improving steadily. He had gotten some inspiration from his spatial storage necklace and learned how to use mana better intuitively. Using items, however, wasn't close to the same as having to manipulate the mana yourself. It was as if the system pretty much did everything for you. You just had to think about what you wanted.

On the topic of items, he had tried hard to locate more lockboxes but had ended up with not even a single common-rarity item or token. The area seemed to have been entirely scoured by other survivors, which was likely also the reason why nearly no beasts remained. He remembered before the dungeon that if one looked for beasts, you found them within minutes. Now he was happy if he saw two small groups within an hour.

Jake knew this meant he would have to move inward soon. He hoped to get a skill, either increasing his speed or his defenses at 20. Beasts were naturally not his concern; in fact, he hoped to meet beasts stronger than himself, as those below 25 were a bit boring.

Walking through the forest, Jake still enjoyed the atmosphere, something he doubted most did, considering that some war was apparently going on. But he liked it. Perhaps the confinement of the dungeon was still at the forefront of his mind, but he loved how open it was. The weird "immortal birds of ambiance" even appeared endearing now. Yeah, those were still a thing, somehow dodging every single arrow effortlessly. He couldn't even use Identify on them.

As an extension of that, if he had to mention one thing he hated about the new world and the tutorial more than anything, it was the lack of information. Jake liked to know things. While instinct was good most of the time, that didn't mean knowledge wasn't just as important.

So not knowing anything was annoying him endlessly. Not knowing how his parents were or if they were even alive, the state of his other family members, how the world was currently looking outside... what would happen to all the animals on Earth. All of this was disregarding his general lack of knowledge about the system and the tutorial itself.

Furthermore, he was fully aware that he knew far more than most. Heck, he was still carrying an entire library's worth of books around with him. He hadn't really had the time or desire to read since leaving the dungeon, but at least he had the option.

Everyone else had to be far more in the dark than himself. Unless Jake had missed another massive happening besides the whole faction war going on, they should all be utterly clueless as to how pretty much everything worked. Which kind of made Jake think that for a tutorial, this place sure sucked at teaching them anything.

Though despite that, Jake still thought he was doing pretty well. A bit less well after meeting that William fellow, he thought he was pretty strong on average. Looking at this status, it sure also amplified that thought.

Status
Name: Jake Thayne
Race: [Human (E) – lvl 31]
Class: [Archer – lvl 19]
Profession: [Prodigious Alchemist of the Malefic Viper – lvl 44]
Health Points (HP): 2986/3100
Mana Points (MP): 3248/3680
Stamina: 694/1040
Stats
Strength: 105
Agility: 126
Endurance: 104
Vitality: 310
Toughness: 157
Wisdom: 368
Intelligence: 107
Perception: 247
Willpower: 180
Free Points: 0

Titles: [Forerunner of the New World], [Bloodline Patriarch], [Holder of a Primordial's True Blessing], [Dungeoneer I], [Dungeon Pioneer I]

Class Skills: [Basic One-Handed Weapon (Inferior], [Basic Stealth (Inferior)], [Advanced Archery (Common)], [Archer's Eye (Common)], [Powershot (Uncommon)], [Basic Twin-Fang Style (Uncommon)]
Profession Skills: [Herbology (Common)], [Brew Potion (Common)], [Concoct Poison (Common)], [Alchemist's Purification (Common)], [Alchemical Flame (Common)], [Toxicology (Uncommon)], [Cultivate Toxin (Uncommon)], [Malefic Viper's Poison (Rare)], [Palate of the Malefic Viper (Rare)], [Touch of the Malefic Viper (Rare)], [Sense of the Malefic Viper (Rare)], [Blood of the Malefic Viper (Epic)]
Blessing: [True Blessing of the Malefic Viper (Blessing - True)]
Race Skills: [Endless Tongues of the Myriad Races (Unique)], [Identify (Common)], [Meditate (Common)], [Shroud of the Primordial (Divine)]
Bloodline: [Bloodline of the Primal Hunter (Bloodline Ability - Unique)]

His stats had experienced significant growth, especially his Agility and Strength, now both being above 100. He had decided to put all his Free Points into Strength and Agility, trying to get them to an acceptable level. It was a bit sad that Wisdom, his highest stat by quite a bit, did nothing for him in direct combat. He had his Touch of the Malefic Viper, but he only used that in emergencies, as he prioritized using his daggers and bow for now.

He had also collected quite an amount of tutorial points.

TP Collected: 313,920

He called it quite the number, but compared to most everyone in the tutorial, it likely sucked. Which, by the way, was another bullet point on his list of information he would really like to have. What the hell were tutorial points even used for? This was a frustration he very much believed he shared with a lot of others in the tutorial.

He also made a mental note that he had yet to sleep since he left the dungeon. He had made it a habit only to meditate to restore stamina and mana, partly due to the weakness that came from sleeping. It did take him quite a while to mentally filter out the constant feedback from his sphere when he just wanted to rest his head. Yet, at the same time, he didn't want to completely cut off the outside world, leaving himself vulnerable.

Instead, he had somehow managed to relegate the sphere solely to his instinct. It was still active, and he had been woken up from his meditation once when a lone beast came close. His sphere had also reached a radius of around fifteen or sixteen meters by now. It was far more potent closer to him than further away.

Most growth, however, had been found in his ability to also feel the mana. After his first level 10 evolution, he had been able to vaguely feel something, while now it was nearly second nature for him to detect it.

After sitting down and meditating for a few hours, both his mana and stamina were fully restored, and his health points had also managed to regenerate passively.

One peculiarity Jake had noticed with how health worked was the interaction between Toughness, Vitality, and—to a lesser extent—Endurance. While Vitality increased health and health regeneration, it didn't mean that they increased one to one. Someone with 100 Vitality and 1000 health would take longer to regenerate from 1% HP than someone who only had 10 Vitality.

Toughness made this process even slower. With higher Toughness, health got harder to lose as the body durability increased. But it also got harder to heal the now tougher body. Jake had also discovered that Endurance did make the body slightly more durable, but far from as much as Toughness. He wasn't exactly sure how it made him more durable, but it clearly did *something*.

Oh, another thing just got on the list of information that I very much hate not having, Jake thought. If the system would be so kind as to just send him a spreadsheet of how exactly stats worked, it would be fantastic.

Shaking off the frustrating feelings, he got up, fully restored, and started hunting for prey once more. It was dark by now, but that didn't really affect him at all. He doubted it really affected anyone by now, as most would have gotten significantly higher Perception just from race levels.

However, the beasts were still docile during the night, making the fights more manageable, but harder to find. At least they sometimes made loud noises during the day.

His sphere continuously scanned his surroundings as he walked and practiced levitating a pen above his hand. Levitating it was easy enough; the difficulty lay in keeping it tethered to his hand while he moved.

After more than two hours, he finally came upon a beast, and as he Identified it, he could only smile.

[Steeltusk Boar – lvl 28]

The big piggy had gone from being an Irontusk to a Steeltusk Boar. Relatively linear evolution tree it had going on there.

This was naturally the evolved version of the first level 10 beast he had ever fought. He felt a strange excitement when staring it down. This had been his first real challenge in the tutorial, and back then, he had faced it together with his entire group of colleagues. They had won after Jake emptied his full quiver in the beast... but not without taking significant damage to their group.

He hoped Joanna had somehow managed to stay alive. Jake realized how much of a dick he had been back then, and not just to her, but pretty much everyone. He felt a lot of regret from how he'd handled things. Not from leaving them and going his own way, but how he'd left.

Shaking his head, Jake dispelled the thoughts. He shouldn't dwell on a past he couldn't change. He could only move forward and attain more power. Only then could he reunite with them. And it wasn't as if there was anything wrong with enjoying that process a bit...

With a smile on his lips, he drew the bone dagger in one hand and a starting dagger for archers in the other. Perhaps this beast would finally give him an exciting fight...

Chapter 43
Big Pig II
Steeltusk Edition

Jake sauntered before the mighty beast. It easily towered over him, reaching the size of a small van. It hadn't grown massively compared to its prior evolution, but Jake could feel the power hidden within its porky body. The boar was built like a tank, with a hide perhaps comparable to one.

As he got closer, the beast seemed to wake from its stupor as it turned toward him, glaring. Perhaps the system was doing its magic since it was night, but it didn't immediately attack. It just stared at him. He instinctively felt that if he moved just a couple of steps closer, the beast would charge with abandon.

The logical move would be to take out his bow and use Powershot with the maximum charge to do massive damage or even kill it with a single attack, but where was the fun in that? Where was the challenge? He didn't even use any poison either.

Instead, he took a step forward and entered its range, and as predicted, the beast squealed as it made its way toward him, a charge he gladly met with his own. A bit stupid in retrospect, but he trusted in his powerful body.

The result was as expected. The beast rammed into him, making him fly backward, but not before landing a good stab with the bone dagger on the snout of the big pig. This did little more than anger it further as it tried trampling him along with everything else in the surroundings.

This time, he decided to dodge as he rolled to the side and started moving around the pig as if dancing. If he had learned one thing, it was that these things had horrible mobility. However, this was highly made up for by the hide on its side being near impenetrable to regular attacks.

All of this was true, for the Irontusk Boar. But the evolved Steeltusk one had more tricks up its sleeve. As Jake moved to the side, the ground beneath him suddenly shifted, nearly making him lose his balance. Simultaneously, the earth itself seemed to help rotate the mighty boar, making it turn far faster than Jake had first calculated.

Forced to move back due to the unforeseen circumstances, Jake was not distraught but happy. The stronger the beast, the more interesting the fight. He could kill the creature far faster and easier if he used poisons, giving him a reliable backup if his pure melee approach failed.

But he would be damned if he didn't even try. Training dual-wielding alone was all well and good, but it was nothing compared to the experience one would get in live combat.

Which was the ultimate reason why he had chosen to engage in this dance of death. Totally nothing to do with having a bit of fun with the first beast above level 25.

The moving ground made his dance difficult, his steps sometimes not finding the expected foothold, but he nevertheless managed to avoid the tusks time after time. He knew that even with his durable body, it would hurt like hell to get impaled.

An issue that quickly materialized was the weakness of the starting knife he used. Against the formidable defenses of the boar, it couldn't even leave a mark with his slashes. Only when he stabbed did he manage to barely leave a mark. Even the bone dagger only managed to make light cuts. The enchantment was doing work, though, making each of those small cuts bleed far more and for longer than usual.

Minutes passed as Jake dodged and weaved, stabbed, and cut, while the beast furiously tried to pin him down and skewer him. As the damage to the creature increased, so did its fury and bloodlust. With little warning, the beast's eyes suddenly started to emit a red glow, and the entire boar gave off a similar red aura.

Jake felt his danger sense flare up as he raised his arms to block. With a squeal of fury, the boar turned its head and hit him with one of its tusks, sending him airborne for a few moments. However, the boar was far from done, as the very earth seemed to reach up and grab hold of him as the beast began a full-power charge straight at him.

With no way to move, he tossed his two daggers into the air and prepared to meet the beast. Its size was both a strength and a weakness, as Jake managed to slide between the two tusks aiming at him and instead have the snout of the beast crash into him.

He felt all air leave his lungs as he managed to grab hold of the boar, avoiding getting trampled beneath it. Using berserk movements, the beast tried to shake him off, but Jake kept hold and managed to somehow get up on its back.

Through his sphere, he managed to locate the bone dagger and, with an unprecedented level of skill, weaved a string of mana that nudged the blade to fall toward his hand. He felt like a warrior from a long time ago in a galaxy far, far away as he caught the dagger and shanked it down into the back of the beast.

The beast's response was to throw itself to the side, attempting to squash him beneath it. Jake pulled himself up by the hide of the massive creature and avoided finding himself between the ground and a van-sized pig.

He kept delivering stab after stab until, finally, he was forced to let go and jump off, as the beast started rolling around while at the same time manipulating the earth itself to try and get him off. The beast's berserk state was still active, making it promptly stop rolling around and continue its reckless assault.

Jake could, however, feel that the beast had started getting slower. Blood was everywhere by now—on the creature, the ground, and even himself. Dozens of bloody holes covered its hide, still oozing out blood.

With the beast's speed reduced, and Jake having adapted to the shifting ground, the fight had gotten significantly more straightforward. He dodged and jumped around the beast, landing cut after cut, as it increasingly grew desperate in its attempts to lock him down.

After several minutes, the beast had only managed to inflict a couple of minor injuries on Jake, the worst one being a long gash on one of his shoulders. Jake called it a minor injury, though before the system, it would, without a doubt, have required a trip to the emergency room. But his high Vitality kept him in top shape, and he felt that his health was still in good condition.

A few minutes later, the beast finally collapsed from its wounds, no longer able to muster any strength to fight back. The ground manipulation kept going even after the creature couldn't move, as it continuously tried to hit Jake with pitifully weak attacks.

Jake was starting to feel bad for it, and finally pulled out his bow and fired a Powershot into the head of the unmoving beast, ending its life instantly.

You have slain [Steeltusk Boar – lvl 28] – Experienced earned. 16,000 TP earned

'DING!' Class: [Archer] has reached level 20 – Stat points allocated, +1 Free Point

'DING!' Race: [Human (E)] has reached level 32 – Stat points allocated, +5 Free Points

Despite the less than satisfying ending, Jake had still very much enjoyed the fight. There was just something about fighting a powerful enemy.

Looking at his health points, he found them only having been reduced by a sixth. Far less than he had lost during the short exchange with the metal-manipulating caster, which showed that other humans indeed were the real danger of this tutorial.

Despite him barely losing any health, his cloak once again didn't avoid suffering catastrophic damage. Luckily, the Self-Repair enchantment had remained active even after being utterly ruined by William's final attack, but now it was once more tattered.

He had also discovered that if he injected mana into the cloak, the repair function would speed up significantly. It still took its time, though. Speaking of injecting mana into items, that was another important thing he had explored considerably over the last few days.

Most materials could be made stronger by injecting mana into them. The primary reason why the trees were so strong was their ability to absorb the ambient mana. The same was true for nearly anything, even something completely nonliving. Stones, metals, even the properties of the air itself, changed and were amplified by mana.

Without injecting mana into his bow, for example, it would without a doubt break when using Powershot. He was still in the early stages of practice, but he believed that it should be possible to also improve already-enchanted items somehow. Currently, he couldn't inject any mana into his bone dagger. Despite not being enchanted, the normal archer dagger also rejected most of the mana he tried injecting.

Of all his items, only the ones with Self-Repair and his bow accepted mana injection. He could use mana with his other things, like his spatial necklace, but that was not really injection per se. Mana injection was more like shooting electricity directly into a bar of metal to heat it up—and eventually make it melt, if too much was injected.

However, for his necklace, it was like you injected that mana into a transformer, which then correctly applied the mana to fulfill the desired function, such as taking an item in or out of storage. As to how this metaphorical transformer worked... That was way above Jake's paygrade.

He was learning a lot about mana these days, but he was also very actively studying it. Before he met with the Malefic Viper, he had taken a lot of its properties for granted. He had seen it as just the system doing its thing and saw no further reason to question it. And even if he did question how things worked, he couldn't do anything with the mana then.

But now he actively questioned everything he could. He experimented happily with mana manipulation at all times, and his control had vastly improved without a doubt. His little trick of pulling the bone dagger to himself during the fight was more than proof of that. Also, it felt really awesome to do. Could he have just deposited it in his necklace and not thrown it into the air? Sure, he *could've*, but the other way was way cooler.

The fact that no skill had appeared or been made available regarding mana manipulation was a bit weird to him, though. He could clearly levitate objects and do things akin to telekinesis, and yet no skills had come.

Then again, he didn't have a skill related to manipulating stamina or health points either. He had tried controlling those two sources of energy and found it way harder. He could kind of control his vital energy to focus on specific areas, as he had done during the final part of the Challenge Dungeon, but Jake couldn't shape it as he could with mana.

Stamina, on the other hand, was a dead end so far. He had theorized that he should be able to use it to enhance his own body somehow, as it was known as the inner energy. The fact that nearly all physical skills used stamina to function proved that stamina could significantly affect the body.

Of course, it could just be the system doing system things. One energy could exhibit the properties of another, after all. In the end, stamina, health, and mana were all just different forms of energy. Not to say that one could necessarily combine all three to make something more powerful. *In before that's how you make divine energy or something like that*, he joked to himself.

Exiting his thoughts, he entered the system menus.

> ***Archer class skills available***

Checking the list, he found the usual suspects he had been offered at level 10. While some of them still appealed to him, especially the Active Camouflage skill, he chose to ignore them all for now. He had been offered two new skills of interest, though—both of them fell into the evasion type. The first skill was a bit weird.

> **[Disengaging Shot (Common)] – An arrow may not only be shot to wound or kill, but also as a tool of escape. Allows the Archer to shoot an arrow that directs and amplifies all kinetic energy into a backward force. Must have a suitable weapon to use. Adds a minor bonus to the effect of Agility when dodging using Disengaging Shot.**

One immediate drawback was the fact that it required a bow and arrow. This, of course, limited the ability quite a lot. He couldn't use it in melee with his daggers, and he couldn't use it in split-second emergency situations as he would have to actually shoot an arrow to activate it.

On the positive side, though, it would be godly when kiting. Depending on the stamina requirements, Jake would be able to use it continuously to quite literally blow himself around the battlefield. He couldn't help but imagine himself trying to fly through the air by repeatedly shooting arrows toward the ground. That would sure as hell be cool... though likely very stupid-looking if even feasible.

Moving on to the second skill, the first thing that struck him was the name.

> [Basic Shadow Vault of Umbra (Uncommon)] – The power of shadows is an often used tool for anyone looking to escape. Tapping in to the Records of Umbra, embrace the shadows for a brief moment, becoming ethereal. Allows the Archer to momentarily become one with the shadows. Can only be used in straight lines. Adds a small bonus to the effect of Agility and Wisdom when using Basic Shadow Vault of Umbra.

The skill was somehow related to something or someone called Umbra. Thinking about it, he checked out his bracers.

> [Leather Bracers of the Novice Rogue (Uncommon)] – A pair of leather bracers made of fine leather, originally designed for new initiates in the Order of Umbra. Enchantments: Self-Repair. +5 Agility, +3 Strength. Increases the effectiveness of all stealth skills, further amplified while remaining hidden in the shadows.
>
> Requirements: Lvl 5+ in any class or humanoid race. Stealth-based skill.

Had he somehow managed to acquire Records related to some entity named Umbra solely through using bracers holding the name?

He understood why he'd gotten skills related to the Malefic Viper, as the profession was quite literally named after him. Could the mere act of having those bracers somehow influence him enough to open up entirely new skill options to him? He was honestly a bit taken aback at the prospect. He kind of assumed that Umbra was a god... Would it then be considered blasphemy to take the skill when he already had the Malefic Viper ones?

Well... at least the Malefic Viper didn't seem like the sort of person to care much about that, and the skill was looking very juicy. The fact that it made use of his high Wisdom was also a huge bonus. He also assumed the skill made use of both mana and stamina... but he couldn't know before taking it.

As a basic skill, it was also very appetizing. Basic implied plenty of room for improvement, AKA skill upgrades. Jake had improved his archery skill through being good at archery, so would he be able to improve that skill too by being good at... Shadow Vaulting?

The description of Shadow Vault's effects was also quite honestly very awesome-sounding. To become one with shadows and dodge around sounded very fantasy-like, but more importantly than that, it sounded pretty damn handy.

Ultimately, the choice of skill was a no-brainer. One required a bow and was kind of gimmicky, and the other one literally allowed him to dodge like a shadow without any immediate drawbacks. With that in mind, he picked it.

> *Gained Skill*: [Basic Shadow Vault of Umbra (Uncommon)] – The power of shadows is an often used tool for anyone looking to escape. Tapping in to the Records of Umbra, embrace the shadows for a brief moment, becoming ethereal. Allows the Archer to momentarily become one with the shadows. Can only be used in straight lines. Adds a small bonus to the effect of Agility and Wisdom when using Basic Shadow Vault of Umbra.

Jake instantly felt the knowledge stream into his mind. Vaguely, he also felt like the dark night became several shades darker as the information was implanted.

A few seconds passed, and everything returned to normal, as Jake now had a vague idea of how the skill worked and how to activate it. Needless to say, it was testing time!

Chapter 44
"Partners"

William listened to the woman talk on and on about the importance of others. His parents were also there, both off to his side, a chair's width too far away for it to ever be considered close. His mother was still a mess, and his father stoic.

His crying mother told of how hard it was, how it felt like she had lost both her sons. Something William naturally took offense to. How could you compare that defective product that they had called brother to him, a fully functional and overall excellent person?

But he didn't show it on his face, of course. He had never quite mastered the act of fake-crying, so he just looked down and pretended to be sad. He was sure it was fooling everyone, even the boar sleeping in the corner.

The woman, a therapist, was the only one who knew what had truly happened, what he had done. William had accepted this, as from what he had read, she wasn't required to report on past crimes committed, only suspected future ones.

The fact that his parents insisted that he "didn't know better" and "didn't do it on purpose" likely also helped. Of course, he was more than happy to reinforce that misconception, or at least he had tried to, but the damn woman in front of him was sharp and had seen through his act.

She also knew he wasn't actually sad currently, but he had to play it off to his parents, at least, as they were the ones sitting on the giant cookie jars. And his therapist had given him good advice on how he should focus more on other people's perception of his actions. He had to admit that a lot of her arguments had logical consistency, so he followed them.

William saw the therapist as one of the few people he had ever grown to respect. She was smart and, without a doubt, the best manipulator he had ever seen. She could speak entirely differently with him, his parents, Richard sleeping on the recliner, and when he and his parents were together. It was terrific, and a great learning opportunity for him.

His father, still stoic as ever, asked while petting the badger on his head, "So the medicine is working? We want to make sure everything is all right before we take any further steps."

"Yes, they are helping greatly," the therapist said. "We have even been able to lower the dosage recently as we are making great strides. I do also believe William has more tutorial points than Richard." She smiled.

William just sat there, listening, but was still a bit annoyed at the insinuation that he was somehow not complete. Yet he had to accept that to others, he perhaps did appear to lack something. He could make up for that by acting like he did have that *something*, but not always and not to everyone.

"William, do you have anything to say?" she said as she turned to him.

He had trained his response, and with as much faux sadness as possible, he stammered out, "I am sorry... I really didn't know how much it would hurt everyone... I promise I will get better, and nothing like that will ever happen again."

His mother teared up even more at that, and even his father slackened his worried facial expression slightly. If only he could've thrown some fake tears in and not been covered in blood, it would have been perfect.

"And, William, what about that other thing we talked about?" the kind therapist said as she smiled at him once more.

A bit confused, William wondered, *What else?* She rarely ever addressed him during these sessions to begin with, but what else did they talk about?

No, this entire situation was wrong. What was going on? He looked questioningly at The Smith standing at his side, but he just shook his head, as confused as William himself.

"You know what I mean, William. That other thing we talked about you lacking." The smile on her face was now gone. A dark aura began spreading from her as a giant sphere of darkness ripped the ceiling apart. "We talked about how weak you are, William. How pathetic you are. So broken and weak... unable to ever truly grasp for power."

As she finished, the door was kicked in, a cloaked man with a weapon rushing toward him. He couldn't react before he was stabbed in the chest by the dagger of bone.

The archer simply looked down at him as he fell to the floor, completely paralyzed. Those eyes stared at him like he was some defenseless critter. He couldn't move; he couldn't breathe. He felt life slowly seep out of his body as he lay there, absolutely powerless. His chest was rotting as the poison spread, the laughing face of Casper staring down at him mockingly from within the sphere of darkness above.

He tried to scream as he sat up in a makeshift bed in a cabin. His heart was pounding, and cold sweat covered his entire body.

Due to his scream, the door opened swiftly and the healer Caroline entered. William couldn't help himself from shaking... He didn't want anyone to see him right now. He felt weak.

"William, how are you?" Caroline asked, but she looked and spoke to him differently than usual. Her voice wasn't warm and friendly, but a bit cold.

William did everything he could to calm himself down. He was too shaken to linger on Caroline's changed demeanor. "Ye... yeah. I am fine. I am just tired, and I feel like shit."

He closed his eyes and tried to gather his thoughts. He had lost. Lost and nearly died in the process. What the fuck was that archer? What the fuck was up with him and his stats? Who in their right mind makes a build entirely centered around Perception and defensive stats? Also, the poison... It wasn't purely physical, but magical and far more potent than the venom from the badgers. Did he even have magic?

As William was gathering his thoughts, Richard entered the cabin too. The young caster didn't even think about it, as he was too stuck in his own head. He did perk up when a barrier surrounded the cabin, however.

"Huh?" he exclaimed, confused as he looked up and saw the cold eyes of Caroline and Richard on him.

"So, what happened?" Richard asked.

William looked back and forth between the two as he put on his innocent teenager mask.

"I went to look for that Casper fellow in case he needed help, bu—»

"Cut the bullshit; we know you didn't," Richard interrupted. "You went to kill him like you've killed so many others. This ridiculous farce is over, so stop spewing out garbage and tell me *exactly* what happened."

Once more, William was surprised. *What*? He knew? How? Richard had been fooled for so long. Caroline too. When did he—

"Did you think I wouldn't know? You weren't exactly subtle, William. You are powerful, yes, but you are also young and inexperienced. A powerful weapon that I have let run rampant for too long." Richard paused before continuing. "I know your type. I am not some shrink who thinks you're lesser for what you are. You are a brilliant young man with endless potential to be the perfect soldier, but every soldier needs a commander—a guide to let you reach your full potential. With your intelligence, you know the benefits of a support system."

William looked with confusion at the man, perhaps even more than before. He looked... serious. What?

He had never been in this position before.

"When?" was all he could manage to stammer out.

"I was onto you the first day we met. Did you think I wouldn't notice a living weapon waltz into my camp?"

The young caster wasn't sure what to do at this very moment. William didn't feel like they were about to attack him, and quite honestly, he still felt too weak to fight, which was weird, as all of his resource pools were full.

"What do you want? You want me to play soldier?" He tried to look stoic. He had to at least put up a front.

"No, I want you to play super-soldier. I am proposing a partnership. I will be at the back, supporting you to reach for higher power, and you will help me be the leader of this camp—an agreement of mutual benefits. I know you want tutorial points and levels, and my death would offer you plenty... but what I can provide you with while alive is far more valuable."

William felt pleased with the man's attitude. *So that is why he hasn't done anything for so long.* There was actually someone smart enough to recognize his worth. *Fucking finally.*

"Fine," he agreed. This was good, right?

"Great!" Richard said with a happy smile as he went over and patted the young man's shoulder. "You cannot begin to comprehend how glad I am to have you as a partner. I couldn't imagine anyone better. Caroline, make sure he is in top condition."

"Of course, boss!" Caroline said with a smile as she went over to heal the young man. William didn't feel much from what she did, but he did sense a bit of strength return. "I have done all I can; the rest is just fatigue. It should be all good in a few hours!"

"Alright, then, let's give William time to rest," Richard said with a happy nod.

"That's it?" William asked, confused. Were they just going to leave him here unattended?

"We can find out which idiot attacked you when you are in top condition. Just find me or send someone. We're partners now; I can't tell you what to do." He then exited the room with Caroline, the barrier disappearing along with her.

William wasn't exactly sure what had just happened. He was pretty sure it was a good thing, though.

Outside the cabin, Richard walked with Caroline; his smile had changed to one of disdain.

Richard had walked in with one of two purposes, and he had already discussed the plan with Caroline beforehand.

The first scenario was getting information out of William about who'd attacked him by acting stoic and pressing him. Then Richard would take advantage of his still-weakened state and just finish off the kid. With him fully healed from earlier, Richard theorized he would get all of his tutorial points and full experience. Caroline may have also gotten some, but that was fine. Caroline was one of his people, after all.

The second scenario was what had played out. William was vulnerable and open to manipulation. Despite how powerful he believed himself to be, he was shaken from whatever had just happened. The broken kid was even more broken than before, so Richard took advantage of that. He stroked his ego and got in. At the final moments, his skill had made him aware that William was now "loyal" to him. His quest confirmed the same thing, going up a single percentage point.

Not that he hadn't been unknowingly loyal for a long time. Richard had purposely sent the less "loyal" groups to areas the scout informed him William was in. As predictable as he was, William would then kill them. In Richard's mind, this was a win-win. He would have people who weren't loyal to him killed, or he would lose an attack dog.

He had only needed to do this three times total before he just led his people entirely away from William. For a long time, Richard had hoped that the idiot would just get himself killed against Hayden's men, but sadly, that hadn't happened. William, in all his arrogance, was, in the end, still a coward. If he knew a party was strong, he would avoid them entirely. It was almost comical how every time Richard went out, William would go in the exact opposite direction.

As to why he'd decided to bring William in now? Because he was vulnerable enough. Richard could feel his weakness the second he saw him. A broken child, unsure of himself, so Richard gave him the recognition he so dearly craved at that moment. He began by first establishing that he was in power by putting William down and then extending an offer of partnership, to appear like he really needed him. The kid had eaten it raw.

His loyalty was fickle, the foundation a fucking mess, but it was enough for now.

All of the crafters were already considered loyal to Richard. Perhaps loyalty was the wrong term, but his skill and quest sure counted them. If he had to guess, then he would say it was more reliance than loyalty. Ultimately, he now considered them his people. The only one who didn't give him the response was The Smith, but he could handle that in time. It wasn't like he needed *everyone* to be loyal either.

Jacob was another example of this. He shifted loyalty nearly daily. It was peculiar, but Richard never got any sense of danger from the man. The same was true for that guy Bertram, who followed Jacob around at all times. He had never displayed loyalty even once toward Richard, yet he was clearly a trustworthy man who had undying loyalty toward Jacob. Again, it wasn't really a problem, as he clearly cared for Caroline, and Caroline was undoubtedly loyal.

It was necessary to have William converted or dead. All Richard now had left was Hayden and his party and a possible third threat, AKA what had attacked William.

Oh, and on a final note for William... While he was a useful dog, he wasn't exactly a good dog. A bit too feral for Richard's taste. A wild dog couldn't just be tamed that quickly, after all. You could feed it and keep it loyal for a while, but Richard wasn't under any illusions that William wouldn't end up backstabbing him at some point.

Against Hayden, William would be a helpful tool. It was the only reason he'd even bothered to convert him today. But once Hayden and his camp were either assimilated or decimated...

The mad dog would have to be put down.

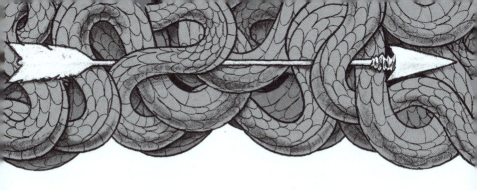

Chapter 45
Shadow Vault & Instincts

In a small corner of the tutorial forest, a very peculiar thing was happening. A man was repeatedly jumping around, more times than not finding himself smashing face-first into a tree. He seemed to turn into something resembling a shadow, quickly moving forward and then turning back to his normal tangible form with every jump.

This weird man was, naturally, Jake testing out his newly acquired Basic Shadow Vault of Umbra. The skill took quite a bit getting used to, which was the reason why he needed to practice it as much as he did.

The skill was quite simple, actually. With little to no warning or preparation, Jake could speed up his movement in any direction he was currently moving, turning into a shadow-like substance, and then appear once more whenever he reached his designated target, or when the uptime of the skill ran out.

When he was a shadow, no physical object could touch him, instantly making Jake want to try phasing through walls. Sadly, that hope was quickly squashed. While he could phase through small things, he had no way of getting through a tree, for example. If he thought back to his fight with that caster William, he also doubted he could get past the wall of iron. He found that objects with a high mana density were harder to phase through, and a conjured wall had to be very mana-dense.

He could, however, phase through smaller objects. So dodging through the swing of a sword, a thrown dagger, or an arrow was entirely possible. Though he did notice that it increased mana consumption when he did so.

The reason he kept crashing into things was the speed increase and the disorienting effect of suddenly accelerating. It was like suddenly stepping on an escalator going far above what any safety standard would ever permit.

One moment he would move normally, and the next suddenly accelerate several times that speed for less than a second. The skill itself wasn't teleportation, after all, but just swift movement. However, to the untrained eye, it could easily appear as if he had just teleported when he used the skill at maximum output.

The fact that he took on the characteristics of a shadow only made it more challenging to use. It was like suddenly becoming weightless, and everything just felt... off. The direct-line movement also made it even more confusing.

So, he trained. As one says, practice makes perfect. While he wasn't exactly aiming for perfection on his first day with the skill, he needed to be at least able to use it without accidentally getting himself killed during combat. He could totally see himself crashing into something far more dangerous than a tree.

The damage he took to both his health and mana pools when he crashed into objects like trees was already quite insane, to begin with. The sudden momentum coming to an instant stop made his mana instantly drain by several hundred points, and his health points drop even more.

One lucky thing with the skill was that it also phased all his equipment. Even if he had a bow in his hand, it too took on a shadowy look. He tried it with a couple of different things and found that pretty much anything he touched would get Shadow Vaulted with him. It did increase both mana and stamina consumption of the skill, though.

He also discovered, with some experimenting, that the enchantment with his boots did indeed reduce stamina expenditure. And despite it saying it was only by a "small" amount, it turned out to be quite significant. It wasn't just a straight-up percentage decrease, but had some more advanced math behind it.

If he did a small vault, consuming only 5 stamina with the boots as an example, the cost got reduced by a whopping 3 points. In other words, a 60% reduction. However, if he did a more extended vault, consuming 30 stamina, the boots would only reduce it by 10 points or so, AKA around a 33% reduction.

His maximum consumption from a single vault so far had been 78 stamina, and then it had reduced cost by 17, which was a weird 22% or so reduction. Quite honestly, the math behind it stumped him, and he decided just to write it off as the system doing system things.

There clearly was a pattern somewhere. He doubted it would just be entirely random. Jake just didn't see the value in crunching the math and trying to discover the formula. Without it, he already had a good feeling for how much stamina he was consuming, and he didn't exactly have time to calculate much during combat. Especially not with a defensive skill.

The vault also consumed mana, where no reduction was available. The cost was around the same as the stamina counterpart—not counting the reduction. The mana expenditure got a lot higher, however, if he phased through objects of any kind. Luckily, Wisdom was still his highest stat by quite a bit, and he didn't really use much mana during normal combat. So, despite the relatively high cost of dodging through objects, he could manage.

He couldn't help but think of how useless the skill would feel if he only had his Archer class, however. The mana consumption would drain him in only a few vaults, leaving him with a dead skill. But with his current resource pools, he could easily make tens of high-powered jumps. If he could avoid smashing his head into things, that is.

But he was getting better. And fast. In only a few hours, he had gotten the short jumps down and was quickly able to move a few meters back and forth in fluid movements. The long vaults were still quite hard, but that too was improving drastically for every minute.

Honestly, his Bloodline abilities felt like a total cheat here too. His sphere was utterly unaffected by him turning all shadowy and kept him completely aware of his surroundings. He "knew" when he was about to hit something, and he seemed to slowly be able to train his instinct to understand the skill better.

A vital distinction had to be made between moving on instinct and moving deliberately with thoughts behind every action. If Jake tried to dodge a sword swing intentionally, he first had to register the weapon approaching, then he had to decide to evade, and then the method he would use to avoid it. If he decided to use Shadow Vault, he would have to use the skill, and all the decisions related to that, like which way to dodge, how far, and how fast.

If it was done instinctually, however, only the first step was needed. And that was more than handled by Jake's overpowered danger perception. By then, he simply had to not fight what he already instinctively wanted to do and vault. It was like he just "knew" what was best to do without deliberating it.

Everyone would naturally rely on instinct there. A boxer blocks based on intuition; when someone throws something at you, you lift your hand to block instinctively. Jake just took the entire concept to another level. He didn't just raise his hand to block something thrown; he would catch it out of the air and fling it back if it was an attack. Of course, his instincts weren't flawless.

Relying so much on only his instincts could also easily backfire. Jake wasn't omniscient, and feints had a considerable effect on him. His instinctual reactions also ultimately relied on himself. If he was attacked by a skill he could in no way understand, his instinct wouldn't know how to respond appropriately either. His danger perception did help quite a bit there, but it too had many flaws.

If he had to bring up an example, it would be during the fight with William. The final attack had hit him hard.

He had been showered with pieces of metal and shot back, taking a lot of damage. His instinct hadn't managed to react, and his danger perception had only activated at the final moment.

The same was true for the daggers that William controlled. Their ethereal movements were hard to understand, making his instinct only able to try and keep up with their attack pattern. His danger perception made him aware of them at all times, but felt more like a constant buzzing telling him that those daggers were dangerous.

The way he had won the fight had also been straight-up against his instincts. To dodge or block an attack was the most natural thing to do, so his instinct naturally screamed at him to do so. Instead, he had chosen to ignore the attacks and get hit, ultimately gaining an opening to win.

If he listened solely to his instincts during that fight, he would likely never have had the chance to land a hit before either he or the caster ran out of resources. While he would undoubtedly have won that battle of endurance, he didn't believe the other party would be stupid enough to stick around long enough to run out. Though, of course, Jake could be wrong.

There was also the fact that five daggers in the back barely fazed him. They'd penetrated a few centimeters into his flesh, dealing barely any real damage. With his high Vitality, he could have taken dozens of those daggers, the only real problem being the pain.

Pain his instincts naturally wanted to avoid. Pain is just the body's way of saying, "Dude, you should stop doing that."

In the end, his instincts were only a guide or an emergency tool for when his thoughts couldn't keep up. It did also have aspects he couldn't at all understand, however. It seemed to, at times, make him aware of things. It allowed him to get vague feelings around things, such as how strong a beast was compared to himself or how much damage a specific attack would do before it even hit him.

Many warriors of the multiverse likely could do these things. Sensing the power level of others wasn't a new concept at all. Learning how much damage something would do also seemed like a relatively simple ability if one had enough experience on the battlefield.

Even beasts were able to determine how dangerous attacks were. Jake saw several of them avoid the more damaging attacks while just tanking the weaker ones. Of course, it depended entirely on the beast.

In the end, he could only sigh at how many unknowns there were. Bloodlines and their associated abilities were only for the holder of the Bloodline to truly understand. The system offered no advice, only a simple explanation of the Bloodline. And even that had many examples of holding minor flaws or lacking information.

Not that Jake had any complaints about his Bloodline. He wasn't delusional. He knew it was his greatest weapon. He knew it was the only thing he had not been granted by the system, something that belonged to him and him alone.

As he sat there, relaxing, he heard some noise above him and felt like something was looking at him. He focused on his sphere and saw one of the weird-ass birds staring down at him. It was rare they got so close... In fact, this was the first time one of them had ever entered his sphere, and...

Birds aren't real. The Sphere of Perception confirmed that.

When he focused on the bird, all jokes aside, he didn't see a physical animal but pure energy. A mana density that was just... utterly insane. Jake couldn't even find the words to describe how ridiculous it was.

Jake felt confused, but he didn't let it show. He still felt a gaze upon him. It was clearly originating from the bird, and yet it wasn't...

It made him think... Who or what was observing him? The birds were clearly just mediums of some kind... scouts. Based on their mana density, it wasn't related to any of the survivors. It felt far closer to the power shown by the Malefic Viper than himself.

Was a god behind those birds? If so, why? Did the system allow a god to directly observe like this? Could the god interfere? He didn't think it was the system itself making them; it appeared far too omnipotent to need conjured super-birds to keep an eye on people.

Also... those birds had been around since day one. Like they were native to this place where the tutorial took place... like whatever or whoever had placed them here knew that it was a tutorial area. *Wait...*

Jake had been under an assumption for a long time... one that he was beginning to doubt. *Who has ever said that the system created the tutorials? What if a god did?*

Clearly, gods could interfere with the tutorial. Heck, the Viper had placed a dungeon there. Who could say that other gods or powerful entities weren't also influencing things? Who could say a god didn't also create this outside

SHADOW VAULT & INSTINCTS

area? Maybe even the rules? Or did a god work with the system to do all these things? Some kind of collaboration?

But most importantly, he thought, why the fuck am I sitting here thinking about stuff I can't, in any way, shape, or form, find out at the moment—but can just ask the Viper about next time we meet—instead of being productive?

So with that, he returned to what was truly important. Trying not to Shadow Vault into trees.

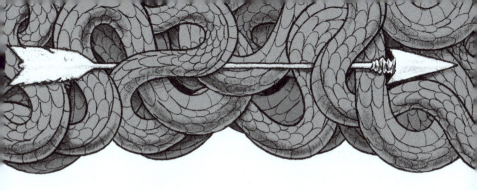

Chapter 46
Unexpected Encounter (1/3)

For so long, they had waited, generation after generation, era after era. Their hope never died, their conviction eternal. Yet the branches died out one by one. Now only a single hall remained, the once glorious order corroded by the march of time.

For only the gods were immortal. Only the gods could stand against time and preserve what was. Perhaps the only reason why his hall had survived so long was that they had one such god among them.

Here, in this world, they were still respected. They had power, after all. But outside, in the other universes, their once mighty order was nearly forgotten. The Lord Protector, the god who watched over them in place of their Patron, had no desire to leave. So they could only wait. Wait for the day of his return.

The current Hall Master was one of those waiting. She had been in her position for many generations, and like the many predecessors, she too was patient, never losing faith. Every year, she dreamed of their Patron's return.

And every year, she found herself saddened when nothing happened.

If not for the Lord Protector and the grand legacy left behind, perhaps even they would have forgotten the Malefic One. Many, even today, still doubted he would ever return. But she believed that the Patron was out there, and as long as they waited, as long as they remained forever faithful, the Malefic One was sure to reemerge.

Suddenly, she was awakened from her meditation by an old man teleporting into her chamber. He wore a black robe with a snake's motif on it, one similar to her own. However, his snake was not giving off the same aura as the one on hers. One had to distinguish ranks, after all.

"What do you disturb my meditation for?" the Hall Master asked, slightly annoyed. If this were another petty squabble with the Brimstone Conglomerate, heads would roll.

"Honored Hall Master, the Lord Protector has ordered you to his realm—immediately," the man said, bowing deeply.

The Hall Master kneaded her brows, feeling a mix between excitement and fear. This was only the second time she would meet the Lord Protector. The only other time had been during her inauguration as Hall Master, and even then, it was only him making an appearance briefly. She knew that the Hall Master before her had also only met him twice, the first being his own inauguration and the second being when he reached the peak of mortality. The Lord Protector didn't even bother to show up at the funeral.

"I shall go at once," she answered as she teleported out of her chamber. She couldn't teleport straight to the

UNEXPECTED ENCOUNTER (1/3)

entrance of the Lord Protector's realm, but instead had to walk the majority of the way due to all the protective wards and spells put up through the ages. A minor inconvenience compared to the security provided.

As she walked further and further down toward the entrance, her nervousness only grew. But at the same time, so did her hope. Had it perhaps finally happened?

Unlike most other grand orders or churches like theirs, the Malefic Order did not build grand castles or towers that breached the skies. Instead, they built into the ground, making vast networks of caves, which wasn't to say that the splendor of their order in any way could be belittled. The gloriousness and grandness of their halls were among the best. Caves could easily be far more extensive than some landmasses, especially with a bit of space magic mixed in.

The entrance to the Lord Protector's realm finally entered her sight after only a few minutes of descending. The portal was unadorned and straightforward, being merely an archway of stone with a portal in it. Taking a deep breath, she stepped through.

This was her first time in the Lord Protector's realm, and her expectations were most certainly met. The realm was not very large, perhaps only the space of a few smaller planets. But numerous reptilian creatures lived on the vast landmass that floated beneath her. Very few buildings stood on the entire continent, and only a single one was of any note—the Lord Protector's abode, she assumed.

"Come, child, come quickly!"

She heard the venerated voice of the Lord Protector as she promptly teleported to the source. The god sounded... emotional.

After teleporting, she found the Lord Protector all alone, a gleam in his eyes as he stared at a colossal obelisk made of black stone. The Hall Master had never seen this obelisk before, but she instantly knew what it was. And she knew what this meant.

On the obelisk, a rune had lit up—the only rune on it. A profound green aura shrouded the obelisk, making even the Lord Protector's own aura seem weak in comparison. The rune represented a single message. A message they had been waiting for oh so patiently for oh so long.

The Malefic Viper was coming.

The Hall Master could only tighten her knuckles as she started shaking from excitement. Their Patron, their one true god, was coming back to them. After eras of waiting, the Malefic One would finally return and once more bring glory to their order. Her eternal faith, their undying belief, had not been misplaced.

But instantly, she was brought back to reality. *Oh no!* So many preparations had to be made! They had to get everything in the absolute best of conditions. She had to brief all the other leaders and minor branches around their world. There was so much! She only hoped paradoxically that the Great One would perhaps take a few more days before he—

> "HELLO, LITTLE SNAPPY! MISSED ME!?"

UNEXPECTED ENCOUNTER (1/3)

Old habits die hard. A common phrase for most, one would imagine. But Jake had never thought that a "habit" could get old after less than a month. Without even thinking about it, he had found himself munching on mushrooms. Much to his horror, he even found enjoyment in it. The mana gained was a nice bonus too.

One thing led to another, and now Jake found himself sitting beneath a tree with a mixing bowl in his hand, moss and mushrooms floating in the purified water. After his fight with the boar and a lot of practice with his new Shadow Vault skill, he was excited to find new strong opponents to test himself against.

But after hours of looking around, he only came across a few weak beasts, none of them even breaking level 20. Barely worth getting out of bed for. So instead, he had gotten bored and started doing a bit of alchemy. It helped calm his nerves, and he needed to practice using his Alchemical Flame anyway.

He had already mixed a few common-rarity poisons and considered if he should start learning how to make stamina potions. He hadn't needed them during the Challenge Dungeon, as he only used stamina passively, but with his new Archer skills, that had changed significantly.

He hadn't gotten a level, but it wasn't surprising, considering he had only done alchemy for a few hours, and the concoctions were some he had trained many times before. He still had plenty of ingredients left in his spatial necklace, so he didn't really worry about running out anytime soon.

As he was about to begin another concoction, he sensed someone looking at him. At first, he thought it was one of the not-bird-birds, but it wasn't. Raising his head abruptly and turning to the side, he activated Archer's Eye instinctively and saw a man standing at the top of a hill wearing an archer's cloak similar to his own.

Shortly after, he saw four other figures appear around the archer. From the looks of it, three different kinds of the warrior class and a caster. Jake, with his high Perception, used Identify on each of them, as they didn't seem keen on approaching him quite yet either. They were likely also trying to Identify him.

[Human – lvl 19]
[Human – lvl 20]
[Human – lvl 18]
[Human – lvl 21]
[Human – lvl 20]

They were all lower than the caster that called himself William, but that wasn't grounds to underestimate them. There were five of them, and one of them had a rather mean-looking two-handed sword. That warrior also happened to be the one at level 21 and was even wearing plate armor. Armor Jake guessed was enchanted, either by upgrading it with a token or just by finding it.

From a quick glance, he noticed that they all seemed to have relatively decent gear. The archer's bow even looked quite a bit nicer than his own. All of their armor or cloaks were for sure upgraded, none of them looking like they only had what one started the tutorial with.

From what he could see, there were four men and one woman. He couldn't see their faces properly, but from their posture, they were all clearly on edge—a perfectly understandable response to seeing Jake, a solitary, unidentifiable human in the middle of nowhere. If possible, Jake wanted to avoid conflict and just move on with his day. Then again, information would be useful, as he had some doubts about the validity of what William said, considering the guy did turn out to be a backstabbing bastard.

Jake, seeing no reason for conflict, acted like he put the mixing bowl beneath his robe as he deposited it into his spatial storage. No reason to openly advertise that he had it, after all. He then got up and started walking toward the five people in as nonthreatening manner as he could. Which is to say he walked with both hands held out in front of him, showing he wasn't armed. Something he could change in the blink of an eye with his spatial storage.

The warrior with the two-hander went a step forward from the group and yelled, "Who are you? Why are you alone out here? And what was that in your hand before?"

Jake, seeing no reason to lie—but not exactly feeling like sharing much—told them the truth for the most part. "I am just an archer, and I am alone because I kind of like it that way. Also, it was just a bowl earlier, see?" He pulled out the bowl once more, making sure to make it seem like he'd taken it out from beneath his cloak.

However, they seemed to care little for the bowl, as their gazes all sharpened when he refused to give his name.

"Are you Jake?" the caster asked as she stepped forward, glaring at him with quite a bit of hostility.

Jake was a bit taken aback at the question. The only ones in the tutorial who knew his name were the ones his colleagues had shared it with. Richard also knew it without a doubt, and while he wasn't exactly on friendly terms with Richard, he doubted the man would still have people out hunting for him after so long. Besides, if they knew his colleagues, it was more than worth the risk to strike up a conversation.

"Yeah, where did you hear my name?" he asked, hoping to finally get some helpful info.

What he got instead was a bolt of ice followed by an arrow. The three warriors didn't stand still either—they all charged the instant they'd confirmed his identity.

Jake took a moment to react, as he barely managed to jump to the side to avoid the ranged attacks because of his danger sense. *What the hell is wrong with them?* he asked himself as he saw the eyes of the opposing party.

The hostility was almost palpable as the caster yelled, "This is for Mickey, you fucking psycho!"

"Don't lose your cool and let him run!" the warrior with the big sword said in a stern tone before he sped up, a green glow swirling around his body.

Jake only got more and more confused. *Who the fuck is Mickey?* But he didn't have time to contemplate further. He jumped backward, dodging the first swing of the warrior. This had to be some kind of misunderstanding. Perhaps another guy named Jake had killed that guy? It wasn't out of the question for more people named Jake to be in a twelve-hundred-person group.

"Listen, I think there is some kind of misunderstanding here! I didn't kill anyone named Mickey as far as I recall! Please, just calm down! There is no reason for us to fight." As Jake spoke, he kept dodging the blows of the warrior.

UNEXPECTED ENCOUNTER (1/3)

"Don't listen to him! Richard warned that he tried shit like this versus the metal mage!" one of the other warriors, an upgraded light warrior as far as he could see, warned.

Jake, at the mention of those two, instantly sharpened his gaze. So, William and Richard did work together. And it seemed like that caster wasn't happy about their last bout at all, even now sending people after him.

Everything suddenly seemed a lot clearer to Jake. They weren't here for revenge for some guy named Micky; they were here to kill him. Heck, maybe Mickey was a guy from the squad Richard had sent after him so long ago. Not that any of it mattered. In his mind, these five were now unquestionably marked as enemies. Yet he wasn't about to give up trying to get something useful out of them.

"So, you are with Richard and that metal caster, William," he said. "Tell me, do you know of other survivors in his camp? Names such as Jacob, Casper, or Joanna?"

An effort that went unrewarded, as they all simply continued their assault. *Fine,* Jake thought, *have it your way*.

They were slower and weaker than him in pretty much every way. Sure, the warrior without a doubt had higher Strength than him, but all in all, he still saw them as weak. Compared to William, none of them had shown anything that could genuinely threaten him. Well, he would be in for a lot of hurt if he let that massive two-hander hit him, but no way he was going to let that happen.

Having decided to stop being diplomatic, he no longer held back. He quickly summoned his bow and Shadow

Vaulted backward, much to the onlookers' shock as they saw him turn shadowy and fly backward.

With bow in hand, he decided to go for the weaker ones first. As he was preparing to shoot the caster, however, an arrow with far more power than he expected headed his way, allowing him only narrowly to avoid it. Part of his cloak was still ripped apart from the wind pressure alone. *Powershot, shit.*

A quick glance informed him that the archer had started charging another Powershot, making Jake instantly switch his focus to him. He knew the strength of that skill, but also its massive weakness.

Nocking an arrow, he shot it toward the archer, but his attack instead struck a wall of ice that popped up before it. Cursing, Jake could only dodge once more as the two other warriors reached him, one the light warrior and the other a medium warrior, from what he could see. Both upgraded classes too, of course.

With his weak defenses, the light warrior became his next target, as he quickly dismissed his bow and drew his bone dagger along with another random archer one. With no time to poison anything, he had to make do. The warrior was faster than Jake with his movements, but Jake had a small edge in Strength and a relatively large advantage in technique with his Twin-Fang Style, insane Perception, and instincts.

Positioning himself to block the archer and caster's line of sight, he dodged the medium warrior's sword as he closed in on the light warrior. With slight panic, the man tried to jump back as he threw small knives at Jake. Knives he decided to ignore. He just let them hit his body.

The cloak blocked nearly everything, only leaving a few meaningless scratches on his tough body.

However, the warrior was far less durable than Jake. Surprised that Jake just tanked the attack, he took several cuts across the chest with the bone dagger before Jake tried to finish him off by plunging his other dagger into his neck. Sadly, he had no time to assess if the man was a goner, as the two remaining warriors had reached him once more.

Shadow Vaulting away, he once more drew his bow and started bombarding both of them with arrows. The heavy warrior manipulated the aura around his body to block them, with the medium warrior choosing to dodge instead. A dodging attempt he failed, as an arrow nailed him in the leg.

Seeing his opportunity, Jake managed to land two more arrows on the man before he had to Shadow Vault once more as another Powershot came his way.

With some distance, he withdrew a bottle of Necrotic Poison and retreated behind a tree, still keeping an eye on the warriors that were within his Sphere of Perception. He had bought himself some time to apply the poison as he saw the party try and save their comrades. He had confidence in the damage on the light warrior being lethal.

However, the medium warrior seemed to already be getting up, his wounds healing rapidly. Not natural health points rapidly, but a self-healing skill rapidly. Something that wouldn't happen again that easily with poison in the mix. More than a dozen arrows now soaked in some of his most potent common-rarity poison went back into the quiver.

Okay, round two.

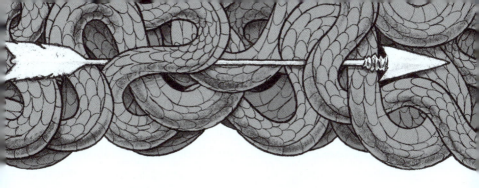

Chapter 47
Unexpected Encounter (2/3)

If simply taken as an archer, Jake wasn't anything overly impressive. He was relatively strong and fast due to his many levels in his race, but he was still a bit behind those with evolved classes. He still got an edge during combat due to his lack of hesitation and powerful Bloodline, though. But overall, fighting an entire team with class levels higher than his own wouldn't end well. If one disregarded his other primary source of power, that is.

However, if one added his profession, the equation changed. The pure stat amount of Toughness and Vitality it had provided made him far more robust than nearly everyone else, especially in prolonged fights. But without a doubt, his greatest strength currently was his potent toxins. A single arrow or a single cut transformed from a minor wound to almost certain death.

And now he had applied his poison. He hadn't done it from the beginning of the fight for many reasons. First of all, he wasn't sure it would turn into a battle. Secondly, he wanted information more than anything, and if it didn't end in a fight, he would just waste a bottle of poison. Now, however, the time for talking was over.

From behind the tree, he saw his enemies get ready to flank him once more, a tactic he would gladly exploit. Taking a normal, non-poisoned arrow, he nocked it and started charging a Powershot. The skill was weak in open combat, usually, but it had its time to shine. Now was one such time.

With the timing just right, as the medium warrior entered his line of fire, he released the arrow. The man didn't even have time to react before he was hit, the arrow exploding from the impact when it hit his chest. The man wasn't left in a much better state than the arrow, as a huge, gaping hole had blown open in his upper chest, taking with it his heart and lungs. Needless to say, the man was well and truly dead.

Having two down, he switched to poison arrows as he Shadow Vaulted away from the tree once more, seeking refuge behind another. Them being unable to pin him down was a significant advantage that he didn't want to lose. Besides, while the plate-wearing warrior was undoubtedly strong and had formidable defenses, he had gotten that by having far worse mobility. Hence, he would be saved for last.

Two Shadow Vaults later, he discovered that the enemy archer had entered his sphere. And from how he moved, he was not yet aware of Jake's location. Seeing him split up from the ice caster, he made his move.

He stalked the archer with his sphere as a guide while staying out of sight from all three enemies. The other archer moved slowly, only at walking speed, with his bow fully drawn and ready to shoot at any sudden movement. His caution was natural but misplaced. Jake never planned to enter his line of sight, after all.

As the archer entered a small clearing, Jake saw his chance and shot an arrow from directly behind the man. He managed to react only at the very last moment, but still ended up with an arrow hitting him on his upper backside—an annoying but otherwise very easily manageable wound. If the Necrotic Poison was disregarded, that is.

The archer only had time to roll out the way and rip the arrow out before he felt that something was wrong. At first, he felt a weird numbness, followed by intense pain that seemed to spread through his very being. Next, he was hit by the smell—the smell of rotting flesh. The archer yelled in horror, attracting his comrades, who rushed over to him.

Jake had taken refuge behind a tree once more but kept close enough for the dying archer to still be within his sphere. The warrior and caster made it to their dying comrade and were both stopped dead when they saw the archer rolling on the ground, shrieking in an inhuman voice.

As he rolled around, pieces of rotten black flesh fell off. The grisly sight ended before long, as the screaming also died down. It had taken less than half a minute from the arrow hitting to his death. Yet this half a minute was enough to bring endless nightmares to those seeing it.

Before the two, the archer barely resembled a human anymore. The entire back area and most of the upper body had completely rotted away. An entire arm was lying off to the side, having become detached as the archer rolled around.

Even from behind the tree, Jake had to take deep breaths to calm himself. This was the first time he'd seen the actual result of his poison taking effect. The only other time he had done anything like this was when he used Touch of the Malefic Viper on a beast. But this had been a human.

He still vividly remembered the water from the second challenge room that nearly killed him. The feeling of your limbs slowly rotting away, the indescribable pain. He didn't like it. He didn't like it one bit. But poisons were his best weapon.

In the end, the only thing he could calm himself down with was that he hadn't been the aggressor. They had attacked first. He was just defending himself. They were allies of Richard and William, two people who both had attempted to have him killed before. They were his enemies, and to your enemies, you show no mercy.

He remembered a conversation he'd had with the Malefic Viper during his visit to his realm.

The Viper told a story from when he was younger, before he became a god. He spoke of how he had just gotten the ability to assume a humanoid form and how he had tried to enter the world of civilization and become, well... civilized.

The Malefic Viper talked of his naivety back then. He believed that the enlightened humanoid races were not like the beasts he was used to, but would have values above simply striving for more strength. He had gotten close to people, and he had believed them as if he were a gullible child. Beasts didn't lie, after all. They either attacked or retreated. A monster that would first become your friend, only to then stab you in the back, was unheard of to him.

Until it happened. Over wealth, the Malefic Viper was betrayed, and his betrayers attempted to kill him. Of course, even then, his strength was above most of his peers, and he was not so easily thwarted. But yet again, he had believed the man when he claimed it was all a big misunderstanding.

So, he spared him. Spared him out of misplaced compassion and benevolence. A benevolence returned by having the few humanoid friends he had made slaughtered. The man had hired a far more powerful force to take down the Malefic Viper out of something as simple as pure pride. He had made a contract with a powerful king to hunt down the Viper and steal his treasures.

Of course, the Malefic Viper returned this favor by massacring the man and his forces, and then delivering his head to the country of the foolish king. Personally. In retrospect, the Viper confessed it was perhaps an overreaction to let the entire kingdom face his wrath.

It ended up resulting in the destruction of nine planets.

After this entire inhuman massacre, the Malefic Viper was not shunned or hunted. Even if he had killed innocents—women, children, and elderly—he was never admonished for any of it. Instead, he was revered for his power. Praised for his boldness. But more importantly, no one dared to assist anyone in ever betraying him again, as the consequences were now clear as day.

The lesson the Malefic Viper wanted to teach Jake was a few things. The first was to not trust blindly and to not show mercy to one's enemies. The second point was that power ruled supreme. Might makes right, as one says. Additionally, if one shows the cruelty and the ability to

UNEXPECTED ENCOUNTER (2/3)

cross certain lines, your enemies will hesitate and falter the next time they deal with you.

Jake didn't fully agree with this interpretation, as cruelty can also lead to a far stronger response than one predicted. In such cases, the enemy will not be discouraged from fighting but instead be far more resolute in destroying you, throwing all caution to the wind.

And that was precisely the situation Jake now found himself in. After the initial fear wore off, the warrior and ice caster didn't flee or go on the defensive. Instead, they abandoned all signs of caution, as they both yelled obscenities.

"Get the fuck out here, you fucking coward!" the warrior yelled, followed by the ice caster calling him far more insulting things. Not that Jake necessarily disagreed with some of the things they called him. He just honestly didn't care. Allies of William and Richard didn't have any right to teach him anything about decency and honor.

Withdrawing another bottle of poison from his necklace, he prepared himself to strike. Jumping out from behind the tree, he fired an arrow at the delirious woman. As he had expected, the blow was blocked as a shield of ice popped up behind her. Automatically activated, from what he could see.

This, of course, gave away Jake's position, as both turned toward him, rage in their eyes. Spikes of ice started coalescing in the air as the caster stepped out from behind her wall, and the warrior charged toward him, still enveloped in the same green aura.

Jake was fully aware that his regular arrows couldn't break through this green aura, so instead, he threw the bottle he had prepared earlier. While the bottle's speed was slower than an arrow, it was still far too fast for the warrior to avoid.

The bottle struck him as he blocked with his arms, the liquid within splashing all over his upper body. A sizzling sound was heard—that of aura being eroded—and the man retreated as he seemingly focused on protecting himself. Jake was aware that the Necrotic Poison was far weaker thrown like that compared to getting applied to an arrow, but he had to make do.

With the warrior out of the way, Jake made his way toward the ice caster. After only a few steps, the ice spikes she'd begun conjuring earlier made their way toward him, prompting him to make a full-power Shadow Vault straight through the spikes. He felt a considerable drain on his mana as he passed through spike after spike. But the tactic paid off.

He now found himself within only a few meters of the caster, whose facial expression had changed from one of pure anger to one of abject fear. Giving her no quarter, Jake continued his assault by stepping toward her and activating Shadow Vault another time.

Just as he vaulted, a wall of ice started getting summoned, but it was too late. Before the wall could fully form, Jake appeared behind the caster and went for an overhead swing, straight for her head.

In a final gambit, the caster seemed to release all her mana, sending a wave of frost exploding out of her. It hit Jake and froze the ground all around her. Jake, however, did not retreat. He instead pushed forward, bringing down the dagger on the woman.

Her Toughness proved inadequate as the dagger managed to enter the top of her skull. He hadn't poisoned

UNEXPECTED ENCOUNTER (2/3)

the blade, but he knew this blow was lethal either way. The notification hitting him less than a second after his attack landed only confirmed as much.

Not that he had time to look, as one opponent remained. With an explosion of ice and green aura, the wall made by the caster was smashed apart by the warrior charging through it. His armor and body had clear signs of the poisons still lingering, but he had managed to cleanse most of it. This slightly surprised Jake, as it displayed that the mysterious green aura seemed to possess both strong defensive and self-enhancing effects.

When the warrior saw the dead caster with Jake standing over her, his anger reached entirely new levels.

Completely berserk, he started swinging his massive blade back and forth with far more power and speed than before. In the end, this did little for him, as at the same time, all semblance of technique disappeared from his attack, ultimately making it far easier for Jake.

Not backing down, Jake engaged in melee, dodging and weaving around the man as he avoided every single swing. It reminded him of fighting the boar, even if the boar had been both weaker and slower. Though at least the beast had magic to pin Jake down, something the warrior sorely lacked.

The fight continued toward the expected conclusion for a few more minutes as Jake felt the green aura around the man get dimmer and dimmer. His speed and power also gradually slowed down, allowing Jake to land small cuts here and there.

In the end, Jake managed to kick the man's arms when he made a far too predictable downward blow, disarming him. Another kick made the man stumble, as he fell to the ground only a few meters from the caster's corpse.

The fact that he lost his weapon and got knocked down brought some clarity back to the man's eyes, prompting Jake to talk.

"What do Richard and William think they can accomplish by sending people after me like this? Except for donating me experience and tutorial points, that is." Jake saw no reason to be cordial.

"Revenge for what you have done, you fucking lunatic," the man answered with a far calmer voice than Jake had predicted. Though he felt the apparent signs of weakness from his tone. He, too, knew that he was dead no matter what.

"Revenge for what? Killing people Richard sent after me, or for fighting back when that William fellow tried to backstab me?" Jake spoke with a mocking voice. How goddamn ridiculous were these people?

"For killing... everyone... For starting this... war," the man said, his voice getting weaker and weaker.

Jake could only stand there, confused at his words. Something was off. Way off. From how he had said "everyone," it sounded like it certainly wasn't just for those people he had killed sent by Richard. Could it be the three ambushers from the very first night of the tutorial? No, that couldn't be it either.

To make matters even more confusing, he was clearly blamed for starting a war. The war was likely the one William had alluded to between Richard's faction and those other guys. But why the hell was *he* getting blamed for it?

"I didn't do anything!" Jake protested as he looked at the dying man. He didn't hesitate to take out a health potion. "Here, drink this health po—»

Before he could finish, the warrior knocked the potion out of his hand.

"Why wou—" Jake tried again, but the warrior's arm dropped to his side, having used his final vestige of strength to knock away the only thing that could save him.

Jake just stood there. "God fucking dammit," he spoke out loud.

I am pretty sure I would remember starting a goddamn war, Jake thought with much frustration. Had their entire fight indeed been based on some huge misunderstanding? Was it a mistake fighting them?

No. Jake shook his head. Even if it had been a misunderstanding, they had clearly been dead set on fighting him. He had tried to talk, but they had shot his attempt down. He had to remember they were enemies. And he couldn't afford to show mercy to enemies. It was simple...

With a sigh, he sat down on the ground. For now, he wasn't going to think of it. Next time, he would try harder on the diplomacy part. *Focus on what you can.*

And with that, his focus shifted to his notification screen.

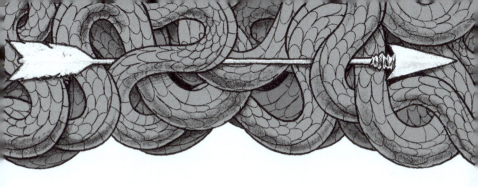

Chapter 48
Unexpected Encounter (3/3)

The Hall Master stood frozen as she slowly turned around. What she saw was a scaled man, looking more human than reptilian. He wore a simple-looking black robe and had what she could only describe as a big, goofy smile on his lips. His long black hair was tied behind his head, revealing his green eyes.

He looked unimpressive, but the aura that he gave off was more powerful than anything she had ever come across. It felt like she stood before the incarnation of death and decay itself. Yet she felt not a shred of fear. The only feeling that inhabited her body was pure joy, combined with a massive dose of nervousness.

«M… master! You have returned! I… I…" the Lord Protector stammered as tears started streaming down his face. He had waited for so long, far longer than any other being in the Order of the Malefic Viper… and he was also the only living member that had ever met the Viper before in person. Well, except for the Viper's disciple, but that guy was a bit looney.

With a step, the Malefic Viper appeared before the Lord Protector and, to the Hall Master's surprise, gave him a big hug.

"I am sorry, little one; it must have been hard for you. You've done well." The Viper began rubbing the head of the Lord Protector, who was now fully bawling his eyes out.

The Hall Master could only stand there, frozen, as she observed. The high and mighty Lord Protector, crying his eyes out, and the Malefic Viper, a being she had only ever heard of in legends, consoling him like he was a small child. She had dreamed of the Malefic Viper's return for so long, but this scenario had never been one she had imagined.

"So, Snappy, who is this young lady?" the Viper finally asked as he stepped away from the Lord Protector, who quickly managed to calm himself down.

The Hall Master was now even more beside herself as both the gods turned their attention to her.

"Ah, this is the newest Hall Master of the Order," the Lord Protector said, as he had now managed to entirely compose himself, returning to his more stoic demeanor that he usually displayed. "She is more or less the highest-ranking member of the Order, as we only have this one hall remaining. I believe she is the descendant of one of the Ladies of the Verdant Lagoon."

"Oh, those girls. That brings back some memories. Good to see they left some nice descendants with the Order. Wonder what they're up to these days." The Malefic Viper stepped closer to the frozen Hall Master. "So, what are you called?"

The Hall Master, now suddenly thrown out of her stupor, managed to get out, "My name? Viridia, my lord!" She did everything she could to compose herself. "May I have the honor of welcoming the Malefic One back to the Order, and apologize for our inadequate performance in the Patron's absence! I swear on my life that—»

"Whoa!" the Malefic Viper said. "Stop, stop, stop! I just asked for your name, that is all. You have nothing to apologize for, geez. I am the one who should apologize to you if anyone was going to. But I already apologized to little Snappy earlier, and I don't make two apologies in a day, so we can't have that. Just relax, okay? Everything is fine. The fact that the Order is still even around is more than impressive in its own right." He raised his hand and gave her a pat on her head, pretty much just petting her.

With a smile, Snappy went over to them and asked, "May I know why Master chose this time to make his return?" He instantly realized that it might have come off wrong. "Not that there is anything wrong with making your return now! It is great, in fact! I am just thinking that with the new universe being integrated and everything... If there was some relation, that's all!"

"Snappy. Relax." The Viper shook his head as he turned and landed a gentle chop on the Lord Protector's head. "And yes, it's entirely related to the new universe. Remember that dungeon I made back in preparation for the second era?"

"The one with the spikes?" the Lord Protector asked. If he recalled, that was the only dungeon yet uncleared. He hadn't lived when it was made, but the Viper had spoken of it in length.

"Yep, that one. Someone actually cleared it."

"Oh! Did Master make a new worthy follower!? Perhaps a great reward was granted for your new follower's performance in the tutorial?" Despite Snappy's glee, they instantly frowned. "Wait, that can't be. The tutorials have yet to conclude."

"I didn't make a follower, no," he answered with a giant, goofy smile. "Believe it or not, I think I made a friend!"

As Jake opened his notifications screen, he was instantly assaulted by a stream of messages.

> *You have slain [Human (F) - lvl 18 / Apprentice Rogue - lvl 26 / Novice Leatherworker – lvl 10] – A small amount of bonus experience earned for killing an enemy with a class above your class level. 425,241 TP earned*
>
> *You have slain [Human (F) - lvl 19 / Apprentice Swordsman - lvl 27 / Novice Smith – lvl 11] A small amount of bonus experience earned for killing an enemy with a class above your class level. 467,111 TP earned*
>
> *You have slain [Human (F) - lvl 20/ Veteran Archer - lvl 28 / Novice Builder – lvl 12] – A small amount of bonus experience earned for killing an enemy with a class above your class level. 489,965 TP earned*
> *You have slain [Human (F) - lvl 20 / Neophyte Ice Witch - lvl 30 / Novice Tailor

lvl 11] – A small amount of bonus experience earned for killing an enemy with a class above your class level. 591,235 TP earned*

You have slain [Human (F) - lvl 21/ Aspiring Blade of Nature - lvl 33 / Novice Smith – lvl 10] – A small amount of bonus experience earned for killing an enemy with a class above your class level. 703,458 TP earned

'DING!' Class: [Archer] has reached level 21 - Stat points allocated, +1 Free Point

'DING!' Class: [Archer] has reached level 22 - Stat points allocated, +1 Free Point

'DING!' Race: [Human (E)] has reached level 33 - Stat points allocated, +5 Free Points

'DING!' Class: [Archer] has reached level 23 - Stat points allocated, +1 Free Point

Jake could honestly only sigh once more at the messages. Three whole levels in his class from the relatively short fight. It was almost criminally more effective than hunting beasts. Even worse was the number of tutorial points earned.

He'd been closing in on 400,000 points before the fight, but now he had over 3,000,000. They had increased more than sevenfold. From the rules, he knew that he had obtained half of the group's points. Half of what they had struggled and put their lives on the line to get, robbed in one swoop.

Looking at the classes on the notifications, he also learned quite a lot. The three first seemed to have rather basic upgrades. Two apprentices and one veteran.

However, he wasn't sure if the veteran was a low-level upgrade or a higher one. He assumed low, as the man had been on the weaker side, honestly.

The last two were the interesting ones. The woman had been a Neophyte Ice Witch. Neophyte made one think it was low level, or that she was just beginning to step on that path. Perhaps Ice Witches were just a really high-tier class? She had been a bit strong, but she was far off compared to the metal caster. Too bad he had failed to kill him to see what his class was called.

The last one, AKA the plate-wearing warrior, had by far the most interesting class. Aspiring Blade of Nature. It reminded Jake of his own Prodigious Alchemist of the Malefic Viper. An unusual adjective before the class seemed to indicate that it was somehow a bit higher level, while the "rank"-based ones, such as apprentice or novice, seemed to be more straightforward paths. "Neophyte" was also likely a "special" adjective. Of course, he seriously doubted it was as simple as that.

And speaking of professions, theirs were extremely uninteresting. All were just novice ranks. Though Jake did confirm the existence of four types of professions besides his own. Tailors, smiths, leatherworkers, and builders.

He had to look at the bright spots of this shitty situation, after all. He couldn't sit there and dwell on what the hell was happening or why they had targeted him. Information was necessary, so he just had to appreciate what he got.

For his Free Points, he split them between Strength and Agility. He still felt that he was either weaker than or on par with others despite his significantly higher race level. He knew that evolved classes would add far more stat points than the basic starting ones. The 6 stat points in total from each Archer level did seem quite pathetic compared to his 20 from Prodigious Alchemist of the Malefic Viper.

Closing the notification window, he got up and exited his meditation. He hadn't been down for long, but he had managed to regenerate a bit of stamina and mana. He was honestly wondering if he even needed sleep anymore. He hadn't felt the need since exiting the Challenge Dungeon. In there, he'd only slept for a few hours once in a while to relax his head. Something that hadn't been necessary yet here in the forest.

Looking at his surroundings, he spotted the big sword dropped by the warrior. It was quite simple-looking but had a relatively nice-looking green gem embedded in the handle. Using Identify on it, he was a bit taken aback.

[Greatsword of Nature (Rare)] – A sword crafted from metal often found in areas with high concentrations of nature-attuned mana. Through the ages, this sword has been filled with the energy of nature itself, giving it the ability to bless its wielder. Enchantments: Energy of Nature's Strength: Absorb and assimilate the powers of nature itself found within the blade, strengthening your inner energy with its properties.

Requirements: Lvl 20+ in any class or race. High nature affinity.

The blade was... great. The enchantment was very interesting. This blade was likely the reason for the man's class and mystical aura. It was somehow inner energy, or stamina, infused with the "energies of nature" as the sword described.

Either way, the sword was good. Jake couldn't help but pick it up. It was a bit heavy, but nothing he couldn't handle. The energy from the warrior was still lingering within the blade, so Jake decided to let it be for now. He could feel it slowly dissipating as he looked at it, after all. In only a few minutes, he should be able to try and claim it as his own.

But the fact that the man had dropped such a weapon made Jake think of something he had entirely disregarded. Looting. It wasn't like beasts dropped loot like in games, but humans sure did. He could take their equipment. It felt dirty and dishonorable... but Jake felt like it would be pure stupidity not to do it.

He needed power; everyone did. The dead won't blame the living for trying to stay alive, he thought to himself. Unless said living person has killed them, of course. So these dead would kind of be pissed at me for taking their stuff... Yeah, not going down that road.

Disregarding that entire train of thought, he went to the warrior and identified his armor. It was common rarity and upgraded just like his cloak was, even with the same enchantment of Self-Repair. As he had plenty of space in his spatial storage, and with the armor self-repairing, he saw no reason not to keep it. Luckily, he didn't have to strip the dead man, as he could directly deposit it the second he felt the man's last vestige of mana leave the armor.

Next, he went to the Ice Witch and identified her items too. He tried to be fast about it, as he honestly still felt very uncomfortable looking at the dead body. The robe was common rarity like the warrior's and his own. She also had a common-rarity wand that he honestly had no interest in.

UNEXPECTED ENCOUNTER (3/3)

But she did have a ring on her finger that yielded a pleasant surprise.

> [Ring of Brilliance (Common)] – A ring with a gem crafted by a skilled jeweler. The mana in the gem grants the user increased mental stats. Enchantment: +10 Intelligence, +10 Wisdom, +5 Willpower.
>
> Requirements: Lvl 15+ in any humanoid race.

Like the armor of the warrior, the ring and wand were stored in his necklace too. He also threw in the robe of the caster without thinking, instantly regretting it as the woman was now half-naked with only ragged clothes beneath that looked like they had been haphazardly sewn together from pre-tutorial clothes.

Quickly, he took out a sheet of cloth he had brought from the dungeon and covered her body. It was as much for himself as for her. He had already decided to burn the corpses, partly as thanks for the equipment, and partly out of a weird sense of respect and to honor them putting up a good fight. It just felt like the right thing to do.

But for now, he moved on to the other corpses. As he walked toward the archer, he took out the ring and started injecting mana into it until he felt a connection form and the warm flow of stats increasing. By that time, he had already arrived before the rather gory-looking archer. The robe was a totally lost cause, and his Identify turned up nothing, indicating it was broken as his poison consumed the man.

But he did find the bow and dagger that the archer had used lying a bit off to the side. He had dropped his bow when Jake first shot him, and while the blade was still a bit... dirty, it must have fallen off early in the process. Identifying both of them, he wasn't surprised, but still happy with the result.

> [Archer's Bow (Common)] – A bow handed out for the tutorial, now upgraded with a token. Has a robust wooden structure and string. Enchantments: Self-Repair.
>
> Requirements: Tutorial Attendee and Archer Class (current or former).
>
> [Archer's Dagger (Common)] – A dagger handed out for the tutorial, now upgraded with a token. Has a sharp edge made of high-quality steel and a strong wooden handle. Enchantments: Self-Repair.
>
> Requirements: Tutorial Attendee and Archer Class (current or former).

His current bow and old dagger were both not upgraded, so two upgraded versions were more than welcome. However, the dagger needed a good cleaning before using it. Something for later, he thought as he deposited both of them into his storage. He could bind them to himself with mana and just have the Self-Repair do the cleaning too.

Next, he checked the rogue and swordsman but found nothing of interest. They both had common-rarity gear, though the rogue did have boots that were also common rarity but offered just a bit of Endurance besides the normal Self-Repair enchantment. Of course, they were utterly useless to Jake as he already had his far better Boots of the Wandering Alchemist.

Having looted what he wanted, he returned to the greatsword that was still on the ground. He couldn't put it in his spatial storage as long as the warrior's energy still resided within.

As expected, the energy was gone entirely after his looting tour. Unable to hold himself back, he tried to bind the sword to himself. But the moment his mana entered, he felt a strong resistance, followed by a retaliatory force that sent a burning sensation up his hand.

Cursing, he drew back his hand. Somehow the sword had communicated to him that he wasn't able to bind it. Apparently, he wasn't attuned to nature, or maybe he didn't have the right affinity or something, going by the requirements. Maybe it had something to do with nature typically seen as related to life, and his current approach to most anything was pretty much the direct opposite of that with his poisons? Or something entirely unrelated, like some innate talent?

Either way, he stored the blade in his spatial necklace. Who knows, maybe he could find someone to use it later on. No matter what, he saw no reason not to keep it around even if he himself had no use for the oversized sword.

With everything gathered, he started preparing their sendoffs. The fight had likely been on the wrong premise and merely the result of a huge, deadly misunderstanding.

The least amount of respect he could give his opponents was to not leave their corpses lying around. He remembered many civilizations used to burn fallen warriors, and even in modern countries, cremation was the norm in many places.

Gathering the bodies, he made sure to transport the half-decomposed archer carefully. Afterward, he gathered some wood and laid all the corpses on top of it. His Alchemical Flame quickly started burning the bodies along with the wood. The flame did nearly nothing to living targets, but due to the ever-present system-fuckery, it worked wonders in breaking down objects or setting things ablaze.

As the pyre burned, Jake decided to continue what he'd been doing before the battle: alchemy. He was getting low on stamina after the many Shadow Vaults, and it was more than about time that he learned how to make stamina potions.

He sat down beside the still-burning pyre, taking out the book on how to make them from his spatial storage. With his new movement skill, he had confidence in escaping pretty much anyone, so he decided to let the pyre serve as a beacon to perhaps draw other survivors to him. The only ones that should see this pyre's smoke would be people already out and about; therefore, it was unlikely to attract anyone.

He clearly needed information. He was filled with questions while having no answers. The risks associated with seeking out Richard or even the faction that opposed him also seemed just too numerous. Once more, due to his lack of information.

A meeting with any of his colleagues would be the best. While they hadn't been the closest of friends, they at least knew him a bit. They should know he wasn't the type to go around randomly attacking people and trying to incite wars.

Jacob especially should know this. That guy had such good insight into other people, so even if he and Jake hadn't known each other for long, he should still be able to reassure others that he wasn't some monster.

Looking at the burning pyre, however, he knew he wasn't exactly helping his own case. He doubted the friends of the squad he had killed would accept him going, "Hey, yeah, sorry I killed your friends, but it was all a big misunderstanding! No hard feelings, right?"

With a big sigh, he half-distractedly read the small book. This entire thing was a fucking mess. Why couldn't it just be easy, killing beasts to get points and humans attacking you being just psycho enemies?

Looking up from the book, he looked toward the sky. He really wished he could ask someone for advice on what exactly to do. His instincts weren't exactly helpful here, as he was sure it would only advise killing anyone who dared raise a weapon against him. It didn't care for motives, thoughts, or morals. It was pure. Simple. Perhaps living just following your instincts would be far easier.

Shaking his head, he decided to cut off all distracting thoughts and focus on his alchemy. Worrying would do him no good. Stamina potions and levels, however, would do him a lot of good.

Keep it simple, Jake thought to himself, *and take the complications as they come.*

TO BE CONTINUED IN

THE PRIMAL HUNTER

VOLUME 3